# NEVER
## Give Up

# HEIDI LIS

Editing by: Emma Mack of Tink's Typos
Editing by: Joanna Villalongo
Interior design by Cassy Roop of Pink Ink Designs
(www.pinkinkdesigns.com)

# CHAPTER
## *One*

Prologue... 5 years earlier

*O*ur study session ended early with, both of us knowing where tonight was heading. We've talked about this night for so long, it is the first time for both of us. Our nerves are getting the best of us as we make small talk sitting on his bed. Knowing Micah has had his share of make out sessions is a bit comforting, at least one of us knows what they are doing. My experience to this point in my life is limited; most of it comes from my romance novels I love to read. Wow, how sad is that?

He's so gentle and caring, never rushing me. The fact that he keeps asking me if I'm okay, has me falling for him even more. He delicately kisses my trembling lips while lying on top of me. Fully clothed, Micah is rocking his body against mine. Somewhere between scorching hot kisses, my eyes glazed over, they are entranced in his icy blue eyes. His sultry smile cascades a blazing streak of fire down my body.

*Removing my shirt over my head, Micah unhooks my bra and takes a nipple into his mouth. No words could ever describe how incredible this feels. The moans escaping my throat help intensify his urge to passionately consume me. I'm drowning in every touch and kiss he unleashes upon me. The minute his teeth graze my skin is the moment my mind spins out of control. A fire in the pit of my stomach erupts into an inferno, the only one I crave, is him. Grasping his shoulders, I strip him of his shirt. My urge to touch him overtakes me as I trace his naked chest, letting my eyes drink in the sight of him. What a sight, Micah with a shirt on is sexy, but Micah shirtless is mind-blowing.*

*He moans, looking as though he is in pain. "Elsa, I love the softness of your body. So perfect." He kisses a trail of wetness licking up one side of my throat just under my ear. "Your body tastes so good, you taste like a peach."* That would be my lotion.

*My slight snickering has him whispering a 'tsk-tsk' before rocking his jean covered erection against mine. Oh my, God, when he hits that spot, I gasp, reaching for him. I had no clue being with him could ever be this good. Locking my hands under his pillow, Micah takes a hold of my hips, raising me slightly, so our hips touch before he sits back on his knees. He's intentionally torturing me with his rock his hard pelvis. Lust-crazed moans escape my lips while the nerves in my body take a back seat to want.*

*"Micah, I'm so close." The words escape my mouth with such intensity as my impending release inches even closer.*

*Glancing up, his larger frame swallows my petite one. He glides his chest against mine, whispering in my ear, "Hang on pretty girl, I've spent way too long waiting to see* you like this. You're so much sexier than in my dreams...and my dreams were pretty damn vivid."

After we are both stripped of our clothes, Micah traces his index finger up my entire body from toe to lips. I'm finally getting a good look at him naked, and I freeze. My eyes widen, praying like hell my body will adjust to him. He catches my scared expression and he tips my chin with his finger.

"Are you sure you want this, pretty girl? Please, say yes, or I need to take a cold shower."

A chuckle escapes my throat as I hold onto his hand, kissing it lightly. "I've never been this sure of anything in my life, but I'm nervous," I whisper at the same time my throat tightens. "I want this to be good for you, too."

No words, instead he takes my hand and brings it to his face. Cupping his cheek, he leans forward to press his lips with mine.

The minute he reaches for a condom he had in his jeans pocket, I close my eyes, praying. I want this more than anything, but the horrific stories I've heard about a girl's first time is damn frightening. Those dreadful thoughts spark a sudden panic attack, without realizing it, I must have bitten my lip because my eyes snap open when Micah is pulling it free with his fingers. At once, I release it, and he seals his lips to mine yet again. This kiss is like no other kiss; it's a kiss to end all kisses.

Softly, he whispers. "I swear I shouldn't Elsa, but I think I'm in love with you."

"Oh Micah, I know I'm in love with you." My eyes instantaneously fill with tears. I have the confirmation for what I had hoped for so long. He loves me.

The look of surprise on his face glazes over as the spark in *his eyes twinkle with his smile. "Really, pretty girl?"*

*I can't help smiling. "Really."*

*"Let me show you how much I love you."*

*My heart stops beating, I forget how to breathe, and I swear time stands still. I'm yearning for him. "Show me."*

*Taking a hold of my lower back, Micah lifts one leg over his hip. Lining himself up, he leans forward, and takes my lips with his own. Once again, I lose myself like I always do when he kisses me. The instant he parts my lips with his tongue, he thrusts into my mouth at the same time he pushes inside my body. Holding onto his shoulders, I cry into his kiss. The burning sensation pales in comparison to how incredibly full I feel. He's consuming me, and I greedily take him in, ignoring the burn. My body quakes with every moan that escape my lips. I pull him closer with every thrust of his hips. The back and forth motions dull my pain as my desires increase tenfold.*

*Our need for one another only intensifies as a sex-crazed Micah props himself on his elbows and begins thrusting like an animal. His lustful moans and tantalizing smile make him even more desirable. I can feel I'm on the brink, as my stomach quivers and my muscles tense before tipping over the edge in euphoria. Quivering under his steady gaze and stronghold, he pushes me straight into oblivion. Not even two seconds later, Micah, with his eyes glazed over, starts shouting my name with his intense release.*

# CHAPTER
## *two*

Present Day

*I*'m still struggling, after all this time, my mind can't stop from remembering. I can't count how many times I've heard that five years is a long time to get over someone, anyone for that matter. No one understands. Here at Burn, my favorite gym, I'm doing the only thing that helps me deal with another day...without him. Months and years come and go, but the pain in my chest is as real as it was the moment my life no longer held any meaning.

Today is another anniversary I wish I didn't have to remember what I've lost, yet the date on the calendar is a constant reminder. I'd rather feel nothing than the sorrow that wants to swallow me whole. As tears descend my cheeks, I aggressively deliver massive blows to the bag I'm releasing my unspent energy on. Even with taped knuckles, my hands ache with each repeated blow. Determined to escape my own mind, I lower my chin, ignoring every sting of pain.

Using the gym was the only way I've learned to help release my inner pain. Typical of most nights, I'm struggling with the waves of torment that consume my mind. With every swing and music blaring in my ears, I'm pushing the images out of my head the best I can. The boy who stole my heart had left me with more than just memories. My life forever changed, and the physical and emotional scars are all I have left of him.

Please. *(Punch)*

Let. *(Punch)*

Me. *(Punch)*

Move. *(Punch)*

On. *(Punch)*

My mind's spinning, my stomach's churning, and my brain is urging me to hit the bag harder each time. My heart is betraying me, reminding me of his baby blues I've never been able to forget. Letting Micah in was as natural as breathing, letting him go was damn near impossible.

All I see are his eyes. *(Punch)*

All I hear are his cries. *(Punch)*

All I remember was being forced to do something I'll never forget. *(Punch...Punch...Punch)*

STANDING IN THE shower, I lower my head and absorb the hot water as it pierces my skin. I embrace the sheer sting for it allows me to escape one pain to seek comfort in another.

*I need to make it through this night. Just need to keep it together for a few more hours, the day is drawing to a close. Breathe; I've nearly survived yet another anniversary.*

TOSSING AND TURNING, sleep is evading me, it's always on this precise date. April 5th is a date forever seared into my brain and stamped in my heart. The hardest of times is at night alone in my bed, it's the time my mind drifts back...remembering like it was only yesterday. The harder I try to leave the past behind me, the more something takes me back to high school. Back, to the day a tall, brown hair, blue-eyed boy transferred to Kennedy High School, stealing my breath from that very first glance.

*Sophomore year started out like any other until a new student from San Diego, California moved here. I was fortunate because I ended up having four classes with him. All of my time spent studying instead of going to parties has paid off. I was ahead in a few subjects while our newest student was behind in others. He was two years older and needed to complete a few core subjects he had not taken at his other school.*

*Each class, I sat wide-eyed, drooling at his good looks. When he introduced himself to the class, every girl admired his presence. I noticed him the minute he walked into the classroom with his rosy cheeks. He walked with an aura of confidence, not a bit timid. The moment he strolled in, a few eyebrows rose, and conversations halted midstream.*

*He had a lovely bronze color to his skin. One you would expect to get from living in sunny California. It was a nice change from our white, pale faces. His vibrant brown hair had light blond streaks, but damn, it was his eyes that halted my breath. Micah's sparkling baby blues vastly contrast with his dark brown eyelashes. They simply command your attention. The minute he announced he liked to surf was not a total shock. His body screamed 'surfer dude.'*

*I lost all rational thoughts while keeping my gaze on him, and the minute he spoke, his voice damn near had me falling out of my seat. His eyes danced around the room until our gazes met, locking onto each other before he lowered his eyes, breaking our connection. The minute his eyes left mine, my breaths halted, and my pulse raced. My eyes however, never moved.*

*"My name is Micah Taylor, I'm from San Diego, California. Not much to say, my parents moved here for work. I have a younger brother, Matt. I love to surf, read literature and have a good time."*

*Right then someone shouted, "You mean you used to love to surf, not happening here in Iowa."*

*The class laughed as Micah responded with a friendly nod of his head. My eyes devoured every inch of him with every word he spoke. It was the obnoxiously loud giggle that echoed in the room that killed my moment. No need to turn around, because sadly, I knew who it was. Sarah Sloan, also known as The Golden Beauty, was like a cat in heat. No mistaking her outburst, she was anything but subtle. Micah sure seemed taken by it, too. The goofy smile I had plastered on my face since I first noticed him, fell away as they shared a lovely smile. Great!*

*Not paying any attention to the rest of the class, I kept staring at the back of his head. He was seated a few rows ahead, and it saddened me. I could see the writing on the wall. It was the same old story, Sarah and her posse swarmed in and devoured any new guy who transferred to our school.*

*No other girl ever stood a chance. Not with them around. With every class Micah and I had together, I learned a bit more about him. His brother Matt was three years younger, and his parents Skylar and Dave Taylor work for a large marketing firm located here in Cedar Rapids. The McIntosh Group was a big deal around here. The second he mentioned he moved on the same street as me, I couldn't help but blush. I happen to chuckle when I learned the large corner stone house at the end of my block is now where Micah called home.*

Shaking my head, I wiped the stray tear as I remembered my first day with him. Stumbling out of bed, I realize I won't be able to sleep anytime soon, so I might as well read. It's my one true escape. Only two pages in, my mind wanders back to the first conversation I ever had with Micah. A faint smile spreads across my face. It's nice to remember him with a smile instead of tears.

*"Now, what's so funny?" Micah whispered leaning closer to me. I never noticed he left the front of the class to sit down next to me. How did that happen?*

*I had to admit I was on cloud nine the minute he mentioned where he lived. I know that house, well.*

*Crap, did I laugh out loud and not realize it? To my embarrassment, I must have. Turning my head his way, I felt my cheeks flush, and my heart race. Opening my mouth though, words just spill out.*

*"Oh, I was just thinking about what you said," shaking away my nerves, I unwittingly groan. "I learn more about you with every class we have together." Needing to break the look he's giving me, I lower my gaze to the floor. His eyes are*

*intense, like they can read my every thought, intense.*

*It's as if he has this magnetic pull on me, because my eyes automatically drift back to his. Once again, his insane baby blues dare me.*

*"Oh yeah? Come on, don't hold out on me. You're my only friend here, what had you laughing?" He continues to stare at me, but now he unleashes his sexy grin.*

*Friend? His sideways smirk only amplifies his hotness. It's not an innocent smile either, nope, it's a panty melting smile. Dimples and all.*

*The effect he is having on me is utterly impossible for me to comprehend. Flustered doesn't even begin to describe it. I'm anxiously trying to find my voice, while I nervously bite the inside of my cheek.*

*Raising my head, I say, "Not to sound weird, but I know which room is most likely your bedroom." Closing my eyes, I try to hold back my laugh. I know how wrong that sounded. Instead of embarrassing myself further, I bite the head of my pencil. Hard.*

*"Well now, that's a new line for sure." He said, with a slight clearing of his throat.*

I can't help but drag my eyes back to his face. His eyes are wide, and his cheeks flushed a lovely shade of pink as his Cheshire cat smile widens. I wonder what he's thinking right now.

*Feeling the need to explain, I'm annoyed that he thinks I'm hitting on him. Was I? Perhaps.*

*"What I meant to say is, my friend used to live there. I've been in your house many times." He's just smirking at me, so I hold my hands up surrendering. "Nothing weird about it, I just know the house well. Which is why I can narrow your*

*room down to two possibilities." I just can't help myself! The thought of me knowing something private about him does put a smile on my face. Thinking of him alone in his room, oh man! I need to stop this daydream.*

*He watches me, casually playing with his lower lip. "Oh, now this is getting good. What's your name, pretty girl?"*

*I kept my stare solely focused on his eyes, speechless. No one ever called me that. My mouth must be open, because he puts his finger under my chin and gently closes it for me.*

*His brow slowly inches upward. "Are you okay, pretty girl?"*

*Pulling me out of my Micah trance, I can't help but shake my head mumbling. "Oh, sorry. Not sure why you're calling me that, but my name is Elsa." I slowly say under my breath. "Everyone calls me El."*

*His eyes squint. "Do you have a last name Elsa, who goes by El?" His voice ever so charming.*

*"Winters. Elsa Winters." I'm still in my Micah trance; his baby blues have me under this powerful spell. Those eyes!*

Hopelessly, I close my book. There is no way I will be able to read right now. My every thought is of him. His eyes I can still see, his voice, I can still hear.

"Jesus Elsa, are you ever going to forget him?" I realize I'm asking myself this same question yet again. Wiping the tears that sting my eyes, I remember the last thing Micah said to me after we had sex our one and only time.

*Kissing me behind my ear, he whispered, "You changed my world, pretty girl."*

Just like that...my dream ends!

I suddenly focus on the noise coming from the room next door. Liza, my roommate, is in her room with her boyfriend. I never heard them come in. I have yet to meet this one. I figured I'd wait to meet him, see if he lasted longer than the last guy did. That poor sap never made it a week. Liza is never alone for long, I have no clue where she keeps finding them.

In all seriousness, the knocking on the wall as her bed bangs against it has me realizing this night is not going to end soon enough. I pick my book back up and curl up for the long night ahead.

# CHAPTER
## *Three*

"Oh shut it. You were so loud with that guy last night, I had to put my pillow over my head." The love fest lasted over an hour, so I was forced to play music and use my pillow to drown them out. My attempt to read did not work.

Liza's face beams. "Pip, he is amazing. More like lick-a-licious, that's a better word." She calls me Pip. It's the nickname she's blessed me with. I don't argue it, like when have I ever won an argument with Liza? Never.

"That's over one word and I'm not sure it's even a word," I say with a slight smirk in my sleepless state. I'm in need of coffee.

In her current dream state, Liza whispers, "Yeah, but it fits him." Her eye's glaze over every time she talks about him.

"Why did he leave so early? Or should I ask, am I ever going to meet this one?" I had to ask. Seeing her so smitten, I really need to see this guy with my own eyes.

With a nod of her head, she says, "Of course you are. It's

just been bad timing so far." Bad timing is what she calls it, but I was wondering if she is doing it on purpose. She must really like this one. She is acting in a different manner that's for sure. This is the first time my roommate has ever acted this way over a guy.

"Get dressed. Let's go get coffee and see Tristan," I say, getting up off the couch. I needed to get some much-needed caffeine, and there's no better place than the Starbucks down the street from our apartment. Tristan is an added bonus. He works there and overtime we've gotten to be good friends.

"Oh heck yes," she frantically replies. "Let's go."

We walk the few blocks instead of driving since it was beautiful outside. The sun is shining, not a cloud in the sky.

Most days, Liza drives me crazy, but she's my only real friend other than Nick. I met Liza the day she started at the Dental Office I work for as a receptionist. Dr. Jeffrey Davis was my actual dentist who hired me while fixing a cavity shortly after I graduated high school. Funny story, he loves to tell it to our patients every chance he gets, hiring me right out of the chair.

Liza and I formed an instant friendship, and as luck would have it, we moved in together a few months later. It was a huge relief because I got to get away from under my parents constant eye. The relationship I have with my parents is strained at best. It's such a long, sad story. Meeting Liza was a blessing, and I would kindly put up with her wild behavior if it means I get to live away from my parents.

Nick, I met a few years back, he's my closest friend other than Liza. I'm not one to hang around many people, I keep to myself, if possible. Liza and Nick are the ones always reminding me I'm twenty-one, not forty-one. Nick's the only one who knows *all* of my secrets. Liza, not so much. I've only told her the basics. A boy had hurt me in the past, and the rest stays guarded in the confines of my heart. If it weren't for a drunken night with Nick a while ago, he would not know all that he does. They say loose lips sink ships. Yeah, that's pretty much true.

Walking into Starbucks, the aroma of coffee engulfs me, and I'm desperate to get my daily cup of Joe. My face lights up when I see my favorite barista, Tristan. His face could light up any room. He's just that kind of person who brightens up your day. He and I hit it off from the first coffee I ordered here. If it weren't for the fact that he likes to hit on my friend Nick, I might have tried to date him myself.

"There's my girl. Double Mocha Latte is coming right up. You look like you need it, I might add." Tristan says, as he is punching my order into the register.

"Thanks, buddy," I yawn, "Liza kept me up all night." I say with an eye roll, slightly joking.

"Oh please, it was so worth it. Sorry, Pip." Liza's nickname for me is definitely an odd one. I swear, the girl has never used my real name. She once told me I reminded her of a pip-squeak, and for that reason it stuck. Go figure!

Liza can't help gloating. She's been on cloud nine ever since she met Ace a few weeks ago. Grabbing my coffee and her tea, we sit by the window. Sitting down, I realize just how tired I am. I'm so tired, my bones ache.

"So you want to know what's weird?" Liza looks at me with her lips puckered up. Something is on her mind.

I stare at her, wondering if I want to answer her. "No idea, but I'm sure you will fill me in, though."

"Well, it is clear that you were totally screwed over by this dick in your past, right?"

I roll my eyes, *not this again.*

With a big sigh, I whisper, "Well, that's not entirely accurate, but whatever." I'm never one to enjoy discussing my past.

"Anyway, Ace was telling me he has had a hard time getting over a girl from his past. He won't talk about her, but he wanted to let me know why he's careful and wants to take things slow."

Okay, this is news to me. She has mentioned how hot he is, and how beautiful he makes her feel. The rest is all new, and I do not understand where she is going with this.

Taking a sip of her tea, she looks off into the distance. "Tell me something about him, Pip. You don't tell me anything about what happened, not even his name. I have never pried but why the hell can't you just get over him?"

My moan lasts longer than I intend. "Oh Liza, there is just too much to relive it all. It's best to leave it where it is."

Without pausing, she asks. "Why did things end?"

Looking into her curious brown eyes, my mind drifts back. That question haunts me to this very day. How our marvelous one night together had changed my life forever. After that evening, things changed drastically. Micah became distant. I knew he never regretted it, but things were not the same. The short explanation I got is he had family issues to work out. Whatever it was, it took him from me. Not a month later, Micah had left. He joined the Air Force Academy earlier than originally planned. I learned he left school, being privately tutored so he could earn his diploma before heading to the academy. He was older than I, and only needed a few more credits to graduate. His father, and his father before him had all been in the military. Dave Taylor had connections in high places from what Micah had mentioned, at one time.

He had his life planned out, and apparently I would not be a part of it. I had to take a back seat to the larger picture. It happened so fast. One minute I'm in his arms, in his bed and the next, I'm on the outside. The girl he said he loved was a girl he needed distance from as he lived his dream. The idea his family expected of him. A note and a brief phone call were all I received. Life stood still, and shock took over. Losing him tore me apart and left me confused. Something did not add up and if losing him wasn't bad enough, I certainly wasn't prepared for the unexpected gift from our one night together.

Loving Micah was easy, hearing him say he loved me was an unexpected blessing. Even more surprising was finding out about the life we created from our love.

Shaking away those memories, I concentrate on Liza, who is eyeing me carefully. Finding my voice, I explain. "He never loved me though, not like he said he did. He moved on." I leave it at that as I fight back my emotions. How could he truly love and then leave?

"You and Ace need to get together and see if you can both help one another move past it all." Hearing her say this, I'm baffled because she is being sincere.

Seriously, there is *no way* I'm sharing my life with a stranger.

"Not happening, let's get out of here." I stand up a bit mortified.

With a wave of my hand at Tristan, we head back home. My phone rings in my purse. Holding it, I glance and see it's Nick calling. He always seems to know when I need him the most. Over the years he's been the one to calm my nerves. He just understands me.

Sighing, I answer, knowing he will help me forget one of the most painful times I had to just relive. "Hello Nick," I say with an amused grin. Just saying his name, I feel better.

"Well, good morning beautiful. Where the hell are you two?" He asks, just as I can see him standing outside our building with the phone up to his ear.

My heart skips as I say, "Heading your way."

# CHAPTER

*Four*

Pulling a shirt over my head, I'm singing the lyrics to *Fight Song* by Rachel Platten, making my way to the kitchen. Nick came in with us when we got back from Starbucks and stayed until his questions were too much for me to handle. I swear, sometimes he needs to learn to back off. Announcing I was going to take a shower, I hoped he would take the hint and leave. It worked.

He pushed me today with lots of personal questions, starting with asking when the last time I spoke with my parents was. To be honest, I'm not sure. Two weeks, maybe. It's an uncomfortable subject to approach with me, and he knows why.

To make matters worse, Nick is their investment banker. That small rift between us is another reason I don't date him. He likes my parents way too much, and he knows the way they treated me back in high school. He knows it all.

"You realize Elsa, they also lost out, it's not only you."

*Their choice, not mine, I scream in my mind.*

That comment from him made me want to punch his lights out. He may think he was trying to be helpful, but I did not take it that way. He was sticking his nose where it was not welcome.

Grabbing water from the refrigerator, I shake off all of those thoughts and sit down next to a grinning Liza who is typing into her phone a mile a minute. "Wow, must be good from the look on your face," I revealed.

"Oh my God, he is so freaking hot." Liza expressed, dropping the phone in her lap. Throwing her head back against the couch, she let out a passionate sigh. "He's getting more brave and sexy in his messages." Licking her finger, she holds it up giving a sizzling sound. "He may be the one."

She can't hide her giddiness for him. Its non-stop talk about the things he makes her feel. A part of me is beyond happy to see her so into this guy, then another part of me feels like I'm missing out. All those firsts you get to have with someone, yeah, I miss those.

Forcing a drink of water, I'm drowning out my slight pang of jealousy. I find it hard to breathe as my chest constricts. "At least one of us is lucky. I can dream of the wild sex I'm not having, through you." Shifting my head, I realize she is not paying any attention at all. She's blushing and typing back a message.

It's time like these that Micah filters in my mind. I have yet to allow myself to date anyone. Part of the problem is, no one has ever appealed to me. Not the way Micah did. I can't seem to escape him, no matter how hard I've tried. Maybe a part of me doesn't want to forget him. Forgetting him might mean I will also forget a part of me that is locked down tight in my heart. That part of my heart, cries out in the middle of the night, just enough to make sure I never forget. It's highly unlikely, but then again, I realize just how much of a broken mess I am.

Liza's fingers freeze as she pauses, it's then I notice she is studying me. I can imagine the look on my face. It's the same look I always have when I remember back to my thoughts that still haunt me.

"You're spacing out again, Pip. Jesus, honey, you need to either let him go, or hunt his ass down. What's it been, four or five years?" Her bitchiness hurts, because she has no clue it's not just him I miss. No, my pain doesn't extend to just him. Her attitude is yet another reason I've not told her about it.

I don't answer her right away. Finding peace to let it all go is not a feat I've been able to carry out yet. She drops it, for now.

"Okay, Ace is taking me out for dinner and drinks. What to wear?" Her puzzled expression diminishes as her eyes go wide, looking straight at me. I know what she's doing, she wants to borrow one of my dresses. I love to buy beautiful clothes. Clothes I never wear, but idiotically enough, when I see a bargain, I have to buy it.

My groan and eye rolling don't even phase her in the least. "Which one do you want?" I say with a deep, weighted sigh.

I'm sure I don't even need to ask, she's been eyeing this one since the day I hung it up in my closet. It's a black, form fitted dress with sequins around the neck and down each side. The plunging neckline is perfect for showing off your chest. Someday I would dare myself to wear it out.

Liza jumped up off the couch screeching. "Oh goodie, the black one."

See? I knew it. The dress is new with the tags still attached. Sometimes I wish we were not around the same size. *Wonder what she would do then?* She's marginally taller than me at around 5'5", this dress would hit my knees, but for her, it will rest higher on her thighs. We also have similar features, the only difference is my chest is larger than hers. Her hair is thick and lustrous as it flows against her back. My hair is long and most days pulled back in a ponytail. I dress for simplicity where Liza goes for style. Her blonde hair to my dark brown. We are close to what matters when you want to swap clothes. Looking at her, she is the perfect image of a Barbie Doll.

"Go on girlfriend, get beautified," I'm happy knowing one of us would get some use out of this spectacular dress.

"Sweet, love you so much. You're the best, ever." She says, before blowing me a kiss.

Her eyes twinkle as the sequins in the dress bounce off the light in my room. "Yeah, yeah, I hear ya. Go get ready." A part of me is excited to see how great she will look in it. All I can think is I sure hope her guy, Ace, is ready for her dressed up in this outfit. When Liza gets all dressed up to go out, she is a total knockout. The girl is gorgeous, witty and damn funny. She's the total package, plus she comes with no baggage. The complete opposite of me.

My phone rings, interrupting my thoughts. My smile widens as I see his name pop up. Yet again, he knows when I need him.

"Hello."

"What's up girl?" Nick is always happy and over the top full of energy. I call him the energizer bunny. Whenever I do, he always responds with, "want to find out for yourself?" I've known him for some time, and his dream is to take our friendship to the next level. I'm the one putting the brakes on it. He's handsome and sweet, but I'm not ready to take that next step with him. He's been my best friend for so long and I don't want to ruin that. My parents have been the other issue. We need to talk about, for sure.

"Not much, we need to talk about what happened earlier." It's a way to remind him how annoyed I was with him earlier today.

"I know, but save it. I'm sitting here waiting for you to call and ask me out on a date, I can make it up to you then?"

I can't help but laugh. "You don't stop, do you? But to be honest, it's nice to know I have you at my beck and call, waiting for me. I'm a lucky girl." Honest to God, this boy is too good to me.

His sudden growl lets me know he's a tad bit frustrated. "That you are. Now if I could just get you to take me up on my offer to take us to the next level, I would be one damn lucky son-of-a-bitch."

With a shake of my head, I wonder if he will ever get it. "That would be a tragedy, Nick. I refuse to ruin what friendship we have for what, sex?" I soften my tone. "You're too important, I can't lose you."

His pause lets me know he's at least pondering what I said. "Damn it El, it won't ruin a damn thing. I'm good for you and you know it. It's him, isn't it? I've never met the jackass, and I hope I never do. Not sure I could keep from beating his ass."

Oh God! "See? Right there, that would ruin it for me. I can't take that chance. Please, just don't...just be you. I need you to be my friend."

"Fine, just know I hate this. You deserve to be happy and have a life. You're like an old lady before your time. Are you happy not having sex? What the hell?"

It's a good thing he is on the phone or I might have punched him for that remark. "Oh, I am NOT. I'm living through Liza. She has enough sex for the both of us." I'm surprised by his display of anger or frustration, not sure which. I do what I always do, turn the conversation away from me to someone else, like Liza.

"TMI, that girl just scares me. Have you heard her stories with this guy, Ace? That poor bastard doesn't stand a chance with her." Nick and Liza's friendship is closer than I even realize. He seems to know more about her latest guy than I do.

I know he's only half kidding, Liza is a wild child who loves to share her sordid stories. I can't help laughing, so hard I have to wipe the tears from my eyes. "Oh stop it, she's getting ready now for a hot date with him."

"And let me guess, she has raided your closet. So she has a hot looking outfit ready for her hot and heavy sex she will have later tonight? Not to mention, when she returns it, you can be left to clean her stained dress. Or should I say your stained dress. The least she could do is wash the damn thing before she returns it. Shit is gross." *What the hell?*

Sadly each word he speaks is the truth, and I wince hearing it. I'm not sure how he knows any of this.

"How the hell do you know she doesn't wash them before she returns them?" Okay, I'm bit horrified. I sound pathetic.

"Ah, well most times I am at your place, and I've seen her toss the clothes on your bedroom floor. Bitch has no clue." He says criticizing.

Running a hand through my hair, clearly frustrated, I let out a heavy sigh. "Listen, Liza lives for herself. It's just the way she is, and I've grown to expect her to act a certain way.

None of which surprises me anymore." Needing to change the subject. "Hey, why don't you come on over, so we can order pizza and watch a movie?"

No, hesitation. "It's a date, good looking."

"Nick, not a date, just a hangout. Now shut it, and get over here. I'm starving, and if you are not here soon, I pick the movie." I know this will drive him insane, it's a guaranteed 'see you soon,' response before he hangs up.

"Shit, on my way, your movie choices suck." Click.

*I knew that would work, and my movie choices don't suck.*

A knock comes from my door, turning around, I find Liza modeling her outfit for the evening. She's leaning against the door frame, with one had on her hip.

"Hey Pip, what do you think?" Her smile is bright as ever.

I whistle. "Wow, you look smoking hot." My mouth is left open as I take in her appearance. She looks damn sexy, her hair's curled with locks spiraled down her back. Her make-up is spot on, and her legs look like they go on for miles. Yeah, her guy...well, he's a lucky man. If he is half as sexy as her, they could set the world on fire.

Leaving my room, she's grabbing her things and getting ready to leave. She quickly turns around to face me. "You know I told Ace all about how awesome you are. He can't wait to meet you."

She's moving so fast, picking up things to add to her purse, I would say she's nervous tonight. Pausing, as if she's remembered something, she holds up her finger, grabbing her heels from the closet.

"Loves the name Pip, he says it's unique." She's leaning over trying to put on her shoe. No clue why she is telling me this.

"Um, okay," I remark slightly embarrassed.

"Liza, that's not my name. You told him my name didn't you?"

"Yeah, I told him Pip, it's your name." She says with a wink.

I give up. "Whatever, I need to get ready. Nick is coming over for a movie and dinner."

Liza all but swoons with an evil grin. "Nice, are you ever going to put that boy out of his misery and screw his brains out?" She asks and I gasp.

Covering my mouth, I swat my hand toward her squealing. "Not. Christ Liza, you know he's my friend, no matter how hard he tries for more."

To avoid another conversation about Nick, I keep my eyes glued to the floor. She pauses, then walks over and puts her arm around my shoulder.

Relaxing my shoulders, I sigh. "Hey, I'm okay. Have fun, rock his world." Raising my head, I glance at her with a grin. It's my way of letting her know I'm fine.

With eyes locked on mine, she puckers her lips. "Um, okay. I will have enough fun for the both of us." Straightening my black dress, it's like a second skin on her. She stands in front of the floor length mirror and applies ruby red lipstick to her lips. In two point five seconds, she will no doubt have it all kissed off her face. I'm watching her, puzzled, as she sticks her index finger into her mouth, wraps her lips tightly around it and pulls it out. When she pushes it back in, my face tightens. *What the hell is she doing?*

Noticing my bewildered expression she says with a shrug of her shoulder. "Oh shit, you wouldn't know this little trick."

*Ouch!* "When you apply your lipstick, push your finger in and out keeping your lips tight. The extra lipstick comes off on your finger and not on your teeth. Simple and works like a dream." Smacking her lips, she seems satisfied with her look, and not a second thought to her insult.

I am clueless where she learned this trick. I nod to agree with her, not caring since I never wear lipstick. Turning I leave the room to order pizza from our phone in the kitchen.

Liza informs me with a huff that Ace is not coming up to the apartment, she is going to meet him at the bar. I'm a bit sad I won't get to meet this handsome stranger, yet again. With the stories I've heard about him, my curiosity is more than piqued. To hear Liza talk, he is this sexy beast. I wave her off and send her on her way. The minute she walks out the door, I finally relax. Liza can be intense.

Soon after she leaves, Nick shows up for movie night. We watched the Hunger Games. I'm a sucker for it. I've even read the books. Sprawled out watching the end of the first movie, my phone beeps with an incoming text.

"Liza." We both say to one another.

Glancing at my phone. "What the hell?" Once again, we say it at the same time. It's a picture...of a guy's ass...like a guy's ass in tight jeans.

My eyes widen when it finally registers. "Oh, my God. She's sending me a picture of Ace's ass." We both blurt out laughing, it's so Liza to do something like this. More than amused, I keep my eyes glued to the picture. I have to admit, it's a sweet ass.

I decide to text back.

**Me: Bet you will grab that ass later. BTW: NICE**

*ASS!*

Two seconds later.

**Liza: It's Ace!**

*No Shit!*

Nick and I roll our eyes, *of course*, it's Ace. Who the hell else would it be? Unless she is snapping pictures of random guys in front of her date. Hearing her talk, Ace is an all-male macho who was in the military. Another reason I want to meet him. I knew Micah went into the Air Force, would Ace know him? No idea, but you never know. I never speak of Micah, not even to Liza.

Hours later, I'm asleep in bed when I hear my phone beep. *Great!*

Of course, it's Liza.

Sleepy eyed, I cover my mouth looking at the picture of a half naked guy sleeping on his stomach. The frame is of his backside, his legs, his ass and half of his muscular back. *Good Lord.*

Half asleep, I yawn typing a message back to her.

**Me: Jump his bones again and go to sleep. Good Lord, he is HOT!**

Great. I roll my eyes, knowing I will go to sleep with these images stuck in my mind. *Oh well, at least one of us is having a good time.*

# CHAPTER
## *Five*

After a week from hell, I'm beyond ready for the weekend. Earlier today, I endured a tense filled conversation with my mother. It boggles my mind that still to this day, she thinks I could just forget about what my she and my father forced me do and believe I'm okay. That my feelings never really mattered or counted. I need a drink after talking with her, and indeed that's what I've planned for tonight. It's Friday and even better pay-day. Right after work, I worked out, hitting the bags to release my pent up frustrations. It was easy, I imagined my mother's face and my anger toward her escaped with every swing of my fists. An hour later, I'm showered up and ready to have fun.

Dancing has always helped me let go, losing myself in the music. Each word and deep, soulful beat, is like a puppet master pulling the strings, and swaying my body to the music.

Liza, Nick and I head out to Blaze. It's a great place to hang out and dance. Tonight I don't mind a crowd, in fact,

I'm more than ready for the bump and grind of bodies on the dance floor.

Sweat beads my face. Slowly trickling down my chest, it pools in my bra. My slightly see-through black shirt does not leave much to the imagination. My girls are busting out, with the help of my black satin push-up bra. Tonight was all about feeling sexy...desired even. In my drunken state, that's exactly how I feel. I sway my hips, bumping and grinding against the sweaty bodies around me. Tonight, I like being around people.

My mother had to remind me, yet again, of the many mistakes I've made in the past. Always hounding me, she never just lets me move on with my life. I blame my bad attitude tonight on her. I've shut my brain off for the night. It's time to let loose.

Liza's dancing next to me, fuming upset that Ace has not shown up yet. He was supposed to meet us here. Presently rubbing up behind me is Nick, taking full advantage of my playful mood. Whatever cologne he has on tonight, well, let's just say it's driving me crazy. Brittany Spears is singing about her being a Naughty Bitchy Sexy girl, and I love it. Her words sway my mind and body.

I let my mind and body take a mini vacation tonight, the years of not allowing myself to feel anything other than regret and sorrow have taken their toll. Tonight, my naughty side joins forces with my dire, sexual frustrations. Right now, they are roaring. Turning to face Nick straight on, I grind my hips against his. Pulling on his shirt, I slam our bodies together in one big huff. Nick's hands wrap around my hips and his face beams, pleasantly surprised.

Nick is taller than me, like most people. He is 5'9, slender, dark hair and has bright green eyes. A total looker and to sweeten the pot, he's wanted me for years. All these years I have denied myself going there with him...until now. I'm wondering what the hell is wrong with me. He's the only one who knows my darkest secrets, yet he still wants me. Why is it tonight, for the very first time, I can see how perfect he is?

He's looking like a piece of steak, and I'm a sweaty lioness in heat. Oh God, let me roar. Just tonight, allow me to be brave enough to follow through with my desires and not regret it in the morning.

Letting my inner goddess explore, Nick leans next to my ear. "El, what the hell has gotten into you?"

Desperately wanting to feel his lips on me, I lean his way. His lips touch my ear and I instantly shiver.

His lips tickle my skin as they curve into a smile. "Oh Jesus, what the hell are you doing? Don't play with fire, El." He says in my ear with a deep sexy moan.

Trying to act sexy, I do my best to dance with confidence, but I don't have a clue what I'm doing. I'm not this girl, but tonight I want to be. Running my hands over his shoulders, I reach the back of his neck, and pull him closer. "Do you like what you see, Nicholas?" I never call him by his full name.

Nick firmly tightens his hands on my hips. "Oh, are you trying to turn me on, you tease?" *Ummm, yes!*

My wild flare earns me a slap on the shoulder from a very puzzled looking Liza. "What the hell are you doing?" She's giving me a puzzled look as if to ask 'have you lost your mind?'

I shrug my shoulder, whatever.

"Okay, Pip. Let's take you to the ladies' room, so you can cool off before you do something you might regret." Pulling on my arm, I'm being hauled off the dance floor. I glance back over my shoulder to look at Nick, who has stopped dancing, and is now running a hand through his messy hair. He looks flustered. *Maybe I can do sexy!*

Pushing the door open, Liza wastes no time, shouting. "What are you doing, are you crazy?"

Really? Her icy tone pisses me off, in my current state of mind. I can't hide my anger. Rolling my eyes, I'm ready to let her have it. Why the hell can't I have fun without being called out for it? "I don't know, but..." throwing my hands up, I slide against the wall. "I just want to be wanted, Liza. Do you know how freaking long it's been since anyone has held me, or hell, even wanted me?"

Her face relaxes and shoulders drop. "Of course I know, but Pip, you let no one near you. Believe me, there are plenty of guys who would love to take you out. What about the guy you have out there?"

I know Liza is talking about Nick without her having to point her finger in his direction.

Instant tears rim my eyes. I ramble. "I heard you the other night with Ace when he dropped you off. You must have thought I was sleeping, but I heard every moan. I *want...* I want that. I want to be touched... kissed. Hell, I want to get fucked. Fast and hard, soft and sweet, I need to *forget.*" I've suddenly lost my mind shouting. "I need to forget *him,* Liza. He doesn't exist... not anymore." Dropping my head, I give in and cry.

Closing the distance, Liza pulls me into a big hug. My outburst and crying fit is drawing unwanted attention as half naked girls stroll in staring at me like I'm a drunken idiot. Hell, I don't even care. I ignore the glares, finally opening up to Liza.

"I did, you know. I've tried to let him go because he's not

coming back." Pulling back from her arms, I look into her piercing, sorrow-filled eyes, and they tear up without delay. It's as if she really gets me.

With a look of determination, she says. "Screw him out of your mind once and for all. Nick cares for you, and it's not like he's ugly. That kid is hotter than hell. I told you long ago to jump his bones, try out the goods' girl." Her face softens. "This may help you. At least it will help with your pent up sexual frustration. Christ girl, five years of sexual frustration? Nick better hang on for dear life." Raising an eyebrow at me, she lets out a giggle.

Her try at making me laugh works. We both stand to dry our eyes, wiping off the smudged mascara we both have

Blotting my eyes, I glance at her in the mirror, saying, "You know, this feels right. Nick has wanted me for a long time. It's a wonder he waited this long. God, I need a drink. My mood killed my happy buzz."

"You must have this potent spell on that boy. Hell, he won't even *look* at any other girl. He's a love sick puppy. Let's go get you a drink for your nerves." She says with an arm around my shoulder.

Liza's phone must have beeped because she all of a sudden jumps a foot off the ground. Her face lights up with a smile. I know who that must be.

Liza lets out a scream. "Yeah, Ace is going to make it, after all. He will be here in an hour." Her smile fades realizing something. "He's going to miss you again, damn it." Holding her phone, she types back. "I'm telling him Pip is on the prowl tonight and is finally getting laid." What?

I gasp! "Don't tell him that, Jesus he will laugh at me when he meets me." Fixing my shirt, I pull myself together. I'm sure

Nick is wondering if I bailed on him. Liza, well, I don't have time to strangle her. I'll leave her to deal with her boy toy.

Gathering my courage to face Nick we make our way out, dodging the people standing around. Just then, Liza shouts from behind me.

"Ace told me to tell you to give him the ride of your life."

Laughing her ass off, she slaps my shoulder. Glancing back, I give her my evil eye. From the sounds of it, Ace is the perfect guy for her. Neither one of them has a filter on their mouths, and they both constantly have sex on the brain.

We find Nick sitting at the bar nursing his beer. When his eyes land on mine, it's as if I'm seeing him for the first time. It's so clear at this moment, I feel this magnetic pull toward him. Not sure if it's the alcohol talking or I have finally told myself it's okay. Feeling more confident I give him my most sexy smile, hoping he understands what I'm trying to say to him. Our eyes communicate, and he gets up and opens his arms for me. Not hesitating, I jump.

Liza laughs from behind me. "Oh, man. Nick, I think you might be in for the night of your life. All of these years of her *not* having sex are about to change." Walking by me, she slaps his shoulder, chuckling. "Take her home, big guy." She moves in and takes his seat at the bar, motioning for the bartender to bring her a beer.

Nick raises an eyebrow as he notices her order a drink. "You need a ride?"

With a sip of her beer, she responds. "Nope, sex on legs will be here soon enough. Maybe next time he will be on time so you can meet him." Her disappointment is all too evident.

"Do you want us to stay and wait for you?" Nick asks her, while holding onto me as I rub my hips against his thigh.

Eyeing my odd behavior, she laughs. "From the look of Pip, she is going to dry hump you right here."

Nick laughs, but then grimaces. "She can hump away, but you might be right. I need to get her home before she sobers up and changes her damn mind."

To protest, I reach out and slap his chest. "First, I'm right here, and secondly, I will not change my mind. We both know this should have happened a long time ago. I'm ready."

Shocked to hear those words from me, his eyes widen. "Shit, I need to get her out of here, and quick." His grimace lingers and then it hits me. He's pulling on the front of his jeans, the source of his discomfort is now visible. The bulge in his pants looks like a python trying to get loose. Sweet Jesus. This boy does not lack in the male department.

Our eyes lower to Nick's crotch when Liza spits out her beer and coughs. "Oh my God, don't let that thing loose in here. Damn Pip, you are in for a night." Liza reaches over to bump Nick's shoulder.. "Just make sure she can walk tomorrow, we're going shopping."

*Very Funny.*

"Oh, I'll take good care of my girl here." The way his eyes light up when he says 'my girl' warms my heart.

"You both realize I'm right here, in the same room with you both. Take me home before I chicken out." I say, directing my attention to a very wound up Nick.

That does the trick. My arm is being pulled out of its socket by Nick, who is making a mad dash for the entrance. Liza was laughing so hard, she yelled at us before the door shuts.

"You go girl; Lord knows you deserve it."

# CHAPTER
## *Six*

*D*esire overtakes my onslaught of nerves, and my body is set ablaze as Nick takes his time peeling me out of my clothes. When I'm down to my matching black bra and panties, he licks his lips, ready to devour me. My gaze slowly connects with his lust filled eyes. My attempts to calm myself diminish the minute his lips fall open. His eyes spark, finally having me where he always dreamt he would. His shaking hands seem unsure where to touch me first.

Tenderly, he places a kiss on my shoulder, as he whispers in my ear, "My God, you're so beautiful." Walking around me, he traces his finger to my neck before delicately trailing it down between my aching breasts. His touch causes shivers to cascade down my spine. The soft touch is foreign, but I ache for more. My eyes drift closed as a flurry of emotions flood my head and my heart. Every touch echoes another set of hands that had softly traced every inch of my body. Unmistakable hands forever cemented in my mind. No matter how long ago it was, I'll always remember. *Oh God, this can't be happening right now.* Five long years have passed. How is it possible I can still remember how *he* felt? It's as if that memorable night has been forever branded in my soul.

I can feel Nick hesitantly pulling away. "I'm so sorry." My tears spring to life.

"Hey," pulling me around to face him. "Baby girl, no tears, not tonight. I won't let him in, not between us, not this evening." I swear, Nick has an ability to sense my flaws, he is just painstakingly sweet and I don't deserve him. I'm baffled as to why he would want a girl who is so hung up on a guy who is no longer in the picture.

My hands hide my face as my voice catches in my throat. "I don't understand why I'm crying, why I can't...forget." I'm so desperate to get over my past, I beg Nick. "Please, forgive me, help me to forget him."

"Hey," letting out a staggered sigh to calm himself, he cups my hands in his. "I knew this might happen. It's okay El, I prepared myself just in case." I gasp and widen my eyes horrified.

"What?"

"Just tell me one thing," he moves closer so we are nose to nose. "Do you want me, Elsa?" The obvious pain in his eyes melts me to my core. We are both hurting. I want Nick, but as much as that is true, it does not stop my brain from remembering...*him.*

I'm abruptly feeling the need to sit down as a wave of light-headedness overwhelms me. With a few calming breaths, I can't help but feel ashamed. "I do, please believe me when I say I do." The moment feels like a bucket of cold water put the flames out. I can't help shaking my head repeatedly as my voice cracks with each tear that falls. "I should have known this wouldn't work out."

Bending forward, Nick wipes away my tears. "Oh, it will work. I'm not stopping. You want me and I need to make you forget him. I need you to realize how good it can be between us. Let me love you, El. Let me be your new beginning, it's time to let him go...for good."

That pretty much sealed it for me. He's right, I need him as much as I want him. It's time for a new beginning. It's time I moved on from *Micah*.

With a flutter in my stomach, I'm hyper-aware of the tingling sensations running rampant when our eyes lock onto one another. As I affectionately, reach out to touch his cheek, he leans in and seals his lips to mine, unleashing all of his warmth and sweetness. His plump lips are all-consuming, and before I know it, his hands wrap around me. Slowly laying me back on my bed, he sits, slowly stripping himself of his shirt. Seeing him this way and knowing what's about to happen, my fingers flex, begging to touch the trail of hair that runs down his chest, dipping below his jeans. My fingertips trace downward to unsnap his jeans. The slight moan that escapes my lips seems to spur him on, lifting his hips into my eager hands.

"Sweet Jesus El, I've wanted you to touch me like this for so long. I'm afraid I'm going to explode the minute I feel you take me in your hands." Nick can't help but cover my hand with his as I lower his zipper sliding into his boxer briefs. He may have expected me to be timid and shy, but I've lacked any sexual contact for years, so right now I'm not shy at all, but that does not ease my nervousness.

Not able to contain my utter surprise, I gasp. "Oh shit,

Nick, you're like...big." I'm so embarrassed. Did I just say that to him?

He belts out a laugh while kissing my neck. "Oh baby, you just wait."

I swallow loudly, "Okay."

In no time at all I'm stripped naked, with Nick looming over me in all his glory. He's quite beautiful. He works out, and it shows. Each muscle is proudly displayed for me to ogle.

"I'm going to take this slow, baby." I know he is trying to assure me because my body is trembling under him.

My hesitant nod has me feeling like I'm a virgin again. I might as well be since I've only had sex once. My other experience was altogether a different situation, I'm not comfortable discussing. Especially not with Nick.

I'm struggling with these memories invading my mind. To push those away, I resort to begging. "Please, I need to feel you."

He positions himself over me while, gazing into my eyes, and we just pause, staring at one another. I'm not sure what he is searching for, but the look he's giving me tells me he will make it good, that he is right for me.

"Do you trust me, El?" His emerald eyes implore me.

Not able to find my voice, I simply nod.

"Do you want me?"

I nod again.

"Thank Christ," he says, with a pant.

Leaning forward, he takes my lips again, bearing his full weight. My arms automatically wrap around him and my legs easily fall open. With the help of his hand, Nick lines himself to my center. Feeling him there, I panic and damn near jump off the bed.

"Hey baby, just feel me. Let go." Repeating this many times in my ear.

A humming noise escapes my throat.

I'm so excited. I know I'm beyond wet, more like drenched because his erection glides with ease, sliding over my clit with every stroke. Arching my back, he takes advantage and sucks a nipple into his mouth while continuing to torture me with his erection sliding up and down my center. This time, I'm losing it. The stars come out, and I scream his name.

"Holy hell, that was hot." He's breathing hard, yet I'm the one who had the over the top orgasm.

Blinking rapidly, I'm gasping for my next breath. "Oh, that was...just wow."

Each moan escaping his mouth is louder than the last in the process of kissing his way up my neck settling on my lips. "Oh baby, you are in for a surprise. Get ready, Elsa." Nick says nervously while sliding on a condom. The minute I see the green wrapper, I tense up...*terrified*. My saving grace this time is I'm on the pill and have been for years. Not that I necessarily needed it, but I'll be damned if I would allow that to happen to me again. My heart would not survive it.

"You okay?" I'm sure the look on my face is nothing less than horrific.

Blinking rapidly, I whisper, "Yeah, of course. It's just...you know."

With a nod of his head, his look tells me he understands exactly what I meant. "Baby, I'll make sure you're okay. I know what you're thinking, I also know you're on the pill. I've seen you take it for years. No worries."

Having him candidly acknowledge my pill routine, enlightens me to how much he knows about me. Lining himself up, he takes his time, kissing my neck. With my thoughts held hostage, I close my eyes fighting what I've been avoiding. I knew whenever I had sex again, Micah would no longer be the only one who would have touched me this way. Deeply, not only in my body, but my soul as well. I've kept that part reserved solely for him. *Maybe that's part of my problem.*

Nick gently pushes inside as tears escape my eyes. I've got so many different emotions swirling in my mind. My sudden panic attack halts my breathing, and I hold onto his arms with an iron grip. Nick continues to push himself into me, an inch at a time.

His body shakes over mine. "Oh shit, Elsa, you're so tight."

Those innocent words sink into my mind, cutting me deep. The slight shred of pain coming from him stretching me does nothing compared to the pain that's tearing my heart in two. Taking every inch of him he has to give, my mind echoes, "Good-bye Micah," as my tears fall for one final goodbye.

# CHAPTER
## *Seven*

 aking a quiet moment to replay my night with Nick, I'm slowly sipping coffee from my favorite mug. My lower body is sore, of course, I knew it would be. Once was not enough for him, he had taken me again before we fell asleep. Emotionally and physically, I'm drained, yet last night was very therapeutic. By allowing Nick in, I'm finally able to let Micah go. I knew it sounded crazy, but to me... it meant everything.

Liza interrupts me when she strolls into the kitchen while sporting the biggest grin possible. I bust out laughing as my tired, weary eyes hit hers.

"Well, well, well... how was it?" Her hushed voice indicates she knew Nick is still here.

Walking by her I bump her shoulder, looking around the corner to see if Nick was in fact still asleep in my room. "Oh, stop it."

"Should I go wake up sleeping beauty and ask him?" My

evil roommate snickers at me.

My cheeks instantly flush. "Hell NO!" I'm shushing her with my hands.

Raising her wicked eyebrow at me, she's snapping her fingers. "Give me the goods, how was good ole' Nick in the sack?"

I nearly choke at her question. Shaking my head, I squint my eyes, as I glare back toward her. "Oh all right," biting my lip, I slightly hesitate. "It was over the top, fantastic. He was amazingly sweet and knows how to make a girl scream." Meeting her gaze, I'm silently asking her 'does that answer your question,' but all I get is bug eyes.

She mouths the word "wow," before whistling. "My oh my. Now *that* is what I'm talking about. So are all the cobwebs cleaned out? Five years is a long ass time to go without getting any action. How sore are you, by the way?"

I'm about to open my mouth with a smart ass response when I freeze, realizing we are no longer alone.

"Hello ladies, talking shop are we?" Nick saunters in, grabs a mug and kisses me on the cheek. "Good morning, beautiful."

Closing my eyes, I breathe him in. My thoughts drift back to last night, even with my mental breakdown, he never once made me feel bad. He never wavered, he stood strong and showed me how much he wanted me. The second time around, he was just as sweet, if not more. I'm a lucky girl.

He must comprehend my daydream, because he lets out a soft laugh. "I am that awesome, aren't I?"

I'm somewhat shocked at how comfortable I feel around him this morning. Seeing how confident and funny, he is, I accidentally spit out my coffee all over him.

He jumps back, shouting out, "Damn that's hot."

Wiping my chin, I can't help chuckling. "Serves you right, sneaking up on us knowing full well we are most likely talking about you. Just be glad my aim hit your arm and not your johnson." My eyes leisurely linger down his body.

Liza laughs, holding her belly. "Pip, who the hell says johnson anymore? You are not some old lady, call it what it is, a dick."

"A 'large dick' or 'johnson' in Pip's case." Nick just has to add in his two cents. It's funny because he only addresses me by my nickname when Liza's around.

Horrified with them laughing at me, I decide to leave the room. "Oh God, you both are sick. I'm off to shower."

Slowly closing the bathroom door, I can hear Liza's soft voice grilling Nick.

"How was she last night?" Liza's trying her best to talk softly, but instead, her voice carries rather loudly.

Nick's voice softens, "She was nervous and upset at first, like I knew she would be. I was patient, took it slow, and had the best night of my life with the girl I'm crazy about."

I can hear what sounds like a slap on someone's back. "You're a good man Nick, not many guys would put up with that shit from a girl."

Liza's words sting even though she's right. What guy would want to sleep with a girl who was crying over another guy when she was naked with him? *Yeah, not many.*

Sighing, I closed the door to take my shower. While I'm rinsing my hair, an idea hits me. It's more of a way to symbolize my new life without ever forgetting my past.

Shopping with Liza today, just got a whole lot busier.

An hour later, showered up we're heading out for our day of shopping. We both got paid yesterday, so we are eager to spend some of our hard-earned money.

Nick left at the same time we did after an awkward goodbye. He grabbed me by my hips, pulled me against him, and crushed his lips to mine to cement last night's activities. The kiss differed from the one's he gave me last night. Long gone were the slow, sweet kisses, this kiss was more urgent and compelling. Fisting my hair in a firm grip, his intense gaze pleads to me.

"Don't forget last night, and don't you dare forget how much it meant."

The sincere honesty in his words meant so much. The only thing I wanted to do was reassure him. "Last night was amazing for me, you were amazing. I should be thanking you for being so patient with me, it had to be weird for you." It hurt admitting this to him.

With a shake of his head, Nick sighed with a one-sided grin. "It was perfect. No regrets. Last night was bigger than just us, I knew that, El. I'm here now, and I'm not going anywhere."

"Thanks," I said snuggling into his big arms.

Liza then interrupts our little love fest. "Christ you two, can you maul each other later? Shopping awaits, chop chop." The girl has zero patience.

Pulling out of his arms, I tell him I'll call him later. He simply replies, "you better."

Liza and I then head off for the Mall, but I had yet to mention the other little thing I decided to do today. Not sure how she'll take it either.

"ARE YOU OUT OF YOUR FREAKING MIND?" Liza is beyond shocked.

I'm calmly hold up my finger. "Umm, no. I'm doing this with or without you. Are you going to come with me?" I say to give her the opportunity to leave.

"Shit, you are serious."

"Dead." My facial expression never changes.

Realizing she will not change my mind, she tosses her hands up in the air. "Well, let's go find a good guy then. Do you know what you want?"

Smiling. "Absolutely."

I'm on a mission trying to locate a man named Jack Daniels. I kid you not, I got his name from a girl at the Gap. Generally speaking, it's pretty odd to get a referral for what I need from a lady who sells clothes for a living. But from the looks of her arms, I would say she is the perfect person to help me out.

Finally, after tracking him down, I'm now sitting in the chair of Jack Daniels, a tattoo guru according to Violet, my sales lady from the Gap. Her arms are a walking advertisement for his work. Quite impressed, I excitedly took his name and number. Lucky for me, he had time, so here I sit.

Getting his equipment ready, he then asks, "Okay, so you're sure this is what you want?"

I'm a bundle of nerves bouncing in the chair, nervous as hell. Grasping the sides of the chair, I hang on with an iron clad grip. Even though I'm anxious, I also know this is what I need to do. "Yeah, it's personal, and it stands for something lost but never forgotten."

He lets out a laugh. "Babe, if you knew how many something lost but not forgotten tattoos I've done in my lifetime, let's just say you'd be amazed. I get it, you know. It's cool, you doing this. It's your way to remember without ever letting go." He keeps his eyes locked on mine. I could not have said it better myself.

Looking over at Liza, he dismisses her with an eye roll. She is making it known she hates this idea, and she doesn't understand why I feel the need to mark my body.

Clearing my throat, I get Jack's attention. "Don't mind her, she doesn't get me."

Shaking his head, he sighs. "Yeah, I get that too."

Clearly agitated, Liza doesn't stop. "Pip, this guy does not deserve to be inked on your body. He's never coming back." Wow, her words are more like venom. I wonder if she'll ever truly understand me.

I can't help fighting back the tears that are screaming at her. "Yeah, Liza, I understand that. The tattoo is not for him, it's for me. Just leave if you don't want to be here with me." I'm irritated and hurt. She's my friend, why can't she support me? I'm getting more support and understanding from Jack and I just met him.

Just then her phone rings. *Thank God!*

"Ace, hey baby. Where are you?" She's even snippy with him. If I'm lucky, maybe she will leave to go meet him.

With a snap of her fingers, she's bitter. "Oh NO, my roommate is now getting a tattoo to remind her of this loser from high school." *No, she did not just say that.*

"LIZA." I'm beyond mad, so I shout at her.

Her voice is inching higher and louder. "Yeah, that's her. I'm not... Oh my God... I *am* here for her. Well, it's been years now, she thinks she needs to do this to get over him. No. No. Oh, okay." She says, shoving her phone in her purse with a huff.

I'm stunned, staring at her so upset right now listening to her one-sided conversation. Jack is nearly ready, and ignoring her the best he can.

Pinching her nose with her fingers, she lets out one final huff. "He thinks I should be more supportive of you. He wants me to tell you how brave you are and good luck." Her incessant eye rolling does not make me feel any better. I'm sure the way her boyfriend stuck up for me is the reason she seems put off.

"Wow. Tell him thanks." I think.

"Okay ladies," Jack turns to Liza, "Miss if you want to talk to your boyfriend, please take it outside."

I'm silently praying she does just that.

She mumbles and stomps off toward the front door. Yes, I can relax for a minute before the real pain begins. The idea of getting poked with needles does not excite me.

A half hour later, Liza strolls back in and thankfully I'm almost done. Jack is going over my home care instructions. To be honest, it wasn't so bad. I might even consider getting another one in the near future. Jack hands me a mirror to look at his masterpiece on my hip. The instant my eyes see it, they flood with tears. It's beyond beautiful and so much better than I ever imagined it could be. Jack is the tattoo guru, it's gorgeous.

"Oh my God, Jack. It's perfect."

He smiles as he cleans up. "Why thank you sweetness, it looks great on you."

Meeting his eyes, the look he gives me tells me he understands the reason for my design. I bet he hears a lot of stories behind the many tattoos he does on a daily basis. For me, it's all about healing and moving forward.

My gaze traces the intricate letters disguised in the design inked on my pale skin. Jack drew up the letters to mold into the design. The idea being I would be the only one knowing the double meaning behind them. A double M weaved sideways to form the wings of the butterfly. Symbolic for the two names forever in my heart. To this day, only a few people know who Micah is. The other letter M, well, that's my secret to tell.

# CHAPTER
## *Eight*

*L*iza's still not speaking when we return home from our day of shopping. We grabbed dinner on the way home. I had no idea that getting poked with needles would wipe me out as much as it had. Dragging my bags to my room, I pull out the beautiful dress I bought. Thanks to my new found lease on life, I'm excited to wear some of my neglected clothes that are hanging in my closet. Getting dressed up and looking pretty for Nick excites me. I want to render him speechless. I'm sure he has to be sick of seeing me in my usual attire of jeans and t-shirts. It's time for a new look, a new attitude, and a new beginning...with Nick Edwards. Who knew the banker, aka my best friend in the world, would be the one who could give me all the firsts I've been missing?

Pulling out my new silver strappy heels, I'm amazed I purchased them. They were astonishingly pricey, but to die for at the same time. It will take me a lot of overtime to pay

them off, but who cares? They were so worth it.

Checking my tattoo out in the mirror, I decided to hop in the shower before we eat dinner. I also need to call Nick before bed. On my way to the bathroom, Liza stops and informs me she's skipping dinner to go out with Ace. *Whatever*.

Turning on the hot water for my shower, I let the room fill up with steam, like my personal sauna. Dropping my clothes, I'm about to get in the shower when I hear our front door slam shut. I left the bathroom door ajar, shrugging off any notion, I'm sure it's just Liza leaving.

I'm about to shut the door when I hear voices. Somewhat surprised, not sure why, but I'm dying to hear what Liza's boyfriend sounds like. Struggling to understand them, I lean my head near the door as softly as I can. Oh my God, here I am eavesdropping, and my eyes go wide when I hear him more clearly. Wow, his voice is a lot deeper in person compared to the few times I've heard him on the phone with Liza. My stomach flip-flops because the sound of his voice surprisingly excites me.

I anxiously inch so close to the door my naked body is flat against it. It's then that I realize things are too quiet. I'm puzzled until the slight knock on the door startles me. Surprisingly, I keep my composure and remain silent, but just in case I have my hand clamped over my mouth.

"Hey, Pip, you in there?" The deep voice gives me instant butterflies.

I'm closing my eyes, cursing how excited his voice makes me feel. "Um...yeah, I'm here. Ace?" Oh God, who else would it be?

"Yeah," he says pausing. "Don't get your tattoo wet okay?"

I swear he sounds so close like he's right up against the

door. A door I'm currently standing behind naked.

"What?" Shit, it's all I can think to say in my moment of sheer panic.

"Just wanted to make sure you keep it covered up, I know it's your first one...that's all. Oh, and it's nice to sort of meet you." He offers a lingering sigh.

*Oh my God, this is so awkward.* "Okay, thank you for the advice... and it's nice to sort of meet you, too." I keep my voice cheery trying not to let my nerves show.

An awkward pause lingers before a hint of a laugh escapes his lips. "Later."

"Sure, later Ace." A wave of uneasiness consumes me, and it's an odd sensation. His voice is so pleasant, but the familiar tone is hard to pinpoint. I quickly dismiss it, chalking it up to nerves. It's just me, I need to let him go. I cannot think every guy out there, is him. It's not Micah. They're not Micah. I'm left to ponder this aching notion taking my shower, extra careful not to get my new tattoo wet.

After I showered up, I ate dinner by myself. I'm grateful Liza went out, at least I didn't have to listen to her all night. Laying in bed, I'm exhausted but I know I need to make a call.

"What are you doing?" I ask a very taciturn Nick.

"Missing you, why am I not with you, again?" Yep, he sounds depressed.

"I have to get to work early tomorrow, and I'm beyond tired. Someone kept me up late last night." I can't help saying with a smirk.

He briskly replies. "Oh, how could anyone do that to you, unless it was because he was devouring your beautiful body?" Depressed Nick is now playful Nick.

I burst out laughing. "That's right, I did have some hot guy in my bed last night."

"Speaking of last night, are you okay with all that happened?" He's so serious, his voice deepens with a hint of anxiety.

"Nick, we talked about this already. Last night was great, but." Softly I close my eyes, praying he understands.

"Yeah, I know you do, El. I'm just happy you are finally giving us a try." His voice is lighter, and I can tell he's smiling. "You're energizer bunny is ready to devour your body again."

It's hard not to smile and laugh when I'm talking to him. "You're the best, always remember that. No matter what happens, you have always been here for me and I appreciate that more than you'll ever know. I know over the years, things have not been pretty, but you never gave up on me. You were a shoulder for me to cry on." I'm on a roll and can't seem to stop the honest things I need him to hear. "You held my hand, dried my tears, and never let me cry alone. You are my best friend, and you are so important to me. It's why I hesitated to take us to the next level."

I knew I was rambling, but telling him this might help ease the news of my tattoo. If I'm lucky, he will merely see a beautiful butterfly, but he's smarter than that. He knows me too well.

"I know and I will always be here for you, no matter what happens with us. Although I see no reason we won't be together, even if we weren't, I'm your best friend."

Hoping like hell he means those words, I'm closing my eyes holding onto them. I whisper, "I'll hold you to that, you know."

"Yeah, I know you will." He replies earnestly.

"Okay, sweet Nick. I'm off to sleep. Dinner tomorrow

night?" Sounds like a good plan, and then I'll tell him about my tattoo.

"Dinner it is. Sleep tight." He acknowledges with some excitement.

"Night, best friend." I think nothing of it, this is how I always said good night to him, this is familiar.

He pauses longer than normal. "Ouch, the best friend comes out, not a good sign."

"Hey, don't interpret that the wrong way. You know I've always said that to you before when we would hang up. It slipped out, I'm sorry." I did not mean to offend him. Boy, this will take time getting used to. I now realize I need to watch what I say to him so not to hurt his feelings.

"Just giving you a hard time, girl. Enough talking, I need to go to sleep. I got a big day at work and a date tomorrow night." The excitement in his voice makes me happy.

"That's the spirit, you buying?"

"Bet your cute ass, anywhere you want to go, girl. I need to show you off. One of the many perks of our new arrangement is I get to have my hands all over you without you smacking me."

We ended the call on a good note and sleep finds me fast.
\*\*\*

Dragging my tired butt out of bed is difficult today. I'm cranky, and it's Monday, to boot. Showering up quickly as I can, I apply the cream to my bad ass tattoo, covering it with some gauze I borrowed from the dental office. Having it rub against my pants all day, did not appeal to me. Not a great way to start off my day.

Liza and I drive together since she will be working late with a patient. I'm off around five, but she has Ace picking her up, so all is good. Making sure we left enough time, we stop off at our favorite Starbucks before work. Like usual, the minute Tristan sees us, he's making our usual orders before we hit the counter.

"Tristan is going to be jealous when he finds out you did the deed with Nick. God, I can't wait to see his face." Liza, the troublemaker, is showing me her evil grin.

"You can't tell him, he will be devastated. Good Lord, Liza, you are too mean." First of all, this all so new to me. I don't want to advertise my love life all over town. And secondly, it might hurt his feelings. Tristan is way too sweet and for some silly reason, he thinks he has a shot with my new love interest. Weird.

"Don't care, this is going to be funny as hell."

Walking to the register, I'm just praying she keeps her mouth shut.

"Hello, my sweetest El and her always grumpy friend, Liza." Tristan then winked with a shrug of his shoulder, rolling his eyes at the always grumpy Liza. A name he's given her. I secretly love it.

I laugh out loud and dare sneak a peek at Liza. Her eyebrow lift tells me I'm in trouble. I cringe, holding my breath.

"Your sweetest girl jumped Nick's bones this weekend. Now how is your day Tristan?"

Ouch. That stung.

His expression freezes.

"Shut the front door, what are you saying? Holy shit... Elsa, you and my Nick? No way."

Using my hands, I'm shushing him to lower his voice. "Ssshhh. Come on, we are all adults here. Don't listen to Liza, let's just forget it." I force a smile and hope he just lets it go.

He replies, cool and calm like. "Double Mocha Latte, extra drizzle order will be held up unless you spill the beans and fast." He smirks with an evil grin that rivals Liza's. He is blackmailing me with...*coffee*! My coffee.

"Really?" I say raising my eyebrow, hand on my hip.

Wiping the counter, he keeps whistling. "Yep, let's have it, sweets. Just tell me yes or no, is he as awesome as he looks?" *Good Lord, shoot me now.*

I concede, I need my coffee. "Yes, now can I have my much-needed coffee... Please?" Batting my eyelashes, I'm smiling, trying to win him over with my sweetness.

Sizing one another up, we both crack up before Liza clears her throat for round two.

"Oh, she got a wild hair up her butt and also got a tattoo this weekend. She was a busy girl, no wonder she's in dire need of caffeine."

"LIZA!" I'm mortified, turning to her before I slap her shoulder.

Leaving Starbucks, I want to murder my best friend. This day is just not starting out well, and it's just beginning. Aargh, maybe the rest of the day will go without another hiccup.

We approach our office, Noelridge Dental. Dr. Davis, a good-looking dentist in his forties, and has an exceptional practice. I run the front office, Liza is his assistant, and we have two hygienists. We're a small office, but we all get along great. The only thing about a small office is everyone knows each other's business. Until this past weekend, it was fine. But now, it's not so great because Liza can't keep her mouth shut. By the end of the day, I know Cindy and Kathy, our hygienists, will also have a count by count rundown of my weekend.

Nick stops by frequently, each and every time he does,

they both drool over him. Yeah, the ladies here are a sucker for a pretty face, and a sweet body. Nick fits that profile just fine. My only horror will be if my boss catches wind of it all, that would be beyond embarrassing. He likes to joke with us girls and always tries to stay current with what's going on in our busy lives. I, however, draw the line at my love life.

Sitting at my desk, I'm trying to catch up on some insurance checks when the office phone rings.

"Noelridge Dental, may I help you?" As I answer the phone, I can see someone from the corner of my eye standing at my desk, ready to check in. Looking up to acknowledge whoever it may be, my eyes about drop out of their sockets. A face that's all too familiar, and it takes me back... a few years at least.

The lady on the end of the phones has asked to schedule an appointment, but I'm finding it difficult to concentrate on her at all. My attention is all too focused on the guy staring back at me with his mouth open wide in astonishment.

In a complete fog, I somehow find a date for my patient. "Mrs. Eckley, we can see you at noon on Thursday. Wonderful, see you then." I'm struggling to finish my conversation, my eyes never leaving the gentleman standing at my desk.

I find it hard to breathe. Scanning the appointment book, I try to locate his name. How is it possible I missed his name?

His sudden throat clearing tells me he's just as shocked.

"I can't believe it's you, Elsa. Wow, you look amazing, by the way." He says rapidly speaking. I think we are both in shock.

The first thing I notice is how deep his voice has gotten. He has grown into his own man. Matt was a looker before, but now he is stunning. His resemblance to Micah is remarkable, and I can't help staring...speechless.

With his raised eyebrow, it's easy to read his curious expression. "Elsa, are you okay?"

*Staring. Pausing. Shocked.*

Finally able to speak, my voice is shaky at best. "Wow, I can't believe you're here. It's been years, how are you, Matt?" When I get to his name, it comes out barely a whisper, like he's unfamiliar somehow.

Of all the things to happen today, this is not one I would have believed. Matt Taylor is standing right in front of me. Standing taller than ever, he looks even better today than he did five years ago. I'm still stunned... and shocked.

Glancing at the schedule, I mumble. "Do you have an appointment?" I correct myself almost instantly. "Of course you do," I'm embarrassed with my lack of professionalism.

"Hey," he looks at me with his head tilted, and eyes furrowed tightly. "Have you seen Micah since he's been back?"

My heart plummets when he speaks his brother's name. I'm sure my eyes are a dead giveaway, they are wide as saucers before I shut them so tight it's painful. For the love of all that is holy, *what the hell?* I'm not prepared for this moment. I've always been bothered with what could happen if I ever ran into Matt or his parents. Luckily, until today I had not. This is just *not my day*!

Swallowing my nerves, I can't let him know how long I've struggled when it came to his brother. "Um...wow, no. I had no idea he was back from where ever he went. No one told me a thing." Hell, no one said shit when I was left to pick up the pieces of my life after Micah left.

Matt tilts his head back like I've offended him. "Your parents mentioned nothing to you?" He eyes me with an odd expression.

The way he is looking at me like I'm missing something is most unnerving. I'm not only confused, I'm baffled. "My parents, no. Why would my parents know anything?" I look at him inwardly saying 'duh,' the only thing they wanted to do was kill Micah for leaving their daughter in a mess. Our parents, never talked. We all lived close, but that was it. No communication, ever.

Matt's frantically running his hand across his forehead. "Well, I told your parents shortly after Micah left. He wanted to make sure I let you know where he was. You weren't home, they said you left for your aunt's house for a while. After that, I never saw you again. Weird." His body language takes on a more relaxed position, laying his arms on the counter. "The way he left was a mess, he really wanted to talk to you. He just felt it was better to leave it alone. The more time that went on, he knew you most likely moved on as well."

"Yeah, weird." My anger overtakes me with the idea Micah once again did what *he* thought was right for *me*, never once asking me what the hell I wanted. Who the hell was he to think *he* knew better? He didn't know shit! A fact proved only a short time after he left. *Me.*

"Okay, not sure when I'll see him, but I will tell him you work here. I know he would love to catch up with you."

Oh please, don't for God's sake. Not a good idea. Not now... *Jesus.* The knot in my stomach feels like a fist to the gut. I can feel my panic attack starting to brew.

"Um, Matt, *not* a good idea. It was a long time ago. A lot has changed, and it's best we don't see one another again." My breathing's calculated, long and slow. I can't do this, I'm struggling to remain calm on the outside because my insides are being torn apart once again. *I really want a redo on this shitty Monday.*

"I'm surprised." Matt's eyes search mine carefully. "He's never forgotten about you. Talks about you, still to this day. He's always wondered what happened to you and even went to your parents house like I did. Only they told him you never forgave him for hurting you, so he decided to let you go."

*What?*

Oh God, what is he telling me? Oh no! My mind is spinning. Micah spoke to my parents. Matt talked to my parents. My parents *never* said one word to me. My mind's not able to comprehend any of this. I was able to finally let go after *five* years. Went as far to get a tattoo to symbolize my finally letting him go, and now I find out he still talks about me. What the fucking hell? This doesn't change a thing. Our time was then, not now. My life is with Nick. I'm sure Micah's changed, and I know I sure have. I honestly never expected to hear or see Micah ever again.

As the tears spill over and down my cheeks, I glance up to see Matt studying my face. Shit. I slowly turn away from him, and clutch my aching chest.

"Excuse me." I stand up and sprint to the restroom. Locking the door my head falls against it with a loud thud. After a few calming breaths, I make my way to the sink. Staring at myself in the mirror, I start to hyperventilate. Splashing cold water on my face, I concentrate on slowing my breathing like I did when I... *shit, not today.* I can't let my mind go back there. It's taken me so long to get to this point, I cannot go back now. Letting out an emotionally packed sigh, it's time I had a talk with myself. Looking in the mirror, my nose flares with each deep intake of air. "You moved on. Get it out of your system. Straighten yourself up, get your ass back out there and pretend like everything is cool."

Like that worked, nope not at all.

Defeated, I walk back to my desk. I'm praying no one caught onto my episode. Blowing out a huff, I notice all is well. Matt is no longer in the waiting area. Thankfully, Lori has taken him back to her room. Phew.

"You okay, Elsa?"

Shit, Dr. Davis is staring at me with concern. I never caught sight of him until he spoke.

"Of course," I force a smile on my somber face. "Sorry, I had to excuse myself." I'm sure the wiping under my eyes, shows how much I'm not okay at all.

"Heard you had a big weekend, Liza has been busy." He jokingly replies.

I groan. "Great. Please don't listen to her, she's on drugs." I blurt it out, not even thinking he is our boss, I'm just so upset that girl can't keep her damn mouth shut.

Slapping my hand over my mouth, I gasp. "Oh, no. No. No. I did not mean that." With my luck, I'd get the girl fired the way my day was going.

The laugh that escapes his lips put me at ease. "Don't worry, I know what you meant. Also, if you need anything, let me know. You're the best front desk girl around, and I will not lose you." He says with a reassuring hand on my shoulder.

Wide-eyed, I just stare at him, bewildered. I'm not thinking about quitting. *What the hell has Liza said, now?* "Thanks, Dr. Davis."

Thankfully, the rest of the day is uneventful. Unfortunately, my mind has been all over the place since Matt showed up out of nowhere. He left with no further incident. I think he felt sorry, because he did not say another word about his brother.

After the way I reacted, I'm sure he saw how shaken up I was.

I'm stuck having a recurring theme plague my every thought. There is a part of my past that has a real connection with Matt, his whole family if I'm honest. The idea that no one in the Taylor family knows is hurting me. I know I can never tell them, and that's what saddens me the most. Even if I could, what would be the point? It's too late.

It's nearing the end of my day and it could not come fast enough. My head has not been right since Matt was here. Liza has been busy most of the day, so I didn't have to worry about her prying too much. It worked out perfectly, I played my bizarre behavior on a bad headache, and she bought it. There was not a snowball's chance in hell, I was telling her who Matt was. Hell, I've never even told her Micah's name. I've kept that part a secret, because I never wanted a long conversation that included his name being brought up over and over again. She never pushed, and I never offered it up.

Cleaning up my desk, I glance up and see Nick walking to the front door from the parking lot. Shit, dinner. Oh man, this is the last thing I need tonight. How the hell do I get out of dinner? Simple. I don't. I suck it up. Nick does not need to find out about this little hiccup.

Opening the door, he says, "Hey beautiful girl, ready for dinner?" His emerald eyes sparkle drinking me in.

Just like that, my frown turns into a smile, a genuine smile. Nick just knows me. He's exactly what I need to forget my crappy day. Straightening out my head, I hold up my finger to let him know I'll be ready soon. "Give me a few and we can head out."

Giving my area a once over, I grab my purse and reach for the door handle. Liza is working late with a patient. They have another hour ahead of them. Knowing her boyfriend is coming to pick her up, I'm ready to go. With my hand on the door, the phone rings, and I ponder on whether to answer it or let it go to the recording. "What now." I let go of the door handle to answer it.

"Noelridge Dental, can I help you?" My voice is marginally stressed.

*An awkward pause follows.*

"Elsa, is that you?"

"Yes, this is Elsa, can I help you?" I'm not paying much attention, because the file on my desk needs filing. Not thinking much else, I turn to do just that saying the alphabet in my head, to make sure the chart is filed correctly.

"Oh my God, this is you." His voice softens to a whisper.

It's then I freeze. A burst of adrenaline blasts my body like a locomotive  My heart slams out of my chest and hits the floor.

*HOLY SHIT. HOLY SHIT. HOLY SHIT.*

"Micah." Saying his name ignites a tingling sensation across my body.

Taking every ounce of strength I have in me, I whisper his name with my eyes squeezed shut. My racing heart feels like it might explode. Damn near knocking the wind out of me, my legs give out. Luckily, my chair catches me. Upon opening my eyes, the first thing I see is Nick standing in the doorway, staring right at me.

# CHAPTER
## *Nine*

My head's spinning, and the awkward silence is almost too much to bear. I'm clueless what to say to him, and by the lack of words coming from him, I can only guess he is feeling the same way. The shock on Nick's face gives way to the look of horror on mine. This day is going to kill me yet. So many emotions are running through my mind. Holding my hand over my mouth, I can feel the tears threatening to escape.

Nick's startled expression abruptly changes to a murderous stare. He's watching me fall apart in front of his eyes. I know the more I crumble apart, the more his look transforms into hatred.

Clearing my mind and throat, I'm desperate to make Micah understand. He's repeatedly asked me to talk with him. With him on the phone, and Nick breathing down my neck, all I want to do is escape.

Fiddling with my necklace, my voice trembles. "Micah,

I'm not sure this is a good idea." My hushed tone carries more like a whisper with every scorchingly hot tear that ebbs my cheeks. Streaming, each tear feels like hot lava, descending, just like my resolve.

Micah's voice breaks into his own set of sobs. "Elsa, I need to talk to you. There are things you don't know, and I need to tell you before you find out another way."

I can hear the anxiety laced with his words. I'm sure he had no idea when he woke up today, he'd ever imagine he'd be talking to me, just like I had no clue I would ever speak to him again. But, here we are. *Five years later.*

Holding the phone next to my ear, I'm struggling to find the right words. Pinching my lower lip, I'm at a loss for words. A part of me just wants to hang up on him, shutting him out. But the other part is desperate to hold onto the phone just to hear his voice.

I simply can't allow this.

"There is nothing you need to say, so please don't contact me again Micah. You have *no* idea, so just please let it go." I say timidly, as a loud sob escapes my throat. Clutching my chest, it feels like it's split wide open. I'm rocking back and forth in my chair. I can faintly hear Nick insisting I hang up the phone over my shoulder.

Micah refuses to listen, he keeps on. "No El, you need to listen to me. For the love of God, please hear me out."

His voice becomes muffled like his hand is covering his phone. "Jesus Christ, how the hell did this happen?" He is talking to someone, no idea who. It's then another male voice speaks, and I conclude it's Matt. Of course. Dammit.

Listening to them talk, I notice Nick is pacing the front room, he comes to my desk tapping his fingers on the counter.

He's beyond mad, more like fuming mad. "Hang up El, there is no need to talk to him. Don't you let him hurt you again." Nick says in a tone the matches the look of his face. Cold, loud, hard and angry.

I disagree with him. "No, he can't hurt me. Not anymore." It's then I realize he must have misinterpreted my notion because he is shouting at me now.

"Enough Elsa, tell him *enough*! You're done with him, once and for all."

My mouth hangs open, I'm surprised by his anger, and the fact he is shouting at my place of work. Holding the phone away from my face, I try to hush him using my hands. "I'm not letting him hurt me again, let me handle this, Nick." I swear the look I'm giving him should alert him to the fact to just how difficult this is. It's freaking natural that I'm shocked, but I don't need him going off the deep end. I'm not stupid, I'm just shocked, surprised maybe, but never an idiot.

At the moment the only stupid thing is all I've shared with Nick about my past with Micah. He knows too much, enough to hurt me by hurting Micah. Nick knows all of my secrets. If he ever got a hold of Micah, I know he would tell him the one secret that would destroy Micah. His primary goal would be to hurt Micah, but in doing so, he would destroy me. I cannot let that happen. It's as if my entire world is gradually falling apart. Knowing what power comes with knowing this secret, hell, I'll protect it with everything I have. I won't let anyone use it as a pawn to hurt someone else. I'll defend it like a lioness protecting her cub. A mother protecting her child.

"Who is that? Is that Nick?" Micah says with pure venom.

Pulling the phone from my face, I stare at it. How the hell does he knows Nick's name? Wait, I just said his name out loud. What the heck, my nerves are shot. I'm not thinking straight. Why the hell would I be? My past showed up today and is slowly chipping away at me. Not sure how much more of me there is to take, because once your heart is shattered, and your soul is shredded, there's not much left. Doesn't matter how strong of a person you are, there is only so much before the only thing left, is an empty shell.

Micah's frantically trying to convince me to hear him out. "Meet me at least once. Please give me a chance to explain things before it becomes a huge mess. I'm begging you, Elsa."

Micah's voice shakes the last bit of my resolve. All of these years he's haunted my dreams, and now he is on the phone begging me. How did this happen?

I need to end this. "No, please just go away. Live your life, I'm trying to do the same with mine." It's not the time nor the place to have this talk with him. Either that or I'm going to faint. Nick is going to smash the phone or better yet, Dr. Davis is going to walk up front. Any of those is not a good thing, the best option is to disconnect the call.

Determined, I'm able to use a hushed, controlled tone. "I have to go, this is not the time or place. I'm at work. Bye!" Lowering the phone, I can hear his voice through the receiver.

"Elsa, please do not hang up on me."

Oops...too late!

Nick and I come back to my place. I'm too worked up to eat or be anywhere in public. To say I'm out of my mind, would not be far from the truth, I'm a wreck. I have no idea what Micah was trying to hint at that he needed to talk about something. It's lost on me, but Nick is beyond pissed. His incessant pacing in my living room is not helping my nerves or resolve.

"Nick, for the love of God, please sit down." I'm damn near hyperventilating sitting on the couch with my arms bouncing, resting on my legs. Lowering my head, I try to calm my erratic breathing. I wasn't kidding when I said, Nick's behavior is not helping me one bit.

"What the fuck is his game, Elsa? Why even bother to call you? And what the hell did he mean to say he needs to talk to you about some huge, potential mess?" Nick's so upset he about hits the wall with his fist.

I'm staring at him like 'how the hell should I know?' Good Lord, it's been five years.

"I told you all I know. Matt was in today, and most likely that is how Micah knew to call me there. Other than that, I'm as clueless as you." I'm so in need of a drink. "It doesn't matter, there is nothing left to say. He left me, end of story. That being said, I know differently, as well as you, but he will never know any part of that, right?" I need him to swear he will keep his mouth shut if he ever has the chance to meet Micah in person.

Nick huffs out a breath sitting down next to me pulling me into his arms. "I'm sorry El, this cannot be easy for you. I just don't want you hurt. Not again, and definitely not by him." He rubs my arms with his hands.

I could not agree with him more. "Yeah, well tell my heart to catch up with my brain would ya?" Ain't that the truth. My head is light years ahead of my aching heart. With strong arms around me, I relax, letting my body slouch. The floodgates are now open, and there is little hope of them stopping anytime soon.

A sigh leaves his lips. "Wonder what he wants to tell you, though," Nick says with little to no emotion. "He's been out of the picture for so long. Now suddenly he wants to talk." I can tell he's tense when his hands slowly tighten around my body. "Well, fuck him."

I'm sure Nick is having some insecurities when it comes to Micah. The one guy I've pined over for the past five years and now suddenly he turns up, and he wants to talk to me.

Wiping my eyes, I sit up to apologize. "I'm so sorry." My words come out in a snotty mess, but I need him to realize I know this is hard for him too. Poor guy finally gets the girl and now the other half of her soul has turned up out of nowhere.

Anguish takes it toll on him. He's obsessively rubbing his hands down his face. "Oh hell, baby, I'm hurt and confused. I don't want this fucker to come in and steal you away from me. He lost you. He gave you up when you needed him the most. I was here for you...for years. It was my shoulder you cried on. My hands comforted you, and my words were the ones you sought solace in. I finally got you. You had finally let me in, and I'm scared as fuck I will lose you. To him. It's always been him." The pain in his voice matches the look on his face, and it hurts me.

His honesty is like a dagger. On one hand, I have the love of my life wanting to talk to me after all this time. On the other, my safety net, Nick, who is strong as steel, is fearful of losing the one person he's wanted for so long. The guy has never wavered from me, all the late night crying, the panic attacks, even the days I just wanted to give up, he was there.

Voices outside our apartment indicate Liza is home, most likely with Ace. Just what I don't need tonight. "Oh shit, I'm in no mood to meet her boyfriend."

Realizing they are coming in, I wipe my eyes and take a few dozen calming breaths. Nick's arms hold onto me tighter, telling me wordlessly it's going to be okay.

"What is it with you tonight? I swear you're acting weird." Liza's sounding like her usual cheerful self. *Not!*

I hear no response, so Nick and I exchange a strange look. Nick had met Ace a few times when I was either at work or not home yet, so it seems I'm the only one yet to meet him.

Going to stand up, I turn to see an agitated Liza stomping her feet. She takes in my appearance; I'm sure I look delightful crying like I have the past few hours.

She stops dead in her tracks. "What the hell is going on here?"

I swear she is ready to punch Nick, thinking he caused my unhappy state. I'm just too damn drained to explain, so I shake my head instead.

Nick, holding his hands up says, "Don't ask me, ask her?"

She pins her puzzled expression on me. Praying this day away, I'm rolling my eyes when I catch the movement behind her. Shit, I damn near forget she's not alone. I go to speak, but I'm rendered speechless as he walks in.

Now in life, you get a few surprises that render you speechless. You might even get a few that knock you on your ass. I would say right now, I got both in one giant puff of smoke.

Several things happen all at once. Not sure what came first, second or even last, but I heard mumbled words, the room started to spin out of control, and I was about to hit the floor. I swear I may have blacked out for a moment, but my hearing is crystal clear.

Liza screeches like she's right next to my ear. "Jesus Christ, what the hell happened to her. Pip, wake the fuck up?"

The next thing I hear is Nick. "Baby, oh shit, I knew this

would happen. Today was just too much. Ace, what the fuck is wrong with you? Liza what the hell is wrong with your dude, over there? He's looking like he just seen a fucking ghost."

"Who the hell knows? He's been weird all day."

Liza's has to be rubbing my arms, I can feel her icy fingers all over me.

It's then I hear it.

*I hear him.*

"Elsa." It's faint, but it's there.

"What did you just say?" No mistaking Liza's 'what the fuck moment.'

I hear a thud followed with a long extended sigh. My head is gradually coming around, and as I try to open my eyes. I'm questioning if I really want to. Feeling Nick's arms around me, and the cold fingers of Liza combing through my hair, it oddly comforts me. The spinning room starts to slow down, and everything is coming into focus. A frantic Nick and wild-eyed Liza are right in my face staring down at me. Leisurely my eyes drift to the person sitting on his knees before me with tears shimmering in his eyes. His expression is distant and lost and instantly, my heart crumbles to pieces. *It's him*, still with the bluest eyes I've ever seen.

After five long years, our eyes are intently locked to one another. My breaths catch in my chest. Staring at him for an overlong moment, I choke back a sob and whisper, "Micah."

Then...I heard two very loud gasps!

# CHAPTER
## *ten*

*I*'m quiet as a church mouse, still stunned I think. That mess, the one Micah was referring to? Yeah, it's definitely a mess. Liza throws up her arms with pure resentment, and is voicing her displeasure so loudly, I'm sure everyone in our building is getting an earful. I can't help thinking our story would make a great TV sitcom. The out of body experience I'm having right now is nothing compared to the continual shouting coming from Liza.

"I don't understand," she idly points out directing her tirade at Micah. "Don't tell me to calm the hell down. Ace, how is it possible my best friend and my boyfriend are a long lost hookup? Why go by Ace? Why not Micah?" She barely stops to take a breath. "Jesus Christ, did you know I hated you? All because of what you did to her." She then throws up hands. "I, of course, had no idea it's actually *you*."

Micah lowers his head giving it a slight shake. So many emotions flicker across his furrowed brows.

I think we all cringe, listening to her unleash her fury. She is missing the fact none of us knew, and we are all just as stunned. While her rant is never ending, the three of us are still stunned speechless. It's Ace, (aka) Micah, getting the worst of it. All the while, he is trying to get her to calm down. But his eyes are directed at me, instead. Sadly, the only thing this does is infuriate her even more.

Micah's still kneeling on the floor, at close quarters with me, nonetheless. His eyes are full of sorrow, and glistening as tears cascade down his cheeks. He admitted to us he used the name 'Ace' while in the Air Force. These days he rarely uses his given name. While he speaks, his ashen eyes are immersed solely with mine, trying to gauge my reactions as I sit and soak in his every word. To say I'm shocked as hell is an understatement. I shake my head in disbelief. My life would be any writer's dream come true. I never knew how complicated or heart-shattering my life would become, but sitting here now, lost in the eyes of the one who shattered my fragile heart, I think it's a tragic love story in the making. My thoughts, and my eyes are stuck, his amazing baby blues entrance me. I've never forgotten how piercing they were. *How is it possible we're here right now?*

This damn day can't come to an end fast enough for me. Who would have guessed that my best friend is with my ex-boyfriend? Nick's hold on me hasn't eased up, he's emanating some serious anger towards the guy he thought was simply Ace, Liza's boyfriend. But he's not, he's the guy who crushed my soul and spirit many years ago. I'm aware Micah is staring at me, and it unsettles me. This intense hold he has on me is frighteningly fierce. One of the many reasons I've avoided prolonged stares into his eyes... I'm afraid of what I may see in them. The way his body is shaking with tears streaming down his face, I think we all know what he is most likely feeling, and a part of me is hopeful for it.

"Mind telling me why you have tears in your eyes?" Nick says to a somber faced Micah.

Nick's less than friendly question to Micah has Liza and me just as curious. I guess we're all wondering why Micah is looking a bit lost. It's his tears that are not so easily explained. *Why is he crying?* He seems just as bewildered as I am. My feelings toward Micah are one thing, and I've concluded he did not feel the same toward me since I have not seen or heard from him in years. He didn't even explain why he broke it off to begin with.

Looking white as a ghost, Micah clears his throat. His hand trembles as it rests on his chin. "I had no idea, how I would feel seeing you again after all this time. It was a shock when Matt told me he saw you today. Then it dawned on me that, you work with Liza. The pieces gradually began to fit together after that." His lips curl, exposing a side smile. "Pip is not just some girl, she happens to be a girl I cared for a long time ago. And still do. Talk about a pleasant shock."

His voice trails off realizing now, all the time Liza referenced me as Pip, I was Elsa. His Elsa, from a long time ago.

"That's all she was to you?" Nick's question is more like than an accusation. "Some girl you once knew? Jesus Christ, you have no idea the hell she's been through for the past five years. You might have had a life, even lived it up, but *not* this girl. She has cried and survived hell, all because of *you!*"

Nick, not being able to contain himself, lets it all out. Micah looks pale like someone punched him in the gut, with every word Nick speaks, his winces. Frankly, I want to crawl in a hole and skip this totally fucked up day. I only wish I had time to process what all of this means, for all of us. We're all connected, one way or another.

Struggling to find my balance, my mind is in a fog. "Listen, just stop. Nick, he doesn't need or care to hear all of that. We were together back in the day, then he went to live his life. It's time I get back to mine. I'm just in shock. He is dating Liza, and I never realized it was him. It changes nothing, he's with Liza, and I'm with you. Now, can we all just get along and forget about the past mistakes." I refuse to let Micah know how much he meant to me and how badly I've struggled. Letting my guard down and openly exposing myself will only end up destroying what's left of my fragile heart.

"Like Hell!" We all snap our heads in Liza's direction. She's more frantic by each passing minute. The more her mind tries to absorb this, the more agitated she becomes.

"Why have you been so hung up on him for so long? Just how close were you two? I, for one, am not comfortable with any of this until I know what happened between you two." She says pointing her finger directly at me.

It's easy to see how hurt Liza is. Her confusion and uneasiness wash over her fidgeting body.

Nick's been muttering under his breath and having a one-sided conversation with himself. "I for one, would love to add some insight into the Elsa and Micah tragedy." Only this time, he makes sure we all hear what he has to say.

I turn to face him head on. The look on my face is daring him. He better not. I make sure my eyes say more than I'll be able to say verbally, in front of Micah. My death glare should do the trick as I openly slam him.

"*Nick!* that is enough. No one needs to hear my story. All of it is mine. I don't need or want to rehash it. Leave it alone." My poor finger is shaking like a leaf against his chest.

"What the hell is he talking about, Elsa?" Micah moves closer to me, eliminating the open space we once had between us. His body is straight as a board, but his chest is heaving deeply, and I swear I can feel his hot breaths as they hit my face. We are standing now, all of us close to one another.

I unintentionally step back from him, not liking the direction this conversation is heading. I'm inwardly praying toward the ceiling. *Breathe Elsa. Calmly cool this situation down, before it spins out of control.*

"Nothing, Micah," I say as I slowly open my praying eyes. I struggle for each breath, "You leaving like you did, hurt me. No need to relive the story, you already know it. Young girl in over her head, in love with a guy who didn't feel the same. That much was plainly evident." Lowering my eyes from his intense glare, I focus on the floor instead. I know if I keep looking at him, I will crumble. Great. Some things never change, his eyes still hold so much power over me.

His loud gasp immediately summons my attention. What I did not expect was his abrupt change in attitude. His nose is flaring with every staggered breath. One hand on rests firmly on his hip while the other rubs his lips, aggressively.

"How do you know I didn't feel the same? I was young, stupid and made mistakes. You were important, some things were just bigger than us and I had to see them through." His blue eyes are pleading with me to believe him, his expression softens with each word. Just hearing him tell me I was important to him is splitting my already aching heart in two.

I shake my head, trying not to let his words affect me, even though they are. "I'm sure you felt you needed to do just that. Matt told me some things today like you went to my parents. I never got a message or knew you ever stopped by." I can't help the tears from escaping, wondering if things would be different today if I had known.

Remembering back to that day, Micah's grin is held at bay when he lightly bites his lower lip. "Yeah, your father was not at all happy when I showed up on your doorstep. He was beyond furious for some reason."

"I know the fucking reason, you prick!" Nick shouts, and I can't help but jump.

My quiet moment when the room felt like it was just Micah and me came to a crashing halt. It pisses me off because Nick is dying to tell him my secret and I can't hide my displeasure.

"*Nick!* Shut your mouth before you say things you can't take back." I've never raised my voice to Nick, but he is pushing me to my limit.

Liza takes a few steps closer to me, questioning. "What the hell, Elsa? What are you hiding? It's obvious Nick knows." She shifts her eyes between me and Nick, waiting for one of us to answer.

My chest constricts and I'm struggling for every breath. I hate the idea of my past being aired out publicly and it may push me back to the one place I've fought so hard to escape. My head starts spinning, and I'm quickly losing what little control I have. Unable to stay upright, Nick takes a hold of me before I hit the floor.

"Nick," Micah says with his hand idly on Nick's chest. "If you know something I should know, man up and tell me. It's pretty evident witnessing Elsa faint, that there is more here than meets the eye." Micah sounds angry and he knows Nick is hiding something. Micah was never one to let things lie, he will keep pushing if he wants to know something bad enough.

Liza, for once, called me Elsa, and that is *not* a good sign. Micah is pressing Nick, who like a rabid dog, is dying to one up Micah and tell him what he knows. I have to stop this madness right *now*. I need to clear my head and find a way to get everyone settled down and out of my apartment.

Tilting my head toward Micah, I aggressively unleash my anxiety. "*NO! NO! NO!* Listen, Micah Taylor, you left me. Whatever I lived through or had to deal with, I did it on my own. I had *no one*. I did the best I could, and it doesn't matter what the hell you want right now, *you're* not getting it!" I'm so angry, my lips curl, and my nails bite in my palms. I need to stand firm. I cannot fall to pieces, at least not yet. And not in front of him.

Pleading with me, Micah holds out his shaky hand. "What are you even saying? Please tell me?" His eyes float desperately looking for any answers he can get.

My limit's reached. Raising the checkered flag, I'm done. "Out, I want you all out of here. Better yet, I'm going to my room. I can't deal with any of this right now. I've got to work tomorrow." Directing my stare at Nick, I need to warn him. "If you open your mouth about me and *my* past, I assure you, we will be finished! My feelings, and my past, they are *mine*. No one else's."

Reaching for my arms, Nick shows his defiant side. "I'm not leaving, Elsa. So get that thought out of your head."

Holding her hands up, Liza's poor body trembles. She's wrecked. "Elsa, what the hell do I do here? My best friend, who I've seen crushed over some guy, just happens to be my boyfriend. What do I do?" Her eyes dart around the room at each of us. She's searching for answers, I simply can't provide.

My heart breaks even more seeing my friend so distraught. Lost in my head, I realize I've not considered what she must be feeling. "Oh Liza, what happened with me was a long time ago. He's with you now and honestly, he hasn't done anything wrong here, not to you. You can't let this affect you and him. Neither of you." Swinging my eyes to Micah, I say. "None of this changes because of me. I'll learn to deal with it. I've made my peace, remember? I need some time myself." I'm at a loss for words. *Who the hell knows what I need about now?* "I'm not sure what to do." I'm so consumed with worry, my nerves are shot to hell. Like Liza, I'm a trembling mess.

"Elsa, can I have a few minutes alone with you. I promise after that I'll leave you alone. One thing is sure, I don't want to come between you and Liza. She loves you, and I can see how much she means to you, as well." Soft and sweet Micah is so hard to resist when he's like this.

How do I resist him? Tell him no? I've never been able to do it, so why start now?

"I'm not sure, Micah. There is not a thing we need to say to one another." I say those words, trying to convince myself that they were true. But the only truth is, I just want to run into his arms and have him hold me. Just one more time. Being this close to the one you have carried a torch for, and loved for so long, is beyond excruciating. His arms are the arms I should not want, but I crave them all the same. His lips, which are asking to talk with me alone, I want to feel them against mine, right or wrong. I want his lips, his arms, hell I want all of him. I know I can't him, but that does not stop me from wanting him. *Thank God, this is all inside my head.*

Taking a step closer, he offers me his hand. "Just let me

explain why I left. The reason I acted the way I did. Just give me that." Leaving his hand extended, he's almost begging, pleading with me to take it. *Damn it.*

Nick's adamantly shaking his head. "Fuck *no!* You're not getting near her alone."

The tension in the room is so thick, it's way beyond awkward. My gaze keeps going from the two men who are dead set on trying to psych one another out. Liza walks next to Micah, touching his arm.

"No Nick, they need to talk. It seems like they both need some closure. Ace, I mean..." She then turns her head to look at Micah. "What the hell do I call you?"

"Ace is great, Micah is okay, too." He's speaking to Liza, but his focus is still on me.

"Okay, well Ace has been weird all day, and now I know why. He needs this. I may hate it, but I also know, Pip's not going to do anything to hurt me." Liza's voice is so sweet, her words of rationale shows how great she is. I may not like the idea, but Liza and Micah might be good for one another. To be honest, I've never seen her so happy, *and it's all due to him.*

"I'm thinking about El. You all believe that this is no big deal, what the hell? I've been living with this," Nick says all the while pointing at me, "with her, how she felt, and how she still feels. Have you even questioned why she has never gotten over you?" He then takes a step toward Micah. "*She* has never gotten over you. You nearly destroyed her. You've turned her life inside out. Five years. It has taken her *five years* to move the hell on. Now you want some alone time with her? WELL FUCK YOU!" Stepping back Nick puts his arm around my shoulder, pulling me, so my back is against his chest.

All this shouting solves nothing. If I give in, I can end this night. Nodding my head, I say, "Fine, all of us can sit down and hear what you have to say. That way, no one will get their feelings hurt. No secrets." The main reason for me wanting to do it this way is so neither Nick or Liza will cause a bigger scene than they already have. Why lie? *I do not want* to be alone with him, a sudden war is being fought in my mind. The longer he is here in front of me, the more I want to sit down and talk to him. I know it's not what I should have felt, but hey, I'm human. And I've wondered for so long about what happened to him. Now, I can find out all of those answers.

"I think there are secrets that *need* to come out. Maybe if we are all honest with one another, real feelings, once and for all, can be understood." Nick is playing with Micah, and by the look on his face, I'm thinking Micah's about ready to lose it. I glance back over my shoulder to jab Nick with my elbow.

He's ignoring me and having a stare down, so I turn and shove his chest as hard as I can, to grab his attention. Yeah, that's right, remember me? "I said NO. Either you respect my wishes or you get the hell out of here."

Liza is solemnly trying to engage Micah. Unfortunately, he is beyond intrigued by all of Nick's less than subtle hints.

I hear Micah protesting, with all of us in the same room just won't work. "Elsa, please let's do this alone. It'll just take a few minutes."

I don't respond to Micah, my attention is solely on Nick, who's beyond irritated. I'm not sure who is pissing him off more. It's a toss up between Micah and me. At this point, I wholeheartedly agree with Micah, we can't do this with Nick in the room. And it will probably be better if Liza's doesn't witness it, either. I'll let Micah fill her in afterward, because I'm not even sure what he wants to tell me. Tossing my hands up, I surrender.

"Fine. My room." I say to Micah, but I keep my eyes locked on Nick's icy glare.

"Like hell!" His eyebrow arches and I swear smoke is rolling out of his ears.

*Oh no, he is not telling me what I can or can't do.* He pushes into me, so there is no space between us. He has some serious height over me, but I'm not budging. He can't intimidate me.

"Nick, either sit with Liza, or leave," reaching up I grab a hold of his chin. "I can't do this with you right now."

"Fine," he angrily replies while I still have his chin in my hand. "I'm not leaving you. Maybe if he did the same years ago, we would not be here right now."

I know he's trying to hurt Micah, but his words still make me wince. He's never hurt me like this before. I know what he is trying to do, he wants to hurt Micah, but damn, if it doesn't sting.

CLOSING MY BEDROOM door, I don't face him. Instead I stare out the window. Gazing up into the night sky, my eyes once again fill with tears, like every night before. Only tonight, I don't need to wonder where Micah is. He's in my room, and I'm scared out of my mind. Having no idea what's running through his head, I'm left contemplating whether or not he thinks I'm nuts for still holding a torch for him after all of this time. My mind even begs to wonder if he's feeling a tenth of what I've felt? I'm not sure but I sure as hell can't ask him.

Breaking the silence, he doesn't hesitate. He inches closer

to me, so very close, but he doesn't touch me. My body shivers at his close proximity. "What happened, El? What did I do to you? I'm so fucking sorry. I've never stopped thinking about you." This time he gently clasps my shoulder. "I'm so confused by whatever Nick is trying to tell me, Elsa, please open up to me." His hot breath connects with the hairs on the back of my neck, and it's so sweet.

It's then he's pulling on my elbow, and the energy that flows from his touch, well, it nearly consumes me. The minute I turn, I'm digging deep, desperately trying to figure out how to protect my heart. I need to distance myself from him. I need to be cold, distant and unaffected by him. I simply need him to leave before it's too late.

Finding my wavering courage, I swallow down the nerves, and push them away. "You said you were going to explain why you left so fast. Why not just tell me? What was so bad Micah, or so hard that would make you turned your back on me?"

to my soul, it's all consuming. I have to ask him the one thing that's bothered me for so long, and while we're being honest, I ask him as softly as I can.

"What happened with your father, Micah? Make me understand why you left the way you did."

Micah's moving us, so we're stretched out on the floor against the foot of my bed. I'm intently listening to him fill in the blanks. It's not a beautiful story, it's more of him telling me how he was forced into fulfilling his father's dream for him. At one time, following in the family's footsteps was Micah's dream, too. The minute it looked like Micah would choose me over the Air Force, it all changed. His father made the choice for him.

His father drilled it in his son's head that I was a sixteen-year-old crush, a girl he would get over. I simply was not his future or his life. Micah told his story of being pulled in two separate directions. His love for me and his family traditions. His father won, he got his wish.

"Why could you not have both, Micah? This is what I don't understand. Why not be with me and be in the Air Force? Why one or the other? Why so cut and dry?" This made no sense to me.

The sigh he lets out, signals more truth is coming. "You were a distraction for me, and my father clearly saw it, predicted it even. He insisted I enter the Air Force, with a clear head, and nothing left behind to mess with my mind. It failed, I never stopped thinking about you, the girl I met in high school. All bubbly, and sweet as hell, in this petite body. My pretty girl." He says my nickname while running his hand tenderly down my cheek.

Listening to his words, and seeing the honest look he is

giving me, I can't help but melt into his arms. My sobs overtake me as he cups my face in his big hands. Micah doesn't hesitate, he takes me into his lap and envelopes me in his arms like a blanket. I don't pull back, instead I go willingly. All of these years of wanting his arms around me, I finally have it. And it's everything I dreamed it would be.

I cry harder, grabbing his shirt as tight as I can. With my face in his neck, I let the years of sorrow escape. His smell is, so familiar. His body is leaner and stronger than it was five years ago, and he's still handsome as hell. He's matured with prominent cheekbones to his chiseled jawline. He looks more refined. He may not be mine anymore, but I need this moment with him. I need to grieve, and in doing so with him here, it's comforting in some bizarre way.

His set of sobs, have him choking up as he says. "My world was not the same without you in it. My head was so messed up, you were becoming my reason to believe in love. I'm so sorry, Elsa. Please forgive me...for being a coward." Kissing my forehead, he lets out a subtle sigh. "Forgive me for giving in to my father. I could have had both, I should have had both, my mistakes have cost me so much."

There is tightness in my chest and, I'm fighting wanting to shout out to him how much his mistakes have cost us both.

"They cost me, you, knowing you have carried all of this pain with you all of these years. I'm such a selfish bastard." He says, rubbing the back of his neck. Tears engulf us both, and I realize Liza was right. We both needed this moment, a moment to remember, reflect and maybe even forgive.

I lower the guard around my heart. "I've never stopped loving you Micah, you were my world. I was sixteen, but you were my being and my reason. Age had nothing to do with that."

Pulling back, my eyes drift into those baby blues. Filled with clear, crystal tears. Before I lose my courage, I'm struggling to find my ability to speak. "Can I ask you something?"

Micah wipes my tears with his thumb, and lets out a relaxed sigh. "Of course you can, pretty girl," he says with a smile.

His damn smile, *oh my*, it's a killer. "Why Ace and not Micah?"

Pausing for a moment, his face masks a look of pain and regret. "You were no longer the one calling my name," he eyes dart to my lips glistening with my tears, "my name was only yours to say. Coming from your lips was the only time I wanted to hear it. You were no longer with me, and I left that part of me with you. Ace was just a replacement, just like every girl since you has been." With his admission, he's searching my eyes for my reaction.

I continue to try to understand what he just said to me, trying to process it all. I'm fascinated, looking at his lips then his eyes, and I gasp at the enormity of their meaning. Our eyes hypnotized with appreciation, locked on one another, with seemingly not a care in the world. Caught up in the moment, I crush my lips to his. The salty taste of our tears melt on my tongue the minute my lips connect with his soft, wet ones. Another giant sob resonates throughout my body, only this time Micah moans, forcefully pulling me against his broad chest. The emotions pour out of each of us, can only be described as carnal. A desperate yearning we both escape in. I've lost all rational thoughts.

Running my hands through his hair, I grab it tight, yanking his head back enough so our lips part. My emotions are thundering past my lips. "I hate you so much, I have hated you for so long. God, I gave you all of me, Micah...I gave you so much, more than you know." My words drift away when our lips reconnect. The chemistry between us is just as potent as it was back then. The moment his strong, firm lips melt against mine, the burning fire in the pit of my stomach ignites. My stomach flutters as my hands tremble with unbridled lust. My connection with Micah is so surreal, it's as if our bodies remember one another. After all this time, our touches seek all the right spots to caress, nibble, and lick.

Both of our bodies ignite sparks as our lips get acquainted once again. Micah cups my ass, pressing me to him and creating just enough friction against his aching need. Every touch sets fire to my throbbing core against his very hard erection. The clothes we are wearing are the only things separating the needs and desires, each of our bodies crave.

The sensuality of his fingers caressing my hair takes me back to the times when we were sitting in his room and our study sessions took a back seat to making out, instead. Remembering what his hands could do to me, emanate more sobs from my chest. My mind reflects back on happier times, but it comes with a price. The agony I felt when he left. That brings about a overwhelming sense of loss.

Sensing my grief, I know my sad sobs will remind him of times better forgotten. Micah gently strokes my cheeks with his thumbs, wiping away my tears. "Shhh, pretty girl, I got you. You're where you should be, where you've always belonged." Our ragged breaths linger, filling the quietness of my room.

The only problem with his words is they also come at a cost, and that cost is waiting patiently in the next room. Our innocent talk has breathed life into passion and lustful kisses.

I just can't win, I'm going to hurt myself and someone else in the process. It's just wrong, but denying my heart what it wants is just devastating.

"Dammit, I'm sorry, El." Micah says breathlessly. "We shouldn't be doing this, I did not bring you in here for that. I just wanted to talk, and try to beg for your forgiveness. In an ideal world, we could all be friends." He knows he's full of shit, I'm not sure why he's even saying it. "Liza is your friend, I'm not sure how to even begin to understand how screwed this situation is." Standing, he walks to my window, and gazes up at the sky. "Shit, I'm so messed up right now, El. I'm feeling things I know I probably shouldn't." *Oh no.*

"Don't say anymore," standing up, I stop him right there. "You're with Liza, and you both seem happy. We are the past, things have to stay there. The only question is, can we be friends from this point forward? Naturally, we're going to be seeing each other." I reluctantly touch my bruising lips, and they feel like fire has been lit upon them. My mind swirls with the idea that maybe Micah and I could truly be together now. Is it possible? Can it happen? Oh my God, why am I even considering this? Of course, we can't. Too much has happened for there to ever be an 'us' again.

He turned around and is staring at me, trying to figure out what I'm thinking. Still in disbelief he's here, the pang of jealousy trickles down my spine. I know how Liza feels about him, but the question is how does he feel about her? Facing the idea that Micah might love Liza, hurts, and the green-eyed monster wants to rear its ugly head. Then there's Nick, what do I even do with him? I want to pull my hair out by its roots as I realize how much of a clusterfuck this situation has become.

Micah's hands open up to me. "Let's try to make this work.

I want to be friends with you, Elsa. I want you in my life, any possible way I can have you and if it's just as friends, then that's fine, but if it's more…"

He closes his hands letting his words trail off. I'm not sure what's going on in his mind.

Stunned and damn nearly speechless, I open my mouth a few times yet nothing comes out. I try again. "What do you mean by that?"

Very slowly, he raises his eyes to meet mine. "Just what I said, if I can't have more, then friend's it is."

"You would want more, with me? Even after all of this time?" I ask, bewildered. I'd be lying if I said that the idea does not excite a part of me, but that same part scares the shit out of me.

"Are you honestly asking me if I still care about you? Come on El, I just told you minutes ago I loved you. You belong in my arms, not his." He says directing his finger towards the living room. "This may be fucked up, but if I had my choice…I would choose you, always you."

With my mouth held open, I gasp holding my trembling fingers to my lips. "What about Liza?" I whisper.

Micah smiles with a deep sigh. "I care for Liza, and up till today, I was developing deeper feelings for her. Then suddenly, the girl I never stopped loving, walked back into my life. Hard to just walk away from that, pretty girl." His eyes dare me, his lips call to me and his head shakes at me.

Sobbing, my voice cracks, "We can't," I say continuing to shake my head as if disagreeing with him wholeheartedly. "You have Liza, and up until last weekend I was alone and sad. I gave you my final goodbye, I finally let Nick inside. Now, I'm confused and pissed and happy as hell you are here in front of me. What the hell am I to do with that, Micah?" I can't help but sit on my bed allowing my body to shake. An inner war consumes me. How do I just turn my feelings off for Nick, but then again, how do I just walk away, knowing Micah is back?

"Show me, Elsa," Micah says with a reluctant sigh.

Confused, I angle my head, unsure of what he meant. "Show you what?"

He then points to his hip. "Your tattoo, what did you get to remember me by?

Oh no, he's getting too close, no way in hell am I showing him that. Not sure why or how he remembers why I got a tattoo, then Liza's conversations remind me how and why.

My eyes gaze long into his, pleading. "I can't Micah, please don't ask that of me. It's more for me than anyone else."

"I'm shattered knowing you've been in so much pain. Baby, I want to make it better. I want you to give me a chance to make it all better."

My head screams at me *'Hell No.'*

"I can't." Knowing my heart is also screaming at me, *'stupid, wake up he is finally here.'*

"I need to wrap my head around all of this, our decisions also affect two great people. Do you remember you're with Liza?"

"Pretty girl, I'm here for you, always. Like I said, even if it's only as friends. I'll be the best goddamn friend you'll ever have. Just know I'm not walking away from you again, not ever...again."

His arm around my shoulder is his way of letting me know he's serious. Resting my head against his chest, I close my eyes and breathe him in deep. The calming effect he has on me, is beyond the best I've felt in five long years.

"Thanks for telling me your story, knowing you did care for me, even though it hurts like hell, means a lot. At least I know I was not crazy." Just knowing he loved me, gives me a small amount of satisfaction.

Breathing deeply, Micah says, "Never crazy. I never went a day without you crossing my mind. Please know that."

"Okay."

"I better go out there before Nick comes storming in here." He says with a slight laugh.

Turning, I move to get a better look at him. "What do we tell them?" I say with a nod of my head toward the living room.

"Nothing," he says with a shake of his head.

"What?" I ask snapping my head back.

"Let's just leave it as we had a talk that was five years overdue. That simple." Micah kisses the top of my head. "Just know, I carry some deep seated feelings for you. I'm here for you Elsa, always."

I tenderly respond. "Thank you for that, Micah." I give him my most genuine smile. For now, I feel okay with all of this.

"Just remember, I'm here for you, if you're ever, ready to pick up the pieces of what we had before. I'm not sure how things will turn out with Liza, knowing you're back in my life. Just know this, none of what happens with her is your fault. I just can't promise she's my future."

I don't reply, because I have no words. There goes my okay feeling. To be honest, my heart is too preoccupied with my unstable emotions to worry about theirs. I have to consider my well-being, first and foremost. Don't get me wrong, I don't want Nick or Liza hurt, but Micah needs to try at least to get me out of his head. Any promises of what could be, need to be forgotten. Too much has happened, and I'm afraid that ship has sailed...long ago.

I agree, it will be harder having him in my life instead of him out of it, but I need to stay strong and remember our lives took different paths for a reason.

I watch him as he slowly opens my door and escapes out closing the door behind him. The minute I hear my door click shut, my tears once again descend. Not a minute later my door re-opens, but a different pair of arms are pulling me against a warm chest. These set of arms, although strong, and inviting, are not the arms I seek. Knowing what is good for you and what your body wants, can be two entirely different things. Moments ago my lips were reminded of what they had missed for so long.

With my eyes clenched tight, I desperately try to hang on to the feelings of Micah's body pressed against mine. *His* lips are caressing mine, *his* hands pressed firmly into my skin, and *his* soft words whispered into my ear. The internal war to push him away is met with my desire and yearning to wrap myself in him, instead. I want to surrender, every ounce of me as I yearn for the chance to have him take control of my body again. My aching heart, combined with the wetness between my legs, only prove how much I want his hands and mouth on every inch of my body. My dream however, is interrupted.

"Are you okay, El? He didn't screw with your head, did he?" Nick's voice is sounding predatory.

A garbled laugh escapes because I was just thinking about Micah screwing with me and it's exactly what I want. Just not the way Nick is talking about. Oh God, I need to get that idea out of my mind, this minute.

Biting my lip, I try to control my heightened arousal. I need to be alone, and I need Nick to leave, so I can think straight.

Mustering a yawn, I let it linger. "I'm okay, just tired and ready to go to bed. I'm mentally exhausted."

"Want me to stay with you, tonight? Liza left with him." He says as hope shines from his eyes.

He says the exact opposite of what I wanted him to say.

Sighing, I realize he's so upset he can't even say his name. "You can call him by his name, Nick. It's Micah, and I'm not going to fall apart every time I hear it." Taking a nice, slow breath, I plead with him. "You go home, I need to be alone."

Pausing a moment, he finally gets it. "Okay," he says nodding at me. "I get it, just call me if you need to talk."

"I will and thank you. Nick, you've always been here for me."

Walking toward the door, he pauses and turns back. "I'll always be here for you." He says as if wanting to say more, but he doesn't. He smiles one last time and walks out.

Finally by myself, I'm suddenly aware how alone I really am. I strip out of my clothes, put on a pair of shorts and a tank, and find my way under my covers. The lights are off, and like every other night, I'm seeking comfort by gazing at the bright, night sky. The moon shadows are like a flash of life, finding home in the depth of the darkness in my life.

I've always found comfort in the darkness. In the shadows, my cries go unnoticed. I can fall apart, and no one is the wiser. Over time, I've found that I'm most comfortable in the dark. I can mask who I am, and I'm not judged, or frowned upon, I don't disappoint anyone, either. It's just me all, alone. Years of being alone, help me guard my heart.

Tonight, I find no comfort in gazing up at the moon. No, tonight I feel stripped, bare and exposed. I'm lost, having no clue how to act around a guy I have loved for so long. How can

I watch him in the arms of my friend, and not come unglued? When he touches her, am I going to be able to smile and be okay with it? It'd be pretty damn hard to tell yourself its okay to not want those hands to yourself instead.

While trying to fall asleep, I'm so afraid, because I've got no idea what to do. I need a plan. A plan to be happy that my friend is in the arms of the guy she adores, knowing I'm in love with him.

As I drift into slumber, I'm being pulled in a different direction. My body jerks, and moans escape my throat. I'm not sure what's going on with me in my dream until I hear it. It's faint, but it's gradually becoming clearer. It's the cry of a newborn. I know that cry, I'm being pulled back to April 5th exactly four years ago today.

# CHAPTER
*twelve*

*O*h God, my muscles ache, and I'm sore. I'm white knuckling the sheets under me with my eyes clenched shut, wishing like hell I had someone with me. The whole time I'm being stitched up I'm silently praying I'll get through this day with my sanity. I'm desperate to have someone hold my hand, telling me everything will be okay. I wished, but looking around at the sterile glances and less than warm smiles, they don't comfort me one bit. My body is shaking like a leaf, every tug of the stitches reminds me how split open I was and it damn near has me hyperventilating.

Hearing his cries, I'm frantically trying to get a look at him. They took him right away, acting as if he's not at all mine. They know he's being given up for adoption, and I'm strangled with the possibility they may never let me see him. His arms and legs move wildly, every cry escaping his mouth is a dagger piercing my heart. He's not just a baby, no, this baby is mine. No matter if it's only for a short time.

*With every tear that descends my cheeks, they are filled with joy and pain, each just as strong having to accept what will never be. I'm alone, frightened, and at the moment, having my heart ripped to shreds. Finding out he's a boy after all this time, hurts a bit more. The idea of knowing Micah has a son unsettles me more. I can picture them together, holding hands, playing ball. Realizing this will never happen, I slowly try to distance my emotions. To survive this alone, I'll have to try like hell to numb every emotion I know will hit me like a tidal wave.*

*The moment he tore his way into the world, he made his presence known. He was energetic and lively. A full head of hair from what few glances I had of him. The nursing staff paid little or no attention to me. They just carried on charting his apgar scores, never once pausing to update me on his condition. Unlike most other mothers in the delivery unit, I've got no husband, no boyfriend, or even a mom with me.*

*No, my parents made this decision for me. They went ballistic when I informed them I was indeed pregnant, at sixteen. Repeatedly, they told me I was too young for the responsibility of raising a child alone. No way could I care for a baby when I was a mere child myself. Micah's leaving, forced my hand to do this by myself. He had left right before I found out. Shocked, surprised and out of my mind scared, I had hoped I could find comfort and understanding, with my parents by my side. Well, I was dead wrong and being an only child, I had no one else. That made me miss my grandparents even more. My grandmother, Faye, she would have stood by my side without question, but my reality was what it was. No close friends, I spent what free time I had with Micah.*

*No amount of time could have prepared me for, the looks on my parents faces. To say I was a disappointment, well that would have been a notch higher from what they felt right then. With not an ounce of understanding, they informed me my baby will be their dirty little secret. They devised up a plan to not embarrass them further. Not a few days later, they stopped bickering with one another and joined forces to isolate me from my life as I knew it.*

*They pulled me out of school, home-schooled me, and by the time I was starting to show, they shipped me to my aunt Peggy's house a mere fifty miles away. They called it a 'six-month vacation.' Who the hell were they kidding? This was no six-month vacation! I was isolated to the four walls of my room, sterile white, of course. Most days I hid away watching television or reading books. When my dear aunt returned home from work, I went straight to my room. Less hassle that way. The days were long, and the nights were even longer. I never felt more alone. They were hiding me until I gave birth and gave my baby to the adoption agency. My aunt, civil at best, was as warm as my parents were. Peggy wholeheartedly agreed with them. To her, I was a loose girl who found herself knocked up by an older boy. When in reality, they had it backwards. I was a girl in love, and yes, although not planned it still happened. Life happens, and not always according to plan, either.*

*I tried time and again to explain to them; that Micah was no boy crush. He was my other half, I knew it, and had even explained it to Micah himself one afternoon. The reason I knew was simple, I've always believed whenever I found my soul mate, my reason for breathing, I would feel it all the way to my bones. It's a feeling not easily pushed aside or thrown away. It's there, and it grows until it reaches your soul, forever leaving its mark. Micah did all of that and more. No amount of time or space between us could ever touch or undo what I felt for Micah Taylor. To put it simply, he was the one. I didn't care if I was sixteen or sixty, I knew it to be true.*

*The hard facts were, a loving couple would teach my little boy all the things Micah and I wouldn't. They would wipe his tears when he cries, teach him to walk and write. In my mind, he would grow up being the spitting image of Micah. Although somewhat sad, it's this thought that comforted me over the last few very lonely months. Our baby could not be with us, but at least he'd be alive. Just knowing he's out there meant that Micah and I existed. We loved one another enough to create him. He's my proof that love does exist.*

*Later that night, my depression and sobs tore through my body in a fit of shakes. Not having one single moment throughout my pregnancy of feeling love or even being wanted has left its mark. Scars on the outside now match the scars on the inside. I've now lost my last connection with him...forever gone. During my last trimester, I spent time running my hands over my basketball of a belly knowing a part of Micah was inside me. This connection and bond kept me comforted when I felt my heart and soul losing its grip on reality.*

*My door gradually opened as my nurse, Alisha Harkins, walked in, pausing to look behind her making sure she came into my room unseen.*

*"Elsa, sweet girl, I could not forgive myself if I let them take your son without you holding him, at least once."*

*Walking over to stand next to my bed, as if it's a natural thing, she hands me the baby cradled in her arms. My eyes* fight back tears of nervousness, and my breathing ceased when I saw the baby in a pink hat. Confused, because my heart wished for a baby, but not this baby. My heart ached for a baby boy. Looking up at her utterly confused, I'm not sure why she mixed up the babies. Did she forget I had a boy? With a shake of my head, looking at her I ask, "I don't understand, why did you bring me this little girl?" Keeping my voice soft making sure not to wake the baby in her arms.

Her eyes welled with tears. "No sweet child, this is your baby. The adoption agency had us put a pink hat on him so you could not pick him if you went to the nursery. It's protocol in situations like these. He's your baby boy. He needed to be sure who is real mommy is before the agency picks him up in the morning."

She barely finished speaking when her tears now matched my own. Knowing she was most likely putting her job on the line, for what...a sixteen-year-old girl? I could not have loved her anymore at this moment. No amount of telling her how thankful I was could ever be enough. No amount of hugs could match it, either.

"Oh my God, you did this for me?" I ask, not taking my eyes off of my baby. "He's so beautiful." I had to admit, he was cute as a button. Gently rocking him in my arms, I trace his little hand with my finger. The instant he feels my touch, he reached out and grabbed a hold. Tightening his grip unleashed a new set of tears and shivers as every emotion I can think of washes over me. He's holding onto my finger as if it's his lifeline, it's a feeling I'll never forget. No one will ever take this moment from us, not my parents, not the doctors, no one. This is my moment to savor, my son, my little boy. Watching him grasping my finger, I freaking love it and my *heart rate spikes to an all-time high.*

*My once flowing tears of sorrow, morphed into happiness. Cradling him close, I kiss his head, and inhale his new born scent. My body easily recognizes him, it aches for him. Tightness burns my midsection, my uterus contracts, and my boobs throb they hurt so badly. I don't waste a minute telling him how much I love him, how much I hate that he's being taken from me. I even break open my heart more, telling him all about his daddy. When Micah's name escapes my lips, I'm haunted by the fact he has no idea he even has a son. Oh, God... Micah... please forgive me for what I'm being forced to do... Know I had no choice.*

*As my mind is consumed with Micah, I look into my son's eyes, and I rely on every ounce of strength I have to tell him the things Micah would never get the chance to. "One day, you will be just like your daddy. He's the most remarkable person I know. He doesn't know about you, but I know he would love you as much as I do." My continual, vast-flowing tears make it difficult to see his cute little face. His cheeks are so big he looks like a cherub. Somewhat chuckling, I remember back to my own baby pictures. I had the same cheeks. He's darling, just damn perfect.*

*Nurse Harkins, hardly says a word, she's allowing us to have this uninterrupted time. Walking out of the room, she periodically comes back to check on us. She even let me feed him, while she takes care of her other patients. She's truly an angel.*

*"Oh sweetie, I see a lot of new mothers every day. Most days, this is the best job to have, to see a new life come into this crazy world. Unfortunately, a few of those new moms I don't have a lot of confidence in. It's hard for me to put*

*into words to explain this the right way. The hardest part is being more excited about the moment when the mother you're helping seems not as overjoyed. Those situations are few, but they do happen. You're the exception, though. It's bittersweet, more of a tragedy. All alone, having no one by your side. I don't know your story, and you don't need to tell me. It's written all over your face, in your eyes, and it spills out of you with every word you say to your son. You would have made an incredible mother, and one day I hope you do. For now, though, God, has another plan. You are doing the best you can child, and I'm so proud of you. Takes a hell of a lot of courage to sit here knowing your time is limited with him, yet you are making sure he knows how much you love him. Keep it with you, always."*

GASPING FOR AIR and drenched with sweat, I sit up straight in bed and reach for my throat. I had not dreamt of that night for a while, but I'm sure seeing Micah is why I'm having it tonight. How do I tell him? Do I tell him or do I never say a word? I've got no clue, and right now, I don't want to think about it. I'm desperate to lie down and remember what it felt like to have him in my arms, having him reach out for my finger. I'm going to do just what Nurse Harkins told me to do... *'keep him with you, always.'*

Closing my eyes, I whisper, "Good night Michael, my baby, my son...always and forever."

# CHAPTER
## Thirteen

Not that big of a surprise, I called in sick the following morning. Liza never made it back home, but I had assumed she made it into work. Dr. Davis was, as ususal, concerned and instructed me to rest. I told him I had been up all night not feeling well. At least, that part was accurate. I spent the whole day in bed with my phone off. No one bothered to check up on me, and I was thankful for it because I needed to be alone.

Unfortunately, the days that followed were not as quiet. Nick called non-stop and saw me every minute he could. Liza was being nice, just not around much. She even kept her distance at work. Everyone at the office could easily pick up on the visible tension between us. I didn't say a word, though. Sometimes saying nothing is best. Micah had left me alone, and to say I'm relieved would be an understatement.

I woke up each day, went to work, even ate dinner with Nick a few nights, mainly because he kept harping at me. Then

I made sure I went to bed alone, further disappointing him. I felt no desire to be close to him, or anyone for that matter. I just needed my space. Little by little, it seemed I was withdrawing back to the darkness I've fought so hard to escape.

I've survived the longest, most awkward week in history. Being forced to eat, sleep and work in this bizarre twist of fate, Liza and I find ourselves in, is beyond mind blowing. The days following that night after Micah left me alone in my room have left me speechless and utterly confused. It seems we are all walking on egg shells, because everyone is afraid of hurting someone else's feelings. Either that or none of us know what the hell to say to each other. I'll go with the last one. I have no clue what to even say to my roommate. She has this nervous energy that is starting to drive me crazy. Nick is standoffish at best, slowly pulling back from me and mostly, I'm letting him.

I'm sure Micah has not mentioned our kiss to Liza, because if he had, she would have said something to me by now. To make it even worse, she invited Micah and Nick over for dinner. Since Liza can only cook grilled cheese sandwiches, I volunteered to cook. But I have an ulterior motive. I figured if I cooked, I'd keep busy. The busier I am, the less likely I would be uncomfortable making small talk with Micah. *Damn, this night's going to suck.* I can only imagine how hard it's going to be being in the same room with him. The only thing my mind can do is remember that damn kiss. I swear my lips still tingle at the memory of his sizzling lip smacking. *Jesus!*

*A knock at the door alerts me, that this most awkward night, is about to begin.*

Staying busy in the kitchen, like I'd planned, is working so far. My damn nerves have me self-conscious, looking over my shoulder constantly while getting the lettuce and tomatoes out of the refrigerator. Letting my favorite song play in my mind, I'm bopping and whistling around the kitchen, not noticing I'm no longer alone.

Rubbing his hands, Nick seems ready to help me out rather than be in the other room. "Oh, can I help you chop the salad?"

I can't help smiling at his pleasant face. He's pretending to be excited, even though, we are all feeling awkward. I'm so glad he's here. He has that calming effect on me. Picking up a knife, he helps me finish the salad. We laugh making small talk. Chopping the last of the celery, I notice he's leaning against the counter, watching my every move. Okay, that's not helping my nerves at all.

I ignore his stare. "I got it, thank you for the help. You can just stand there and stare at me or sit down. It's weird they are watching TV," I whisper, pointing my knife toward the living room. "And you are standing in the kitchen with me."

"Pointing that knife around while thinking about him." Nick sighs rather loudly. "Got to be honest, makes me nervous." He says biting his lower lip to contain his laugh.

His attempt at humor is pretty funny, but then again not.

"No worries," I give him a half turned up smile. "I have no desire to cut anything other than the salad."

"Pfft, please." He says with a roll of his eyes.

Dropping the knife on the counter, I say, "Try to mingle, talk, have some fun." Saying the word fun, just seems odd. Who the hell thinks this is fun, more like torture? At the same time we laugh.

Suddenly, in walks Liza. Well, it's more like stomping her feet. "Okay, this is not working. We are in there, and you two are hiding out in the kitchen. The idea was for us all to get along, and find some common ground. I want us all to be friends here." Addressing Nick, but her eyes are centered on me. What can I say? I'm the cook. I'm where I should be.

Opening my mouth to say something my eyes lock on Micah, who walks up behind Liza, most likely wondering what we are talking about.

"Hey," holding up my hands, I argue. "I'm cooking you all dinner. I'm not hiding or avoiding anyone. If you all want to chat, come on in, but stay out of my way. I've got garlic bread to make."

"Love your garlic bread, El. I remember it, oddly enough." Micah  blurts out . The only issue is the fact it's been years since I made it for him.

All eyes snap to him, and he shrugs it off. "Hey, sorry, but it's true. She made it for me a few times at my house. My whole family ate it."

His explanation adds to the shock and blank expressions staring back at him.

"Look," Micah huffs clearly frustrated. "If we are all going to be around each other, we need to get over the fact that Elsa and I know one another. The depth of our relationship is not relevant."

To hear him say it like that, does make sense, so I nod agreeing. The visible one not agreeing happens to be standing next to me, and he's really not happy. His fists are balled tight, he's shifting his weight side to side, and he looks like he's ready to start a fight. I brace for whatever Nick is going to say.

"Yeah," Nick's immediate growl doesn't surprises me. "If you believe that crock of shit, good for you. Knowing you have slept with both of my friends here, just doesn't settle well with me."

Listening to Nick's honesty, makes this situation sound so much worse. Why did he have to bring that up? We may not even make it to dinner. By the looks of Liza's face, he's got her all wound up.

"Jesus Nick," Liza's so shocked, she slaps his chest. "Thanks for reminding me. For fuck's sake."

It's easy to see her mind's spinning out of control with the fact I had a relationship with her boyfriend. Trust me, I've played it out in my mind. Knowing Micah's been intimate with her after we've been together is a difficult pill to swallow. It doesn't matter how long it's been. I decide to speed things up, getting this night to end without bloodshed. The sooner we eat, the sooner we can call it a night.

Like I predicted it would be, this night is a train wreck in the making. Everyone has stopped talking. It is driving me insane.

"This dinner is just dandy. Exactly what we all needed, feeling the love already." My sarcasm is evident as I butter the bread, adding the garlic heavier than I intended.

Micah laughs so hard and we all look at him like he's lost his mind, but I can't help join in. Of course, Liza and Nick never even smirk.

"Shit, this is classic," Micah says with one last hefty laugh. "Come on you two. Elsa and I are chilled out. If you two were wound up any tighter, you might explode."

Nick's mouth gapes open in shock. "Really, fucking funny dude."

Flicking his hand, Micah dismisses his comment. "Nothing funny man, just trying to see if this shit will work or not." Raising his eyebrow, Micah finishes with a shrug of his shoulder.

Turning to leave the kitchen, Liza looks back over her shoulder, "I've lost my appetite."

I want to yell at her that is was her idea to begin with.

I'm annoyed with everyone, Micah and Nick are glaring at one another in some sort of standoff. I'm trying to keep my composure and not flip out, so I bite my lip so hard, it's on the verge of bleeding. I want to get their attention, so I drop my knife rather loudly. My ploy worked perfectly. All sets of eyes snapped my way.

"Sit the hell down," I sharply say through my teeth. "Everyone is going to eat an incredible meal, and you are all going to love it. We will have regular conversations like we are long lost friends and act like civilized human beings. Suck it up, I have. If anyone is to feel blindsided here, it's ME, but I'm cool as a cucumber, so d.e.a.l. with it." I'm lying through my damn teeth, but I had to lie in order to survive this cluster-fuck of a night.

Continuing with my less than friendly attitude, I add. "Nick, set the table. Liza, grab the salad. Micah, just sit down and enjoy." It seems to work because they all just nod their heads not arguing.

The four of us sitting down at the table is bordering on being as uncomfortable as a routine dental exam. Small talk proceeds, but to be honest, it's merely just pleasantries.

"So Liza, how is work?" Nick asks.

*Seriously?* My mouth hangs open. *He's that uncomfortable he's asking her about work?*

The forced smile she gives in return is just as awkward.

"Good, thanks. How's yours?"

He answers her so kindly, it's sickening. I want to gag, but out of the corner of my eye, I can see Micah biting back a smile, and shaking his head. He's trying to think of something to say, I'm sure of it by his expression.

"El, dinner was fantastic. I'm stuffed." Micah replies with a rub of his stomach. Instead of leaving it at that, his eyes dance around and he's biting his lip to contain a laugh. I fear he's not done, yep, more is coming.

"Thank you for having me for dinner and cooking for all of us." The kind words and sincere smile he gives me damn near melts my heart. "It's a nice thing you did," his happiness fades looking to Nick. "I know you have no desire to be sitting here right now, and to be honest, neither do I. It's fucked no matter what way you look at it."

Nick adds, "You got that right." His remark less than subtle.

I don't dare look anyone in the face. Instead, I stare at my barely eaten plate. My insides are in knots, my nerves are shot and to add insult to injury, Micah rubs my leg under the table. He's sitting to my left, and the instant I feel his warm hand caress my leg, I damn near jump. The minute I make an attempt to move, he clamps his hand down forcing me to stay where I am.

No one notices my sudden movement. Liza's busy rubbing her temples, and Nick is staring at the ceiling, cursing to himself no doubt. No one is looking at Micah or me for that matter. *Thank God!*

"Hey," Micah says, leaving his hand resting on my leg. "It's the truth. My world's been turned upside down. We've all felt it, let's not lie. Now, the question is, can we move past it all?" Pausing for a minute no one says a word, so he continues. "You three have been friends for a long time, and the last thing I want to do is ruin it. If I need to be the one who needs to leave, I will."

"Now that is an idea." Nick says, smacking his hand on the table.

"What are you saying, Ace?" Liza appears to be taken back.

A loud moan escapes Nick's throat. "Can we all just call him by his name? It's stupid he's going by Ace anyway." The way he says 'Ace' is distasteful. I'm sure he did it to get a rise out of Micah.

"What do you mean stupid? What do you have to do with it?" Micah snapped back like I knew he would.

"Shit," Liza said but her eyes linger on him wondering if he'll answer the question.

He doesn't get a chance to answer, because Nick keeps at it.

"Just seems silly to me, man. I don't get it." Throwing his napkin on the table, Nick sighs questioning Micah.

"Elsa has everything to do with it, Liza." Micah says addressing Liza, not Nick. "After I left home, and went into the Academy, I started going by Ace."

"Why?" Her eyes are full of curiosity.

Letting go of my leg, Micah's rubbing the back of his neck. I can tell he's nervous and like an idiot, I want to soothe him. Placing my hand under the table, I gently take hold of his thigh. An innocent gesture meant only to offer him some comfort. The look he gives in return is soft, but as uncertainty takes hold of his baby blues, they furrow with doubt. It's then, I feel his hand covering mine. My heart can't help but accelerate. He intertwines his fingers delicately with mine. Our hands seek comfort in one another, giving each other strength like we always have done. This small gesture is only a fraction of what seems like a natural thing for us, well the old us anyway.

Our unspoken words speak volumes to the very strong connection we have. Our souls, sing a tune familiar only to us. My teeth indent into my lower lip and my eyes pool with tears. Will he tell her the truth why he no longer went by Micah? For her sake, I hope not. For me, I might melt hearing his reason once again.

Searching for the right words, he's studying Liza's questioning eyes, intently. He starts and stops a few times, pausing each time. When he does start to speak, it's soft and sweet.

"When I left, I realized how much I missed the way I felt when El said my name." He says with nothing but pure honesty.

*Oh dear lord, he's going to tell her the truth.* Tightening my fingers in a death hold on his, I'm trying gain his attention to beg him to stop. Not to hurt her with the truth. The only problem is, my gesture could also be taken as a sign of support. That it's okay to tell her the truth. *Shit.* Holding my breath, I brace myself for whatever comes out of his mouth.

"When I left, the old me stayed behind. I wanted to hear my name come from *her* lips. 'Ace' has been a replacement name to go by. I've spent years, remembering the way she echoed my name, knowing it was coming from the sweetest voice I'd ever heard." He speaks so soft and utterly sweet as he bares his soul, being completely honest with her. Micah doesn't lie, even when it would have been easier to do so. How can you not fall under his spell? Seeing him here, hearing his sweet words, having him hold my hand under the table, there are no words to explain what I'm feeling for him right now.

I hold onto his hand for dear life, my body trembles as my tears reach my lips. Desperate to leave, I try to get up and leave the table. I need a breather. Only Micah's not allowing that to happen, he firmly tightens his hold on me under the table. I'm stuck here, so I quickly take my other hand to wipe my cheeks. Nick ends up handing me a napkin. Not to make it obvious because Micah refuses to give up my one hand, I take my other hand to take the napkin from Nick.

"You still love her, don't you?" Liza's question seems like a statement more than a question. Her eyes never leave Micah's visibly shaken face.

Without pause, he graciously answers. "I don't know if I've ever stopped, that part of my heart has been sealed off for years. I never knew if I would ever see her again." His voice cracks forcing him to take a shaky drink. "This week has been one of the hardest of my life, only second to the week I left town...left her." Slowly, his eyes leave her to settle on mine before his charmingly sweet smile hits me.

Resting his arms on the table, Nick leans closer my way. "Are you still in love with him, El?" He asks cordially.

My heads ponders with his question. Not able to concentrate on anything or anybody, I ask myself 'how the hell do I answer this?' *Do I let my brain answer or my heart? Do I even know, myself?* "What?" My lips say the word but it's my eyes that find it hard to focus on Nick's conflicted face.

"Just be honest with me," his words are heartfelt, not an ounce of anger. "We all deserve to know how you feel since Micah pretty much laid out his feelings for you." *How is this possible, is it true? I can't trust myself right now to believe anything, had I heard him right?*

Pain and sorrow are the only emotions I've grown accustomed to living with over the years. Right now, both of those emotions are simmering getting ready to overtake every new tear that escape my eyes. Sobs escape past my throat, and I'm desperately searching for a way to tell them how I'm feeling when I'm not sure myself. To say I'm conflicted is an understatement.

"I don't know how I should be feeling." A whirlwind of emotions flurry in my mind eager to see which one takes the top spot of my heart. Being forced to explain how I suddenly feel after five freaking years, not only hurts, it angers me. It's only been a short time that Micah's been back in my life. They are expecting me to know exactly how I feel. What they don't understand is not everything is cut and dry, black and white... sometimes things are gray.

"I'm not sure." It's the most honest answer I've got. "When you've loved someone like I did, it's not easily forgotten." Snapping my eyes between Nick and Liza, I'm trying not to come across bitchy or rude. Micah is dead silent, but hidden to prying eyes, he's holding onto my hand in a death grip.

I continue.

"Obviously, my pain is no secret, so I can't lie and say I'm fucking great! I'm not, and I don't have an answer for you because I don't know."

"El," Nick tries to soothe me with his hand as he reaches out to rest it on my arm. "No one expects any of us to be fine. But we need to be honest enough to say that everything has changed." He replies, lingering his eyes between the three of us before settling on Micah.

"I knew the minute you entered her life again, everything would change. How could it not? The Elsa that finally got over you and let me in—disappeared the moment she laid eyes on you. The way she looked at you, well a blind man could figure out how much her love still burns for you. I'm not happy about it, but I can't deny my friend the love of her life, either. No matter how fucked I think it is."

"I can't...excuse me." Liza jumps up from the table and rushes out the front door, not bothering to close it on her way out.

Not a second later Micah stands. "Liza, wait." He says nothing else, he followed after her.

Nick's left to stare at his plate, his expression unreadable. That leaves me sitting with my hands in my lap. The warmth my hand once had when Micah held it is now cold, and alone. My tears are flowing strong and the sudden urge to flee overtakes me. I get up from the table, in need of a hot shower. I'm sure Nick will get the hint and leave, at least I hope!

I undress in a hurry and turn the shower on as hot as I can stand it. As I climb in, I let the water pierce my skin, embracing the pain. My hushed cries escape and flow down the drain along with my tears. I can't imagine how many times I've been in this same situation...left crying in the shower. Too many to count.

Wrapped in my towel, I can't help noticing my eyes are puffy and bloodshot. As I dry my hair with my towel, I keep my head down walking to my room without giving a second thought about dinner or the dirty dishes. I'm going to crawl under my covers and stay there for the rest of the weekend. Thankfully, Nick took the hint and left after Liza and Micah's fast departure. It was easy for me to understand how discouraged Nick may be at this point. He can see the writing on the wall, I'm in no means ready to carry on a relationship with him. I need to come to terms with Micah, and what that means. God only knows what's happening between them. I'm sure Liza hearing Micah admit to her that he never stopped loving me, was a hard pill to swallow and I can't blame her. The poor thing is smack dab in the middle of whatever it is between me and Micah.

As darkness fills my room, I'm left unsettled with every tear that escapes my eyes. I glance at my clock, and realize it's been three hours since Liza took off. Leaving like she did, all upset makes me sad. The last thing I want is to hurt her. A part of me can't help taking the blame for it all. I didn't think I could sink any further, but I guess I was wrong.

Just then, I hear my front door open and close...then lock. I relax letting out a sigh, I'm relieved she's home and safe. But scared she may not want to see me, so I decide to stay where I am, and see if she'll come to me.

I'm quiet like a mouse hearing my door slowly swing open. My body's turned away from the door, and my eyes are closed. I'm hoping she'll think I'm asleep, because I don't have the energy to have a long, drawn out talk. Not tonight. I hold my breath, waiting for her to say something or better yet turn around and go to her room.

Yet nothing. I realize I'm mentally ticking off the seconds.

As I let out a hesitant sigh, I feel my bed dip as someone sits down next to me. Guess, I can't hide from this. I turn my head, and can see who crawled into my bed as the brightness of the moon sends a ray of light, hitting my bed. It highlights my visitor perfectly, lightening up *his* face.

"Micah," I whisper in total shock.

"Hey, pretty girl. I had to come back and check up on you."

My eyes squint as I struggle to look over his shoulder. "Where's Liza?"

His head tilts to the side before he sighs. "My place, she is out cold. Had too much to drink, and passed out like a light. I took her keys, and came back here, hoping like hell Nick was not still here."

I let out a timid 'ah.' Answering his prayer, I say, "He left, and I don't expect him back anytime soon."

Micah's eyes widen, registering what my words could potentially mean. "Left as in for good?"

*Yeah, he sounded a little hopeful!*

I nod, with my lips tightly closed. "It was a mistake to think we could ever be more than friends. It wasn't meant to be, he saw it, and so did I." This is the first time since Micah came back into the picture, that I've admitted to anyone, including myself, that Nick and I were never going to work.

"Thank fuck." Micah wastes no time lowering his body to mine. His arms wrap around my shoulders, and he takes my lips in a panty melting kiss. My resolve is beyond shot, so I willingly go to him. I'm not fighting this feeling anymore, I'm going to savor being this close to him again. Snaking his arm under my knees he adjusts our bodies so I'm lying underneath his rock hard body. His moans and my sobs are the only sounds that echo in my room.

With each breath he takes, he's whispers in my ear. "Baby, I've missed you so much."

"Micah." I whisper in a dreamlike state. "Are you really here with me right now?" My wielding emotions with the reality of him being here, swell into loud sobs. My body's trembling as the gravity of this moment finally registers.

Micah takes my hand in his, and plants a sweet kiss. "Yeah, pretty girl, and I'm *never* leaving you again." His words are music to my ears.

*Oh is it possible?*

"How...what about Liza?" With my mind slowly clearing,

all I can see is Liza in my mind and I panic. The thought of hurting her is not a welcome thought.

"Ssshhh," He says pressing a finger to my lips. "Not now, not tonight. This is about us and what we need. What we mean to each other. God. Please, let me love you, El? Jesus. Let me love you like I have dreamt of doing for the past five years."

I'm so lost, his words take me to new heights. My mind's in a fog, and the only thing I can concentrate on is his larger than life body. He's touching me, kissing me, wanting me. I want him, I need him, and my body's yearning to rekindle what we once had.

"Dear Lord Micah, make me remember how good it was. I need you." I'm so desperate and needy. Each aching cry that escapes my throat, is a yearning desire to touch him. I'm so unbelievably desperate to connect with what we once had. How the hell could I ever think, I could ever feel this with anyone else? "I miss what it feels like to be with you, I've never forgotten, though. Micah, I need it again. I need to feel what it feels like to be loved by you. My dreams remember every moment of our night together."

Rocking his body against mine, he places kisses on the tip of my nose. "I've never forgotten, either, it's only you baby. No one could ever take your place in my heart and soul, Elsa. I fucking can't help how much I love you, I never gave up hope of finding you again."

Both of us bare our souls to one another while staring into each other's eyes. I can't help myself. My deep desire is to make sure he understands just how much I've missed him.

"I've lived for so long, never being sure of how you felt about me. And I tried to convince myself that you loved me like I loved you." Going to wipe my tears, Micah beats me to it. Only he kisses each one as it falls. Tilting his head back, he slowly sits back up on his knees, taking in every inch of me. My head falls to the side while my eyes stay locked on his. Each continued sob that escapes my throat sends violent tremors throughout my body. I can't stop now. "I've always loved you...always, Micah." Finally I let my heart win out, admitting this to him.

"Baby, I'm so sorry," he says delicately. "I'll make it up to you, I swear it." He says, slowly lowering himself again until our foreheads gently touch.

Losing myself in the way his body feels pressed against mine, my body suddenly goes stiff. Remembering what happened after he left, there is no way he can make that up to me...to us. Oh God, how do I tell him? How do I let him know that a part of us lives, that we had a child? Pushing him off of me, I scramble, damn near falling off my bed.

"Oh God, Micah. I have to tell you something but I have no idea how. Things happened after you left." My eyes are scrambling with fear. I'm terrified, and struggling not only to find the right words, but my next breath. My chest is tightening, making it difficult for me to breathe.

"I don't want to hear it if it involves Nick. Knowing his hands were on you pisses me off. The mere thought of it makes me want to kick his ass." *I missed this jealous side of him.*

With a slight turn of my head, my body relaxes and I struggle with my next words. "No, not that. I've not been with anyone since you until...last weekend." Like that's not embarrassing to point out.

Hearing my words must resonate with him because he scrambles off the bed. "Are you serious, El? No one since me?"

Okay, he looks rather shocked and I'm not sure why.

I'm feeling a bit awkward, because I'm sure he's had sex plenty of times in the last five years. Taking a big encouraging breath, I close my eyes, "I couldn't do it. No one even came close. Once you've experienced the love of your life, no one can measure up to that." Slowly I open my eyes and smile, not sure how to gauge what his reaction will be.

His smile is so infectious, it nearly steals my next breath. Shivers line my body, and he reaches for my hand, drawing our bodies together. "Come here, pretty girl. Just when I thought you were perfect, you prove that I'm fucking right. No one could ever hold a candle to my pretty girl."

Not to ruin his mood, believe me, I could stay like this all night listening to him tell me how perfect he thinks I am...but! I still need to find the courage to tell him. Not sure he'll think I'm so perfect then.

Holding up my hand, I reluctantly take a step back. "Micah, there is something I need tell you." My eyes are big as saucers, and nervous as hell. Do I have the courage for this conversation?

Micah doesn't respond with words, no, he strips his shirt off. Time for talking is indeed over. Inching closer, he's holding out his hand for mine. As I take his hand, he doesn't waste a second pulling me against him. My mind completely shuts off and I let my desires take over. Seeing him shirtless, only revs my engine and I'm left speechless. His time in the Air Force has been damn good to him. His body is beyond lean and trim with, muscles in all the right places. Not too many, but enough to make it into a magazine.

I'm a mess, and I forget all about the talk I need to have with him. Drinking in the sight of his sheer beauty gives me momentary amnesia, I don't get to stare long because he takes the hem of my shirt and yanks it over my head. With my chest fully exposed, my nipples harden under his stare.

"My God, look at you," he whispers, gazing at my naked chest. "You have grown into a stunning woman." His excited moans fuel my lust-filled desires that are now catching fire and blazing out of control.

Looking at him half naked, short circuits my brain and my ability to breathe. After finding my voice, I nervously admit, "My body has had to make some changes over the past few years." Okay, that is kind of telling him the truth. Since having Michael, my breasts have become fuller, more rounded you could say. My hips are definitely a bit wider, but thankfully, no stretch marks. Those nightly baby oil rubs worked wonders.

His moan lingers. "Well, whatever you did, you look fucking amazing."

*Oh shit*, he has no idea what he's saying.

Going down to kneel in front of me, he gingerly kisses his way down my body. A kiss, a lick, and a nibble an inch at a time. Paying particular attention to each breast, I can't help moaning as I arch my body into his, eagerly awaiting mouth. Bracing myself, he keeps unleashing his brand of torture. To stay on my feet, I have to hold onto his shoulders for dear life. I'm so lost in this incredible feeling, I roll my head back rolling in waves of ecstasy.

His warm touches are soft, yet demanding. Kneading and tantalizing my breasts, he continues leaving a trail of scorchingly hot kisses that take me to new heights. Micah's definition of foreplay is anything that will drive me insane. This little erotic scene is about to get even hotter. Micah pays homage to my belly button by swirling his tongue around it, dipping in a time or two. It's a mildly weird sensation that has me squirming. I'm trying my damnest not to giggle.

Not to deter him from his passionate touches, I rock my hips and let my eyes roll back in my head. Giving into passion, he plays my body like a fine tuned instrument, further igniting my libido. Erupting like an inferno, my blazing desire escalates when his hands rest on my hips. It suddenly dawns on me that his lips have slowed and are inching closer my tattoo. A tattoo I've completely forgotten until now. I tense up as I look down into his eyes. Gently, he traces his finger around it, but careful not to touch it. He is so sweet as he delicately places a kiss over top. No words, no questions...he let it go...and I was so thankful.

Enjoying the feel of his hands, I close my eyes and let out a whispered moan. "Oh Micah, you have no idea how much I have missed you. No idea at all."

He responds by tightening his grip on my hips, breathing heavy. Looking intently, all I see in his face the minute his eyes search mine is heartfelt sorrow. "Baby," he raises his eyes to meet mine. "I've missed you more, need you more. I have to touch and taste you, take you to the moon and back, baby." Tracing the elastic of my shorts, he pulls them down my legs. Inch by slowly aching inch until they reach my ankles. I step out of them, kicking them across the room. Harder than I needed to, but hell, they were in my way of getting what I want.

He laughs, watching the path where my shorts ended up. Raising his sparkling baby blues back to mine, his smile disappears, and raw lust flares in his eyes. "Damn, look at you baby."

Must be my red lacy thong. I just pulled out a random pair after my shower, without a clue that this would be happening tonight. Right now I'm thanking my lucky stars I grabbed a sexy pair leaving my granny pairs for another night.

"Going to taste you now, pretty girl." His voice sexy as hell. He traces a path with his tongue along the elastic of my thong. Micah's foreplay is one for the record books. He is setting my body on fire with just his tongue. He has not even touched me where I need him the most, but damn when he does, I will detonate for sure.

It's been a life long dream to be with him again like this. My body has yearned for him, and ached to remember.

Using his thumbs, he runs them along each side of my panties. Up and down he's inching his thumbs closer to my now drenched core. I'm moaning so loud, my neighbors might hear me, but he couldn't seem to care less. He's taking his sweet time running his nose back and forth as his fingers reach over and rip my red lacy thong to shreds. *Damn, my favorite pair.*

Not wasting another minute, he throws it over his head. I'm fully exposed to him now. Smooth and glistening wet.

"Oh, baby, wet and beyond beautiful. Elsa, all shaved up. Wow, that's perfection." Leaning forward, he breathes in my essence.

Jesus, I'm holding my breath and I'm about to combust. I'm beyond ready, and aching to have him touch me. While holding onto his shoulders, I eagerly open my legs wider, granting him access to the place made just for him.

Parting my lower lips with his thumbs, he flattens his tongue against my aching clit. He does it all the while looking deeply into my eyes.

"Oh, my God!" Stretching to my tippy toes, I dig my nails into his shoulders. I'm so close to having an earth shattering orgasm. Each tremble brings with it a set of violent shivers, that start at the tip of my spine and end at tip of my toes. His tongue ignites a torch in my belly, blazing a path of fire throughout my body. Each swipe of his tongue brings on mewls that come from my soul. I begin shouting out his name and rolling my hips against his mouth at the same time. The more he laps, the wetter I seem to get, my juices are slowly dripping down my legs. My essence erupts into his mouth and he greedily consumes it. This erotic, most private exchange is like a drug, one I can't help wanting more of.

Micah aggressively responds. He's way more intense now holding me in a stronger hold, driving his tongue in and out of my core. He takes long, urgent licks in between driving thrusts and my hips rock, begging for more. Not wanting to lose his hold on me, his strong hands cup my ass, his fingers press into my skin to the point that they will no doubt leave marks.

My overly wet center is pressed against his wanting mouth and needy tongue. The slight bite of pain sends me into oblivion as his teeth pierce my enlarged clit. Stars shoot behind my clenched eyes, and I nearly collapse on top of him. But Micah doesn't waver, he steadies me as his mouth devours all of my sweetness.

Barely able to open my eyes, I stumble, falling into his waiting arms. He stretches his fingers lacing them together. The evidence of my arousal glistens on his chin as his blue eyes twinkle. His hot smile is enough to set me on fire again. Not wanting to waste a minute, I lean forward open my mouth like I'm going to kiss him, but instead, I lick my way from his chin to his greedy lips.

My tongue relishes in the remnants of my pleasure. Turning me on even more. I take ownership of his lips. Nipping and licking, forcing my way on top of him, I'm now in his lap, pushing him back to the floor. His hands rest on my hips as I give him my version of a lap dance. Gyrating my hips in big circles, I grind down right on his erection that is no doubt dying to come out and play. I swivel my body like I have an imaginary stripper pole in front of me.

Soft moans escape his lips. "Elsa, baby."

"Ssshhh." I say, not wanting him to distract my concentration. I'm not sure how women do this for a living.

Slowly he goes to lower his zipper...smiling as he does and my eyes light up. *Now we are getting somewhere.* Pulling him up with me, we lower his zipper together. Pushing his hand away, I take over, wanting to strip him. I lower his jeans and draw out deep, lustful moans from his throat. Desire pools in the depth of his baby blues as they gaze over in pure ecstasy.

His growl is low and sexy. "Pretty girl, I'm not going to last if you keep toying with me. As much as I love your flirtatious side, I'm dying here. I need your body now, deep, and fucking hard. The second time around...we can take it slow and sweet." A grimace of pain etches on his face when he cups his enlarged cock in his hand.

Lowering my gaze from his pained eyes to his hand, a whimper escapes my throat. "Let me take care of you," I say cupping my hand over his. Easing his hold, he drops his hand, replacing it with mine. His jeans were first, but soon his boxers follow as I lower them down his legs. He swiftly kicks them near my panties across the room. Micah's erection is standing tall and proud, and I sweep my tongue over his slit to taste the bead of pre-cum that glistens.

"Ah, I won't make it two seconds if you do that, El. Fuck, you have no idea, how long I've wanted your lips wrapped around me." On his tippy toes, Micah slides his hands through my hair.

"Ssshhh, we got all night, baby." I say as I hold the back of his thighs in a firm hold. "This is about you and me, and tonight is all about us reconnecting." Nice and steady, I take a long lick from root to tip.

"Sweet Jesus," Micah's trembling all over. Cupping my head, he tilts his hips forward. "God, Elsa just please take me in your mouth."

So, I do.

His soft, sweet words are even more earth shattering with the way his lips part and his head tilts back. I've never seen Micah look more beautiful as he does right now. Not waiting another minute, I take him all the way to the back of my throat, struggling not to gag. Instead of taking him an inch at a time, I took him fast, frantically breathing through my nose. I refuse to ruin this moment with gagging or worse yet—throwing up.

"El, if you don't want me to cum in your mouth," his legs shaking along with his voice. "Pull out now!"

I don't listen or answer him. Instead, I straighten myself on my knees, holding onto his thighs tighter allowing myself to relax and suck him back knowing his release is coming. No longer unsure, he cups my head guiding my mouth precisely where he wants it. Thrusting his hips with urgency, he's hissing through his teeth, moaning my name in a deep tone.

"Oh fuck me El, I'm going to cum." He raises up on the tips of his toes, blowing out a rush of air through his gritted teeth.

Cupping his balls, I moan, suck and swirl my tongue, taking all he has to give me.

"Ohhh fucckkkkk yeesssss.Yes.Yes."

His release surges with a trail of his hot essence that streams down my throat. Closing my eyes, I swallow what he offers as he caresses my head with his fingers. Tiny breaths of pleasure leave his lips. And he seems so at ease and relaxed. Me? Not so much. Pleasuring Micah to the point he climaxes was beyond fulfilling, but my need is burning.

Standing, I take ownership of his lips letting our tongues duel, and taste each others desires. We nip, suck and moan to the point that our lips will definitely be bruised when we finish. And that won't be for a long while. The fire in the pit of my stomach blazes, and the burn is spreading like wildfire.

As our lips briefly part, Micah's voice is urgent. "Oh my God, I need to bury myself in you. Let me come home, pretty girl. Let me remember what home feels like."

I'm more than ready. "Yes, Micah. Come home." I whisper sucking his lower lip into my mouth.

# CHAPTER
## *Fourteen*

$\mathcal{M}$ icah walks me backward until the back of my legs hit the bed. With one arm around my hip, he reaches past me, and in one swift move, the covers fly off my bed. I can't help giggling. It's as if we're carefree, like back in high school. Both of us share a nervous laugh, but once I'm laying there, all of my nerves and laughs vanish. As I lay sprawled out on the bed, Micah's eyes feast on my body. The wait is finally over. I invite him home.

My nerves infiltrate my deep desire when I notice Micah reach in his jeans for a condom. Memories flash in my mind and I freeze. My eyes go wide as saucers, remembering the result of our condom failing the first time and I'm living in my own hell at the moment. I'm mentally freaking out, trying to protect my heart and Micah's as well. He has a right to know, the question is *when?* Covering my mouth, a tear or two escapes my eyes.

He intently watches the flow of my tears before a look of

worry washes over his angelic face.

"Baby, what's wrong?" The condom wrapper he's holding is half torn open in his hand.

My mind swimming, and my head is moving side to side. *Great, what do I do now?* "Oh, it's just—all of a sudden it's as if we're back in your room. So many memories." I let my words trail off, not sure how to finish that thought. I want this moment, and I hate myself for reacting this way right now. I need this, so my tears have to stop or else I'll ruin it.

Leaning forward, his finger wipes a stray tear. "You need to be reminded what it feels like to be loved by me, pretty girl. I worship you Elsa, always have. If your dad had told me how to get in touch with you, I would have." The desperation in his eyes tell me he's telling the truth. All the possibilities of what could have been flashed before my eyes.

That is why my story will have to wait for a more appropriate time, not when I'm about to reconnect with the love of my life. I have a failsafe anyway, I'm on the pill. When I tell Micah about our baby, I'll make him understand why I waited to tell him. We need this moment, we need tonight. The minute he brought up my parents, my mind got angry. Tomorrow, I'm going to pay them a visit. Messing with my life again, proves one thing, they don't give a shit about me. They of all people knew how important Micah was to me. They should have told me, given me the choice to see him or not. Once again, they took that choice away from me. Well, this shit has to end.

He is watching me carefully, just being patient, wiping my tears and placing kisses on my shoulder. Leaning into him, a long sigh parts my lips. "I have things I need to tell you. Soon, but I can't right now." Pulling back he looks in my eyes, searching maybe wondering what I need to tell him, but right now he's not asking. He's nodding like he understands. Our eyes stay locked on one another as he laces our fingers together and raises our arms above my head. He's holding me to him, using his body to worship my trembling one. Micah nuzzles my neck, and he licks my jaw beckoning for my lips.

"I can't hold back El, I need you now." Blowing his hot breaths against my body, he finishes with the condom. In record time, Micah is sheathed, lining himself up and inching his way in while he stretches his whole body above mine. His face rests over mine, and his eyes are commanding. Withdrawing just enough, the next push is more urgent, more forceful and finally he's all the way home.

My erratic pants are hard to control. The sting of being stretched and adjusting to the fullness of him, takes me to the edge bordering on pain, but there is so much pleasure. I can't help but close my eyes tight. I'm deepening my breaths, controlling the painful sensations to absorb all of his pleasure.

I faintly hear Micah's sweet pleadings in my ear. "Baby look at me. I need you to look at me."

Feeling him, and hearing him is my slice of heaven. My lips drift open at the same time my eyes do. And we gaze into one another's eyes as he gently slides back inside. The feeling of him sliding, in and out of me, filling and stretching me is so very hard to put into words.

"You feel so good. Elsa, no one has ever made me feel the way you do. No one ever held a candle to you, only you make me feel like this. It's home baby—you're my fucking home." He whispers, kissing, licking and nibbling at my tender skin behind my ear.

When I said all the years ago, he was my soul-mate, hell yes, I meant it. Who the hell says these things if they weren't a part of your soul? Eyes glazed, totally in tune with one another, I take his hands in mine holding on tightly as I buck my hips upward, silently letting him know that I need him deeper.

"Hell yes baby, move with me. Come on pretty girl, show me how much you have missed me." Each time he thrusts forward my moans increase. It's pure heaven.

His enticing words have me on edge, and the urge to let loose is overwhelming.

I cry out. "It feels so good, Micah. I fucking lov..." I stutter, realizing what was naturally going to escape from my lips.

"Tell me Elsa. Tell me what I want to hear!" He's tense, buried all the way inside of me. Holding my hands, he's staring into my eyes, begging me to tell him what he already knows.

I'm scared, though. I bite my lip while shaking my head. I refuse to put words to what I know I feel. Can I open myself up even more than I already have?

"Come on baby, don't make me screw it out of you." I'm so close to tipping over the edge. Shit, he knows how close I am and he's using it against me.

"Oh my God, please just don't stop." He's not getting what he wants, so he has halted all action. I'm not sure how he's able just to stop mid-action, but I'm about ready to take matters into my hands if need be. "You are so mean. You *do* realize I've taken care of myself for years and if I'm forced to, I can do it right now." My slight laugh is cut short because Micah is not playing fair. He's continuing to move, very, very slowly. The mischievous grin on his face, tells me he's enjoying this little cat and mouse game.

Pulling out slightly, he starts to inch forward. Leaving only his tip inside, he freezes. His eyes are sparkling, yet the high eyebrow he's glaring at me with, sends him in a fit of laughs.

"Tell me what I want to hear and I'll give it to you. I'll give it so good. You want that don't you?" His smirk is just as adorable as he is. Too bad he knows it!

Rapidly blinking, I'm writhing trying to get any friction I can. "Yes," I achingly moan, realizing I'll get what I want if I just agree with him.

"Well then, let's have it, sugar," he says, daring me with an edge of cockiness. "I'm dying here, El. My dick wants to explode, and I'm exercising all the self-control I have left. But it's fading, so just please, fucking tell me you love me. Goddammit El, please tell me. I need it. I need it so fucking bad. You own me, El, you've always owned me. Please baby, tell me. Tell me while I'm deep inside of you." His dark piercing eyes beg me. Taking a few extra breaths, Micah slides in slow, making sure his chest glides touching my aching breasts. Eyes never leaving mine he's using every part of his body, to anchor himself to me. And I give in, I will not deny what my heart wants.

"I love you Micah Taylor so fucking much." It's a cry, it's a statement, it's what I feel with every fiber of my being.

"Fuck! Thank you, I love you too, pretty girl. I've always loved you." His thrust is more urgent. He has so much power behind his moves. Totally loving every minute, he's finally letting loose with me. I'm more than happy to go along for the ride of my life.

In perfect sync, our souls search for their impending release. Micah's comes with a hefty grunt and a violent shake. Mine is less hefty, but not any less potent. I feel it building, the way my muscles start to contract, my toes begin to curl, and as it gets more intense, I scream.

"Micah—oh, MICAH!" My release is so potent I tighten my

fingers with his.

Lowering his head, he's breathing frantically and I take this moment to bite his neck as each shake and tremor of my orgasm slowly leaves my body.

"Oh, holy hell, pretty girl." Reaching up to his neck where I had apparently drawn blood with my teeth. He winces a few times, eyeing me playfully. "Are you a vampire now baby, holy crap." A bead of blood appears when he removes his hand from his neck.

"Oh shit," I say mortified. "Sorry,"

He winks with a shrug of his shoulder. "Oh don't be, babe. It's pretty hot." Leaving me with a big grin.

"Pfft, smartass."

Our back and forth is so easy and— normal.

"God, did I ever miss this with you." His chuckle is suddenly more serious and loving as he swipes his thumb across my cheek.

I stay quiet, looking at him with nothing but love.

"Elsa?" He asks with a slight head tilt.

Swallowing hard, I sweetly reply. "Yes."

"Tell me about the tattoo. It's beyond beautiful, but what does a butterfly have to do with me?"

I follow his eyes as they travel to my hip.

I'm unsure how to explain this to him, this is not a conversation I ever thought I would have with him, ever. I know I'm going to have to tell him the truth, just not right now.

Looking away from his intense looking eyes, I shrug my shoulder, "It's more or less a beautiful butterfly, always meant to fly." Part of this is correct, I'm just omitting the rest. Hopefully, that satisfies him.

His slight grin deepens and his eyes dance around it. "I love it, it's unique. The wings, have a shape like a delicate letter M. Did you do that on purpose?" He's tracing the wings recognizing the hidden letters.

Damn, he's good. Not much ever could get by him.

With tears stinging my eyes I aching say, "Yeah, can't believe you picked up on that." Maybe it's easier to make out than I had hoped it would be. I think he's more than pleased with the smile that stretches his lips. Moving his eyes from my tattoo they settle back on mine. He seems content and completely satisfied.

Laying next to me flat on his back, our shoulders touch. We turn our heads at the same time and look each other in the eye. The moonlight is just enough to make out his strong features. "I love the idea of my initial being marked on your body, babe. So much, that I'm going to make love to you again. This time, I'm going to adore you an inch at a time." Leaning my way, his lips ghost over mine as he whispers, "Treasure it."

*Oh God.*

"Yes, please." I reply.

The next hour is spent with Micah slowing making love to me and taking his time to worship every inch.

Both of us are covered in sweat and breathing heavy. We are so exhausted, we don't care that the sheet is barely covering us. I'm on my side and Micah is tucked snugly behind me. With his arm on my hip, he laces his fingers with mine. Getting lost in my own thoughts, I gaze out the window, trying to find answers...for what? I'm not sure. I don't want to over think things, but at the same time, I'm worried about what I need to do. How do I tell him the truth, without running the risk of losing him?

His sudden kiss on my shoulder snaps my attention back to him. "You know, I'm not leaving you again. I'll deal with Liza tomorrow. She can see the writing on the wall, she told me that earlier." He pauses for a second, running his nose along my shoulder blade, and suddenly tenses. "Tell Nick to keep his hands off of what's mine. What has always been mine."

A smile forms on my lips, the idea of Micah all possessive, well, it's an awesome feeling.

"No worries, *Ace*," I say sarcastically using his nickname.

That earns me a slight nudge of his chin on my shoulder. "Hey, no way pretty girl," no amusement in his tone. Tilting my chin with his finger, he says, "You call me Micah. My name was always yours to say. I love hearing you say my name." Softly he brings his lips to mine.

Peering in his eyes, I say. "I missed you."

It's easy to see how he enjoys hearing these words. His eyes grow wide, and his smile is just as bright. "I missed you too, pretty girl."

My yawn draws a lingering one from Micah. Seems like I'm not the only one exhausted. "I need sleep, you've worn me out. Hope I can walk tomorrow." I'm half kidding, of course. The megawatt smile I get in return tells me he likes that idea.

"Getting to sleep next to you, nothing could get any better. God, I've missed holding you like this." Micah whispers in my ear.

Before drifting off to sleep, my mind is troubled with what's to come over the next few days. One thing's for sure, they will not be dull. Figuring a way to deal with Liza and Nick is one thing. My parents, are a nightmare in the making. Wrapped up in Micah's strong arms, I realize this is the first time in five years I've felt this good. I won't be having a bad dream tonight, not a chance.

# CHAPTER
## *Fifteen*

Waking up the next morning I'm aware without opening my eyes, he's not sleeping next to me. I miss his warmth, my bed feels oddly cold and lonely. Dreading it, I peel my eyes open looking at the spot he laid claim to last night. The only thing there now are wrinkled sheets, but no warm body. I notice, however, he left a note on the pillow. Our night before plays out in my mind, and a goofy smile spreads on my cheeks. I pick up the letter and read.

*Hope you slept well, Sunshine. You looked so peaceful, I did not have the heart to wake you. I need to go check up on Liza before she wakes. I know we have a lot to deal with, but we will do these things together. Liza, however, is my issue, I will talk with her. Believe in me to handle this, please. Looking forward to seeing you, kissing you. Getting up to leave you cuddled in my arms was not an easy thing to do. I love you, pretty girl. Having you in my life again, is a dream come true. You are my light, always burning bright. Sleep well, talk soon...*

*Love,*

*Micah*

Oh my, I read it twice, each time fighting back the happy tears. Having Micah in my life again and knowing I have a second chance at happiness is more than I could have ever wished for. The only thing I know for sure is, I refuse to waste a single minute. Unfortunately, waking up today means, I have to deal with the aftermath. First I need coffee and a hot shower, then I can tackle what needs to be done. Preferably, one at a time. Micah said he would talk to Liza, and I'll gladly let him. Nick will have to wait until after I talk with my parents, because I've got a lot to say. They are my top priority for the day.

Showered up, I'm in the kitchen when I hear keys at the door. Shit, it has to be Liza. I'm not sure what kind of storm is heading my way, so I try to act busy. I pretend to wipe the counter as quickly as I can to clean up after last night's disastrous dinner party. When she stumbles in, I keep my eyes trained on the counter, but not a second later, they automatically swing her way. I know the second my eyes find hers. The expression she is giving me tells me she had a long talk with Micah this morning. Nervously, she's fidgeting with her hands. Anxious myself, I'm biting my lower lip, holding my nonexistent breath.

This will play out one of two ways, she will either go ape shit on me, or will ignore me all together. The longer we stare at one another, it's quiet, too quiet, and my eyes wrinkle with worry. No matter what, I refuse to be upset with whatever she decides to say to me. She's innocent in all of this, just like I am. I never asked for things to play out as they have.

Her eyes shift upward taking in a big breath. "So it seems, I never stood a chance. Not with you back in his life." Her hands tremble wiping the falling tears. I'm struggling with the fact I want to reach out and comfort her. Wishing like hell I could run to her and give her a much-needed hug, I'm smart enough to know that it's the last thing on earth she would want. I'm torn for the first time in a very long time, my happiness will come at the cost of my dear friend's loss.

Taking a step forward, I hold out a trembling hand. "Liza."

Looking a bit shocked as I approach her, she at once shoots her hand up. "No, don't. I know. It's easy to see how much he loves you. The pain in his eyes, when we talked, brought me to tears. Not for me either—for him." Turning from me, Liza kept talking. She walked to the couch and sat, with her head falling to the back of the sofa. Closing her eyes tightly, she continues to talk while I stay where I am. "He kept talking like he had held all of these feelings inside for a very long time. I had no clue the torch he was carrying for you. I knew there was a girl from his past that he cared for deeply, but holy shit. Hearing him say the words, I not only felt the love he has for you, I could see it in his eyes."

Shaking her head side to side, she turns to look my way. "You know what was weird? He opened his heart and talked to me as if we've been friends for years, but all of it had to do with his feelings for you. I hate to admit I was in awe."

Her expression changes like she's conflicted, hell, I think we all are at this point.

She stops talking as I take a few strides to sit next to her. Any other day this would be a normal thing for us, amazing how one day can change it all.

Tapping my knee with her finger, a slight smile formed amidst her tears. "I can see it in you, too. When you first saw him, it's as if a light had come back into your life. I may hate it, but I can't deny what is in front of me either. I will never have him—he was never truly mine."

My eyes are glistening, her pain and slight jealousy is easy for me to pick up on. I'm at a complete loss with what I should say.

"I'm so sorry," I whisper letting my tears fall, to be honest, I wasn't expecting this conversation to go so calmly.

She's rubbing tops of her jeans looking uncomfortable. "Why, are you sorry? Because the love of your life came back? You have no reason to be sorry. I can't hate you, or even him. Jesus, you two are soul mates destined to be with one another. Hell if I can understand it."

Standing up, she walks next to the window and pauses a minute before she slaps the wall, clearly frustrated. *Is it possible for us to maintain a friendship?*

"How are we going to do this, Liza?" I ask because this has to be the most bizarre situation ever. "We live together; we work together. How can I be with him and not hurt you?" I've asked myself this question, again and again.

My eyes plead with her as she leans her back against the wall. Her eyes furrow in my direction. Letting out an extended sigh, she says, "You won't. I've made peace with this screwed up situation. I won't lie and say it doesn't hurt like a bitch, but I honestly don't want a guy who is so hung up on another girl."

She has a great point and one I still am having a hard time believing myself. All these years, I never knew his real feelings. The only problem is I have so much to tell him, but first I need to convince myself he is with me for good, that he won't leave me again.

"Liza," I say needing my friend more than ever. "I'm a bit lost here. My life is crashing down around me. I'm not sure how to handle it or him. How do I let him in after all of this time?" I'm confused, scared and out of mind for even asking her this question, but she's my only real friend, outside of Nick.

Moving from the wall, she walks kneeling in front of me. She's nervous but lays her head in my lap. She's being the friend I desperately need right now. I'm selfish for even asking, but I need her.

"Easy," she admits. "You let him in. Come to terms with the past five years, and move on. Why sit and stew on the past, it's over, can't change it." Pulling back, she searches my face. "Work on the now, you've got a second chance with him. Take it and run. Hell, most of us never find what you have with him. You had it once, lost it, but now you have it back." Her smile is genuine and this has to be hard for her to admit.

"I still love him," I let my guard down, telling her the truth.

"Honey," she pauses. "It's obvious you do. If it were anyone else, I would put up a fight for him. Since it's you, it makes it easier. Just do *not* tell me anything sexual, that would just be cruel."

We both laugh, cry and hug.

My arms are around her, patting her back. "Okay, no sharing sex stories. Good idea."

Both of us are wiping our eyes, trying to figure out why we're laughing, and crying instead of yelling and screaming at one another. Liza keeps joking, it's her way of dealing with the hurt that is so evident in her eyes. I laugh with her because if I'm honest...I'm relieved as hell I still have my friend. She makes a few comments about us both living together, working together, and the guy she has been sleeping with is now my new guy who was my old guy. *WAIT... WHAT?*

We both sit, deciding we're going to take it one day at a time. Figure it out as we go.

"We just move on, try not to dwell on it. I may not sit and be here front and center with you two for a while, but in time maybe." She says.

"Thank you so much, Liza... for not hating me. I am sorry you had to be in the middle of it. Some story, huh?"

"Yeah," her reply lingers with an extended sigh. "One I hope not to live through again. I see, I'm going to have to play nursemaid to Nick because he's going to need someone. That boy is all screwed up right now."

Shit, she had to mention Nick. Her facial expression is alarming. Her eyes widen and her lop sided grin feeds into my fears. I can only imagine how he's feeling.

"Ugh, I can't even think about him right now. I'm having a hard enough time wrapping my head around it all." Lowering my head, the truth in her words hit home.

"Oh!" She suddenly perks up. "If I sleep with him, that would undoubtedly help." She's laughing so hard she snorts.

I crack up, slightly mortified. Her sleeping with Nick would be another guy who we've both slept with. That's a frightening thought.

"Well, at least you are laughing instead of crying. Listen, don't worry about Nick. He's a big boy, and he knows more than anyone when it comes to Ace...I mean Micah." She says frowning as she corrected herself. I can tell she's wondering what the hell she should call him by.

She lowers her gaze. "Christ, I see I never knew him. All along, he wasn't who I thought he was. That right there tells me, we would have never lasted."

We both stay quiet with her admission. What can we say.

Her phone beeps with an incoming text. We both get big-eyed wondering who it could be. I'm nervous it could be Micah, and why he would be texting her. I'm sure she feels about the same. Her face mimics my thoughts.

Scrolling through her phone, she relaxes her shoulders. "Nick, he wants to meet for coffee." Texting him back, she explains. "Nice, now he can cry on my shoulder. Well, might as well get this over with." She says while walking into the kitchen that for the most part, is cleaned up from last night. Thankfully.

Just when I was ready to ask her to tell Nick how sorry I am, my phone beeps. I'm afraid to look at it, the idea of Micah texting me with Liza in the room makes me nervous. In no way do I want to rub the fact he is texting me in her face.

She easily reads my anxiety. Resting her hand over mine, she's cool as a cucumber. "It's okay, it's most likely him. I will go and shower, you lovebirds get caught up."

With that, she leaves me with my beeping phone. I'm baffled at how cool she's acting. Heck, it's a lot better than I would be I imagine. Glancing downward, my stomach flutters with butterflies, knowing it's Micah texting me.

**Micah:** *Pretty girl, all is well with Liza. Had a long talk. Missing you terribly. Need to see you, hold you, preferably all night long. This time, I'm not leaving. It's Saturday, let me bring you dinner, and we can watch a movie or talk. So much, we need to discuss. Don't say NO... you know you want to. Only YES, Elsa.*

On cloud nine, I'm smugly shaking my head to text him back.

*Me: Sounds Great, look forward to it. Going to stop by my parents today and set some things straight. Bring alcohol. I might need it. LOL*

Two seconds later.

*Micah: Want me to go with you?*

Oh hell!

*Me: NO! I need to do this alone. Long over due... trust ME!*

*Micah: Are you sure baby? I don't want you to get upset... NO MORE!*

*Me: I'm sure, but thanks. After a few nights with me, you might want to leave again (just kidding) XXOO*

*Micah: Not funny, Elsa! Never. I want you always. Let me know when you're done. I mean it. Not a minute later, that way I can be on my way to you. You know nothing about me anymore. Need to catch you up.*

*Me: Yes, you are a bit of a mystery to me. Like where do you work? What are your favorite things? How are your parents? WOW... lots.*

*Micah: Hey, no worries. We have time, baby.*

*Me: Yes, we do. Okay. Off to get this over with. Wish me luck!*

*Micah: Be careful, luv you pretty girl*

*Me: Um... thanks. Luv you too <3*

Driving to my parents, my stomach's in knots. I'm not entirely sure what I'm going to say to them. Calling them beforehand was a good idea since my dad had a golf date scheduled. Thankfully he canceled since he knew I was coming. Gripping the steering wheel, I'm playing out my conversation with them in my head.

I want to shout, yell, scream, and holler. But knowing that none of that will help, I need to find a way not to get that upset. My mom asked me over and over why the urgency when I called, but I gave her no indication the reason for my visit. If I gave them an idea as to why I want to see them, they would use the time it takes me to get there to formulate a defense, it's what they do.

Pulling into the driveway, all of my anger I had bottled up ready to unleash on them is slowly wavering. Sitting in my car, looking at the white two story house, I feel like I'm the girl back in high school. Thirty minutes ago I couldn't wait to get here, right now I'm dying to leave. Slamming my car door, I'm somewhat choked up knowing how differently things could have been if my parents would have just told me Micah or even Matt came to see me. All my heartache, all my pain, and yet, they said nothing. Angrily, I'm biting back tears. More upset than ever for what grief they put me through. Mentally cursing them, I unintentionally slam the front door and I'm engulfed with the smell of cinnamon rolls and coffee. Yep, my mom, is pulling out all the stops today. My two favorite things. Question is, why on earth did she make them? Perhaps her way of bribing me in some way. Well, the only thing it does it make me more upset. Maybe she was already knows my visit was going to be less than pleasant.

Mom comes around the corner of the kitchen, smiling from ear to ear, and pulls me into an embrace. She's a few inches taller than me, but we do resemble one another. Same hair and eye color, even the round shape of our faces. Looking at her I can get the idea how I'll look when I'm older.

"Hello mother, how are you?" I say placing a timid pat on her back. She's tense, because we normally aren't a touchy-feely family. That all changed when I was sixteen.

She's rubbing my back, giddy as ever. "I'm so happy you came home for a visit." She's pointing to the counter. "Got coffee and cinnamon rolls just for you."

Her over joyous welcome is a nice touch, but it's not her usual style. Yep, she knows something is up.

"Well, there she is." My dad says sweetly, walking in behind me. My dad is a tall, thin man. He's aged well. Both my parents are in their sixties, but for the most part are in decent health. He's not built by any means, just in good shape.

Turning my head around, I'm not sure if I want to cry or smile. "Dad." I don't say more than that, and he takes notice.

Tilting his head, he draws me against him. "I'm better now that you are here. You don't stop by much anymore." The slight hesitant pause he had before he spoke was odd. The fact I never asked him how he was is another odd thing.

*I wonder why!*

This small talk goes on for some time. We sip our coffee, nibble on the cinnamon rolls, but time for small talk is closing... quickly.

"Um, I need to speak with you both about something. Some of which, you may not want to talk about." My eyes go between them waiting to see any emotion from them.

My dad's eyebrows arch and my mother stares at her coffee, but her eyes twitch a few times.

"Okay," his word lingers as his eyes show slight concern. He starts tapping his finger against his coffee cup.

"Why did you never tell me that Matt or Micah came to see me? That they talked with you, why not tell me? Why lie?" I keep my questions coming not even waiting for an answer.

My dad's face reddens; he's not happy or prepared. Accusingly, he keeps his glare on me. "What lie? I told you no lies, I call it watching out for your best interests. Like always. I've done it before and will do it again if need be." He said that so fast and matter of fact, it's like he's rehearsed it before hand.

Damn, he's not pulling any punches.

Tearing my eyes from him, I ponder what my dear mother might add to this conversation. She's tight-lipped. I'm staring at her and like always she's avoiding me.

"Mother, what do you have to say?" My eyes stare intently on her twitching face. She's trying to control her emotions, like an actress.

Sipping her coffee she seems totally relaxed. She adds a soft smile nodding her head. Finally she settles her eyes with mine. "Elsa, we do what we need to do. It's as easy as that," she politely says, straightening her posture. "That boy has been nothing but trouble for you."

With that, she's back to sipping her coffee. The only thing I want to do is go over and slap the cup from her hands. That might help me keep her attention for once. Like always, they think they know best.

"Like hell," I accuse. "You want to control my life. I'm an adult for Christ's sakes."

My dad doesn't even pause; he's on his feet in an instant. "Like back when you were sixteen? Come on Elsa, this boy is no good." His finger is in my face when he shouts.

I mimic his standing position with my own finger pointing

at him. "Who the hell gives you the right to tell me who I can and cannot see?"

"Obviously, we need to. Seems the only choice you can make is a poor one. Do you know the embarrassment we felt? Our sixteen-year-old pregnant daughter. Do you Elsa? Put yourself in our shoes for once?"

I'm rendered speechless. There is no talking with these people. They don't get it, never did. Why I thought I could reason with them was a big mistake. I can't do this anymore, I don't need their approval. Not sure why, or what I even hoped I would accomplish with them, but whatever it was, I'm not going to get it. I know if I told them Micah was in my life again, it would throw them for a loop.

It's not worth the trouble. Storming toward the front door, I hold it open, so the screen is the only thing standing in my way of getting the hell out of here. But, I pause, turn around and let my mouth have its way first.

One hand on the door, my other is clenched tight. Not caring if the neighbors can hear me, I shout, "You know, did it ever occur to you to put yourselves in my shoes? Do you have any idea what I've been going through for five long years? Any IDEA?" I'm shaking with rage, but the lack of compassion in their faces, haunt me. "No, all you see is yourselves! It's a pity, all I needed from you was compassion and a bit of understanding!" My shouting is now a whisper spelling out what I needed from them all along.

"Listen little lady," my dad says taking a step forward. "You have no idea what life is all about. Your little high school fling was nothing." He dismisses me with the flip of his hand.

"Nothing?" I'm back to raising my voice. "I loved him! I still love him, *you* just don't get it! YOU should have told me he came looking for me. *I* should have been the one to decide if I wanted to see him or not." This time I look in my mother's eyes. "Not you two!"

My dear mother is holding onto my dad's shoulder, maybe to hold him back. "Elsa, you were always such a fool when it came to him. You let an older boy take advantage of your innocence." Rolling her eyes, her voice goes low. "Look where it got you. That's not love honey, that is pathetic."

*So not expecting that!*

Tears sting my eyes, I had no idea they harbored such horrible feelings. Not an ounce of love and understanding, no, it's the look of distaste and pity.

Resting against the door, I realize they stopped loving me the day I stood in this exact hall telling them I was pregnant and scared out of my mind. Seeking help and a bit of understanding—only to find none of it was the last thing I expected when I told them the news.

"You both, to this day, just don't get me." I'm not sure why I feel the need to explain, but I do it. "If you had listened to me even once back then, you would have known I loved him. We were young, careful even, but I was never forced into anything." I'm near speechless, looking at these people who are my parents but right now I realize they are nothing more than strangers.

My dad's posture straightens, and his look runs colder if that's even possible.

"Okay, miss high and mighty. What would have happened? If you would have talked to Micah? Or do I assume you have since we are having this conversation today?" He walks closer, but his voice keeps getting louder. "Did you tell that boy he left you high and dry, pregnant with his kid?" He pauses a second before an evil smirk takes over his face. "Who is the one hiding secrets now?"

My head snaps like I've just been slapped, and I damn near spit fire. "I'm not hiding this, or lying to him. I will tell him when the time is right."

"Is that so?" My dad all but gloats as his eyes squint and his evil grin reappears. No idea why.

"What the fuck?"

That's all I hear coming from behind me. It's him—he's here and my dad knew it. He must have seen him, and he—he set me up. Oh my God, how could he do this?

A look of horror flashes across my face, and I gasp before my hand clamps over my mouth. I turn to see Micah and his brother Matt standing, eyes wide, with a look of shock washes over their faces.

Oh NO!!

"Micah." It pains me knowing what he heard. How awful it is for him to find out this way. Desperate to get to him, I about pull the damn screen door off its hinges.

He backs up a step, holding his hands up. "Tell me what—what the hell is your dad talking about, Elsa?" Eyes wide with shock, he keeps his eyes locked with my dad's.

I step forward, pleading with him. "Micah, please not now. Let's go back to my place and talk, privately."

Tilting his head back looking toward the sky, he's cursing. "Elsa, tell me what. *What* the hell is he talking about?" His shock now erupts into anger. He's not getting the answers he's looking for.

"Micah," I cry, losing every ounce of energy I had left. I can't fight him and my parents at the same time. The only one who will lose is *me*.

Micah's eyes widen. "HOLY SHIT, it's starting to make sense now. My God, Elsa were you really pregnant?" Planting his feet wide apart, his hands are clenched and shaking.

I'm not sure how anyone can go from confusion, shock and now anger in a matter of two seconds, but he sure did. What I know is my parents are not saying a word for a change. Matt is still in shock, he's frozen to his spot, and I'm just at a loss for words. To say I'm hurt is an understatement. I'm confused and annoyed. My parents, yet again, take a hold of a situation and do what they saw fit, not caring if it hurts me in the process. It seems my feelings were never their top priority.

Shock has set in and I'm a trembling mess. Big ugly cries escape from me as I turn to see the smug faces of my parents. Watching Micah come unglued only seems to amuse them.

Mustering the strength, I'm digging deep to find my voice. "Are you happy now? You did this on purpose! You *knew* he was behind me," I say, controlling my sobs. "I hate you both now more than ever. It was *my* story to tell, not yours." I'm not only sickened, I feel more hopeless than ever before. How dare they make me feel ashamed, when all along all they have ever done is made me feel worthless.

Micah's still raising his voice, still shouting as shock has settled in. He's being held back by a struggling Matt. Micah no doubt is stronger than his brother. He's wounded, heartbroken and feels betrayed.

"What the hell, Elsa," he keeps saying it over and over followed by a string of, "what the fuck?"

I need him to calm himself so he can begin to understand. My instinct is to run into his arms and hold him tight, but right now I'm afraid he'd reject me. I'm not strong enough for that today. It's going to take a small miracle for me to fix this.

"What do you want me to say, Micah?" I shout back with my patience starting to run thin. I'm on the brink of losing it."Not here. Please?" I continue to beg, "let's go talk, I'll tell you—all of it." *Just take my hand Micah...just hear me out.*

Stretching out my hand I invite him to come with me. I need him more than ever. This is not the way I wanted him to find out. But he now knows the truth. I'm desperate for him to reel in his emotions long enough so I can explain. Oh God, I want the chance to tell him my side of this story. How can he be mad at me? He was the one who left; I was the one dealing with a baby. Surely, he will see this...*wouldn't he?*

His lips snarl, his nose flares, and he's not backing down an inch. I can see my hope of reaching him slipping away. He's far to seething mad to ration with.

Dejected, he is looking at my outstretched hands like they are most vile. "Tell me right God Damned *now!*" His says with his lips pressed tightly, and his eyes narrowing on me. It's not a welcome feeling. It's potent and I'm feeling more insecure by the minute.

The guttural roar of his voice is even more threatening with his angry stance. Standing tall, defiant, and ready to explode, he's way beyond reasoning with. Matt is all but shouting, trying to get him to calm his ass down. Taking a glance over at my parents, they stare with a smug expression on both of their faces.

"Hey bro,' don't lose it now. Take a few deep breaths, and go talk with El. You two need to talk this out man." Matt is toe to toe with his brother, forcing Micah to back down. I know Micah would never hurt his brother, but he's not thinking clearly. I'm fearful Matt's going to get punched in the face. *Please listen to Matt, I silently pray.*

Matt's the only adult right now, *finally* a voice of reason.

Unfortunately, Micah's not hearing him at all when he pushes back. "FUCK THAT, I want to know why the hell I never knew? Why keep it from me, Elsa?"

He's not stopping, he keeps pushing, but doesn't stop for a second to hear me out. I knew he'd be upset, but not at me. If he would just take a second to step back and breathe. He doesn't, he's yelling at my parents, he's shouting to the sky... and he's back to yelling at me.

Frustrated, hurt and getting more disgusted by the minute, I let him have it. What am I going to lose? They are all pushing me past my melting point. Micah's anger is misplaced, it should be at my parents, not me. "Are you kidding me right now! Seriously?" Holding my hands up, I don't even know how to deal with him right now. This nitpicking he's doing with me is beyond ridiculous.

"Yeah," this time he's dropped his shouting to a mild yell. "I guess I am." His body relaxes some as he lowers his shoulders. Matt is standing close to him, and my parents are still on the front steps, quiet, but ever so smug looking. Their faces void of any compassion.

Sagging my shoulders, I close my eyes tight, fighting back the sting of pain this is causing me. "You left Micah; I had no idea where you were. I found out after you left *me*. After you broke it off with *me*."

Opening my eyes, I'm pleading for his understanding. My throat is sore from all the shouting. I'm sure the neighbors by now have come to see what's happening at the Winter's household.

My finger shakes violently as I lift it right at Micah's chest. We are close, but I left some space all the same. The moment

I've always feared is being played out in front of my eyes. My parents are present, Micah is beyond furious and poor Matt looks confused as hell. If I could just wish myself away.

He takes two steps back. "Come on Elsa, you could have told Matt or my parents." This time his face and body language looks drained. Crossing his arms he appears to be in more control of his emotions at the moment.

The calmer side of him is much more pleasant than the screaming lunatic from a few minutes ago, but he still has a sour edge to his voice.

The husky voice of my dad startles us all. "Listen kid, you knocked my little girl up and took off. Like hell, would I let her embarrass herself, or us, with that announcement?" My dad's distaste for Micah is rearing its ugly head, he's even telling him how much I embarrassed them. Ouch!

Matt's relaxed behavior has taken on a sudden change as he's now swearing and kicking the grass. He's in disbelief. It's one thing to know he has a nephew, but hearing how my parents felt towards me is chilling in itself. He's struggling to catch a breath with his hands on his knees. He's visibly shaken to his core.

Walking up to my dad, Micah's mellow mood is gone, replaced with bewilderment. "Are you serious? It was my kid you were talking about, let alone your daughter. I loved her, she was everything to me!" He says deadpan.

Not backing down, my dad strikes back. "Funny way of showing it." He's pushing Micah's buttons and I wish he would just, shut the hell up. I wouldn't blame Micah for taking a swing at dear old dad.

"Yeah," Micah asks him. "You think you know me or what I had to do?... you don't." Turning his body, the look I get from

Micah scares me shitless. It's like he just ate something sour. "So what Elsa, you got rid of my kid... you aborted it?"

I froze not sure if I'm mortified or shellshocked?

I'll go with utterly shocked. And sickened. Stumbling to my knees, I feeling like the wind was just knocked out of me. My chest constricts while I grab my throat struggling to breathe. "*WHAT*, you think I got an abortion?" That idea is so vile I taste it in the back of my throat. He believes that's what I did. It must be because the look he is giving me—says it all. His anger is because he thinks I got rid of his child. Of all the things, this is the lowest I've ever been. Losing Micah, giving up Michael, none of it compares to how I feel right now. This is a new low.

Through tear filled eyes, I drift my gaze between each and every one of them. Matt, who I thought might understand me the most, looks uncomfortable at best. His eyes look helpless. My mother is chatting in my dad's ear. I don't even get their attention it seems. Then lastly, I hold my breath to look directly at Micah. He's detached from any emotion, he simply is studying me. My look, my body language, any sign or clue.

Eyes raised, he roars, "Well, *where* is my kid then?"

It's hard not to hate him with everything I got right now. I understand he's dealing with emotions he has no clue how to handle, but he keeps pushing me and pushing me. If we were alone, that would be one thing. But, to do it here with my parents...it's not the right time or place for this.

Oh *My God*! His lack of having a normal conversation with me pisses me off. Like now, he's carrying on with his theatrical groaning, and continual questions. He never pauses enough for me to answer. Okay, Micah you want it right now...well fine!

On wobbly legs I go to stand. "Fuck you, Micah. Maybe if I knew how to get in touch with you, I would have told you. I had NO ONE! NO, ONE!" I scream so loud, my damn throat cracks. I can't keep up with wiping away my tears, so I let them fall. I'm focused on enlightening Micah. He wanted this. "I was ALL ALONE, my parents were embarrassed by me, their daughter. I was forced to live with my aunt for six months. I had to give him up for adoption and then return home to tell everyone I was on a six-month *vacation*." Retelling my past feels like it should be someone else's horrid past, but sadly it's mine. Makes it that much more vile.

"Jesus Christ," Matt says under his breath.

"What the hell?" Micah can barely form the words. "This is so fucked up." He wipes his face with his hands, in disbelief, and shock most likely

"All this time..." He stops mid-sentence, searching my eyes. He's looking for the right words to say. I can see the fight in his eyes. He wants to comfort me, but he also needs to come to terms with the fact he has a child. He's just not handling the news well.

Throwing his hands in the air, he shakes his head. Anger washes over him once again. "I've got to get out of here," he says flustered, anxious even. "Elsa, you should have gone to my parents. If they had known you had MY BABY, they would have helped you."

I can see him struggling but the idea I should have gone to his parents is idiotic I was sixteen...not twenty-one.

"Like hell, boy." My dad finally speaks again, like he hasn't done enough damage already.

The tone of his voice, sends shivers down my spine, and the only thing I can do is close my eyes. I halt my next few breaths. It's like a firecracker was lit under Micah, he's going to explode. This cycle is getting us nowhere. What's the point.

"You," He's enraged, pointing his finger at my dad. "Shut the hell up! Because of *you* I *never* knew I had a baby. You bloody hell should have called my parents. I blame you for this shit." He's not done as his attention swings back to me again. "Elsa I'm so pissed at you. I don't get why you did not go to Matt or my parents. *Fuck* Elsa, a baby?" One minute he's furious, outraged, and more upset than I've ever seen him. Then, all of a sudden when he's finished shouting, a look of loss and remorse takes hold with the way his shoulders curl over his chest. He's conflicted and overwhelmed, that I can understand, but yelling and blaming me is just too much.

God, my patience is running thin hearing the same thing from him.

Matt again tries his best to calm his brother's manic behavior. "Hey man, getting mad at your girl will not help. You're angry, and understandably so, but put yourself in her shoes, brother. Don't forget you left her without her knowing all the facts." *Ah! A voice of reason in this madness.*

"She should have been open and honest with mom and dad, Matt. She decided not to, this is on her and her parents. Who gives them the right to make that decision on my part?" Micah's jerky movements about gives me whiplash. One minute he's talking with his hands, then he changes direction.

A part of me understands where he is coming from, but I wish he could understand how I feel. I hope after he has time to clear his head, he will. Why am I more understanding than him? The only thing I can think is the fact I've lived with this for so long? He's only had a few minutes, and he never had a chance to have a voice in what happened to his child. The fact he keeps talking like I'm not standing right here though, is pissing me off.

He keeps going between Matt and my parents, back and forth this and that. It's like I'm watching a ping pong match. Blame is being thrown around, and now Matt is joining in on the blame game. I'm a bystander at the moment, watching this train wreck play out before my eyes. The sad thing is my name is being tossed around in their arguments, it's like I'm not even around.

Clearing my throat, I want his attention. "I'm right *here*, look at me Micah," I edge my way closer to him.

"Not right now Elsa, not right now." He's still visibly shaken staring at the ground instead of looking directly at me. I'm not getting anywhere, it seems he's more interested in this back and forth with my parents.

My dad's non-stop insulting Micah, with the help of my endearing mother it only upsets Matt more. Which leads to more shouting and yelling between them.

I wonder if they would notice if I left, most likely not. "Screw you all, NONE of you understand what I went through. I'm the one who was pregnant... alone... at sixteen. I had my baby *ALONE*."

"Our baby." He says remorseful.

I have no problem looking Micah in the eyes, but for some reason he has an issue doing the same with me. Too bad.

"Yeah, our baby, but where were you?" I whisper, trying to make my point as calm as I can. His eyes wince but never leave my mine, this time.

No, answer.

I keep going.

"That's right, not with me. No, you took off, with no more

than a few words with why. So why, would I go to your parents? Why, Micah? I had no one. My parents, were embarrassed with their daughter. They were cold, calculated and shipped me off like luggage only to return broken and very much lost. You know what I got when I got home... not a damn thing, no hug, no, I love you's. I got shit, it was as if it never happened. How do you think I felt?" I kept my tone as calm as I could, the sadness in my eyes desperately trying to reach Micah.

The way he's looking at me, it's as if he wants to hug me, but he doesn't. It's his brother that breaks up our silent moment when no one dared speak.

"Oh, Elsa," Matt says to console me. *Not Micah.*

My parents have stopped their insults, instead they are glaring at me like I'm out of my mind. Micah's staring at the ground with his hand behind his neck. He's struggling, hell if he only knew how much we all were. I'm looking at each of them, stunned no one is saying a word. Wow, I'm not sure what I expected, but this sure wasn't it. This time standing right next to Micah who is next to Matt.

"Okay, not a word huh? Let me ask you something, do you know why no one knows, Micah? NO one cared enough to ask me. I had my baby alone, not one visitor, no one. No words of wisdom, no shoulder to cry on. The doctors and nurses wouldn't even look me in the eye, the whole time. I had a beautiful baby boy. But before I could hold him, even get a good look at him, they took him from me. I was not allowed to see or hold him. I had my insides ripped open, scared and wanting to fucking die."

Peering off in the distance, no one says a word. I take the chance to tell not only Micah but my parents as well since they never bothered to ask me themselves.

"I had one nurse who took pity on me, felt so sorry I had no one who cared enough to sit with me. A sixteen-year-old scared girl should never have to face that, alone. She put her job on the line and brought me a baby in a pink hat, that night. Crying and scared, she told me they put him in a pink hat so I would NOT know it was him. Shitty right? But she let me hold him, feed him and spend some time with him before the agency came and took him the next morning." I'm completely wrecked, and exhausted retelling my story.

"That is so fucked." It's all Micah says. So I keep going.

"I named him...I named your son." With my head held high, I proudly tell him. My parents never even knew.

He gasps. "What?" The pain and sorrow is apparent with his tight jaw, and harsh squint.

"I named him as he held my finger. I even took a picture. He was the most beautiful baby boy, ever." My voice cracks at the same time my chin quivers.

My mom's eyes fill with tears. "Elsa, you never told us?"

*Yeah, I wonder why?*

"Why the hell would I?" I turn in disbelief to face them. "You disowned me the minute you found out. You made me give him up, I had no say."

My mother huffs. "For God Sake Elsa, you were sixteen years old. You knew nothing about raising a child." My mother's voice cold as ever. My new nickname for her is the ice queen.

I've heard this so many times. I'm rubbing my eyebrow like I'm warding off a headache. I sigh. "Maybe so but the way you both treated me, it was awful, and I've never forgotten or will ever forget. I hate what you made me do. Especially the way you treated me when I needed you the most."

Micah's not only agitated with me but my parents, too. He stares at me for a long moment breathing heavily. His voice cracks, "Why, Elsa? I just don't understand why you did not go to my parents? You were so stupid not to. They would have helped you. They would have called me. And you and I could have our son RIGHT NOW."

I flinch with the intensity and resentment in his voice. But right now, he's pushed me too far.

"*Stupid!* What the hell do you know? Stop asking me why I didn't go to your parents." Trying to relieve some of my tension, I roll my shoulders. I know this will hurt him, but oh well. "You fucked up, *you left.*"

"I HAD TO, I had no choice." Micah finally admits.

And here I go.

"And I HAD to give up my baby, I had no choice." I don't back down. I square my shoulders and stand tall. Hell you had no choice, but then again either did I!

"I don't know what the hell to think or feel?" Micah's pacing back and forth, talking with himself.

I'm incapable of calming him right now. If I stay things will continue to the point of one of us will say something we will both regret. To say I'm angry, hell yes I am, but I'm also heartbroken.

Biting my lip, I'll help him out. "I'll make it easy on you. *GO.TO.HELL.*"

Stomping my way to my car, I don't even take one last glance at my parents. Over my shoulder, feeling dejected, I holler, "All of you...can go to hell."

# CHAPTER
## *Sixteen*

Throwing my car in reverse, I can see Micah yelling at me to stop. I think he's realized he has pushed me too far. I pay no attention to him or my parents who stood in the same spot, just staring at me as I drive away. Matt is the only one looking up at the sky, searching for answers he most likely will never find. I should know I've done it for years.

Screeching my tires, my anger has me so worked up my body is trembling from head to toe. I so badly want to yell, hit something, or just drown myself in vodka. Any of the three would work, but the idea of liquor numbing this crushing feeling in my chest seems to be the winner.

Growing up in Cedar Rapids, Iowa does not leave much to choose from when it comes to bars. After driving around for what seems like forever, I ended up at a dive on the South part of town. The Pink Safari, an out of the way place with pink flamingo's decorating the outside seemed liked the perfect place to drown myself. No one would think to look for me here. Micah and I need time to cool off. Only then can we talk rationally. Right now, emotions are at an all time high. He needs time to process this, alone.

My damn phone was blowing up with calls and messages. Walking into the bar, I glance once more at my phone seeing it's Micah's missed calls and texts. With a shake of my head, I press the off button. When I wanted to talk, he didn't. Now he wants to talk, and I don't.

Swearing under my breath, I head for the bar to grab a seat when I'm greeted.

"What can I get ya, little lady?" What a voice it was, I glanced up to see a real life cowboy, no shit. Hat and all, he looked the part.

Amused, and completely surprised, I sigh, "Gin and Tonic please." Never would have guessed a cowboy would work in a place with pink flamingos' but hey, who am I to judge? I get a hot cowboy to serve me drinks. Lucky girl.

Smiling he slaps his hand to the bar. "Yes ma'am, coming right up."

Mixing my drink, I just watch cowboy go to work. My mind suddenly wonders, where was this guy years ago?

"Here ya go, sweet thing." Placing my drink on a napkin, he slides it to me until my fingers touch his.

"Thank you." I whisper.

"You okay? Looks like you've been crying? None of my business, but sure hate to see a cute thing like you all sad." The sincerity in his voice is nice and a welcome relief to Micah's shouting. I wished Micah could have spoken to me like this, hell, to know he cared would have been nice, too. I knew he'd be mad and upset, but not downright mean and cold. No way, that was just uncalled for.

Sadly, I say. "I've had a bit of a bad day."

Nodding, he lifts a corner of his hat. "I'm a great listener, you need to let it out, name's Caleb."

Country boy through and though. His voice matches the whole cowboy theme he has going on. Watching him, I can't help taking him in. With a voice like Garth Brooks, and a body you would expect a cowboy to have, Caleb, was hot. Tanned skin, defined muscles, tight shirt, snug jeans. Glancing over the bar, yep, even cowboy boots. Wow! Now, I do realize he knows I'm checking him out, but who gives a shit. The smile he's trying to hide doesn't work so he cracks up laughing back at me.

"Thanks Caleb, appreciate it, but..." I say taking a nice long drink, letting it burn my throat, "You don't need to hear my sad story. No reason we both need to be feeling down."

"Way I see it, I need to cheer you up. You need to be smiling, not crying. Assume over some dick, am I right?" The twinkle in his questioning eye draws out a chuckle.

Nodding, I agree. "I will admit, I do feel better after talking with you for all of five minutes. You must be a miracle worker, because if you would've seen my mood just before I walked in these doors," I say pointing toward the door. "Well, let's just say I was ready to hit something or someone."

"Pfft, if that's what you need, take a swing my way. I'm a big boy, I can take it." Caleb says with a sexy wink.

Instantly, I spit my gin out. "See? Miracle worker. I thank you for that... sir."

"Ouch, Sir. No.No.No. That will not do...Caleb will work just fine. Sir would be my father, and he's not here." He says with a wink.

"Caleb, you are a sweet talker, aren't ya?" I say with a meek eyebrow raise.

He chuckles. "Been told that a time or two, I guess."

Small talk continued for several hours, along with several more drinks. More customers came and went and a group of what I assume are Caleb groupies came in half dressed, giggling like school girls. Rolling my eyes at their attempt to flirt, he kept ignoring them, laughing with me instead.

"Wow." I mouthed to him as the girls kept at it.

Walking next to me, he leans against the bar. "Yeah, got my own groupies, haven't you heard? Sweet thing, I thought you would become one of them." He's flirting and bites his tongue between his teeth while raising both eyebrows at me, waiting for me to respond.

Taking another drink, I only shake my head. "Pfft, no way, dear Caleb, you seem to be doing just fine. I am in no way the type of girl you need."

"Now, I beg to differ with you on that." Pressing his lips together he moans...out loud. "I would say you are exactly my type of girl." Leaning into my space, with both of his arms are lying on the bar, he keeps moving toward my face. This is *not* what I need right now.

I'm halfway to not giving a crap about my shitty mood or the disaster of my life at the moment. I have this hot looking cowboy who is being nice and flirty with me. To him I'm not a disappointment, not a failure, not a bad person. I am just a sad, cute girl he is making smile with every glance and wink. To hell with it, I'm going to play along. I need to laugh. No harm done, just friendly flirting back and forth.

An hour later while I continue to watch Caleb serve drinks,

I stupidly reach for my phone. I'm bored, so I turn it on. I've lost count of, the number of drinks I've consumed and looking at the time, I see it's way passed dinner. Shit, I missed lunch, too. No wonder I'm close to being three sheets right now. Barely able to roll my eyes, I sway to the music that is playing on the sound system. My cowboy Caleb, is playing a favorite song of his, I would assume. Garth Brooks', *Friends in Low Places* has me singing and rocking side to side. Paying no attention to him, I see twenty-seven missed calls from Micah, twelve missed calls from Liza, and ten from Nick. Lord almighty, I have thirty texts, mostly from Micah. Wow...and nothing from my parents. Go figure!

"Whatcha' doing, sweet thing?" Caleb appears next to me, sitting at the bar stool on my right, smiling from ear to ear.

"Oh, looking at the bitch fest who is trying to figure out where I am." I slur my words laughing. I know none of it is funny, but right now, I can't help laughing.

Glancing down at my phone, he sees a text message from Micah. Pulling it toward him, he reads it.

"Wow," he whistles, "this Micah seems really worried about you?"

I try to lick my lips but my mouth is dry as a bone. I dismiss hearing him say Micah is worried about me. "Oh, I'm sure he is, he didn't want to talk earlier. No, he wanted to yell at me and blame me for it all. I begged, and he refused to talk. Well, now I refuse."

"That's a shame. Sweet thing like you deserves to be heard. If you were begging to talk to me, I would gladly give you my undivided attention without question." He then bumps his shoulder with mine.

I lean into him, whispering, "Yeah, if you knew the whole

situation, you might think differently."

"Try me." He replies.

What is it with alcohol and confessing your deepest darkest secrets? No clue, but after he tells me to try him. Well, I do, I lay it all out for him. The ashen look on his face lets me know he wishes he'd never asked.

"Jesus Christ, how the hell could he be mad at you? He should be begging you for forgiveness. Darlin' he's a dick, sorry, but he is a straight up dick."

I have no clue how long he sat next to me, the bar was pretty empty which most likely explains why he spent so much time hanging around me.

"Yeah, whatever. Begging for my forgiveness was not his priority." I say when my phone beeps again. I ignore, delete and repeat this process for several minutes until it stops. Finally, I sigh with some relief.

Caleb, starts switching my drink to water. My sexy cowboy bartender threatened me, it was that, or I was going home with him. I wasn't sure if he wanted me to stop drinking or continue. Yikes, so not ready to go there. On the flip side, it's most likely what I should do. A night with a sexy cowboy might be just what the doctor ordered, but I know deep in my heart I never would. Micah has my heart, always has, always will. Another reason I'm so screwed.

Not long after, I say goodbye to my sexy cowboy. Insisting I would come back and see him, was the only way I was getting out the door alone. Jumping in my seat, I'm exhausted and somewhat sober now. The day crashes down on me, and my phone rings once more.

His name displays on the screen and it grips my heart. I want to cry. How long have I longed for his name to show up?

That he would be calling me, I just wish it was under different circumstances. I have no idea if he can ever forgive me now. The anger and venom in his voice sickened me to the point of feeling alone all over again. After finally making it out of the darkness, I'm afraid of being pushed back inside. Only this time, I don't have the energy to fight it.

Biting my lip, tears hit the screen of my phone as I hold it in my hands. Once again, I press...ignore!

# CHAPTER
## Seventeen

Micah

Where the hell is Elsa? She's ignoring all of my calls and text messages. My damn fingers are sore from typing so much. I'm worried out of my mind but I screwed up. I never should have acted the way I did...*not to her.* It's wasn't right and I know directing my anger at her only hurt her more. I know it won't excuse any of my behavior for earlier, hell, I knew it then, but I was so fucking mad. I couldn't control myself. Holding my tongue was never a thing I was good at, especially when it came to my pretty girl.

Damn, finding the girl who stole my heart all of those years ago, had more of an effect on me than I expected. I spent years trying to forget her and what we had. I kept telling myself what my father had drilled into my mind. I was too young and just had my first real crush on a girl. I'd get over it. Like hell!

She was my first. My first after years of almost losing it multiple times. That is more than likely the reason I kept her in my heart. Every year after that and up until now simply refused to let me forget what Elsa Winters meant to me.

*First day of school, this beautiful girl caught my eye. She wasn't into cliques either, and what a relief that was. The school was full of piranhas, trying to sink their teeth into me. Hell, not one of them had an ounce of what my pretty girl had. Elsa had more class in her pinkie finger than those girls had in their whole bodies. She was too sweet to realize what a gem she really was.*

*From day one she caught my eye and has held my attention since. The other's tried like hell to land me, it was funnier than hell watching them attempt to score with me. It was Elsa's pure beauty that made my heart rate spike and hands clammy. Most of my time was spent fighting to keep my damn hands off of her. She was that irresistible.*

*With her I had to go slow as not to spook her, I could tell she was a virgin right away. She blushed so damn easy. Man, when she blushed, my dick took notice. I'd had to adjust myself so often around her, she had to think I had a serious problem. Made me laugh though, if she only knew what kind of problem I had...well I'm sure she would have blushed even more or at least run away.*

*When I finally convinced her to have study dates with me they were more or less an excuse just to be close to her. I came up with more reasons why I needed her help. If she knew I didn't need the help, she might have slapped me silly. She was always so proud of herself when she learned of my test scores. Her face would light up with excitement and the high five's she gave me afterward, well, let's just say I'd do it all over again. She had a way about her that sucked you* in, and made you beg for more. Her sweetness and honesty, damn, just thinking about her still drives me crazy.

I let things get out of hand though; I was getting in too deep with her. Instead of shutting my mouth to my father, I let my feelings for her be known. Even if I hadn't said anything, my parents saw right through me. The not so friendly stares grew into long frustrated talks about planning my life and making sure I was on track to meet and exceed my potential. It all started with the Air Force. My life was all mapped out for me, like my father and his father's before.

Once I wavered in my response to one of my dad's questions, that was all it took for him to set my path in motion earlier than I had expected. The one day I'd planned on taking a different course with my life, was the day I'd made my first mistake. At the time, I wanted a life with Elsa. The Air Force would have to wait, or not happen at all. I was okay with it, I wanted my girl by my side...always.

Dad, not wanting any of it, had sat me down the day after my amazing night with Elsa. Our first time was beyond fantastic, it was earth moving. Damn, her body was perfect. I can still remember the way she quivered as my body took hers. The way we moved in perfect fucking harmony took my breath away.

Early the next morning, I was informed I would be privately tutored to get my last few credits I needed so I could graduate early. Then and only then, I'd be ready for the Air Force Academy. My father, who had friends in high places, pulled a few strings, and the rest is history. I'd receive my education while I was stationed in Seattle, Washington. Hell, I had no idea how he accomplished this plan of his, but he was a smug bastard. He'd move mountains if need be. My *only job was to NOT to disgrace the family name. The Taylor name meant something in the Air Force. Knowing I had zero choice in the decision to go, I sucked it up. What else could I do?*

*Forced into leaving, there was no way in hell I could see Elsa, not now. How could I? I would only end up breaking down and crying in front of her. For a young man going into the military, crying was a sign of weakness.*

*I knew the best thing was to limit my contact with her. For now. I would have Matt go and see her after I had left, and explain things to her. Maybe she would wait for me? I knew full well I couldn't call her from halfway across the country and be able to maintain my focus on what I needed to do. Selfish or not, Elsa Winters would be a distraction for me, one I could not afford. My father drilled that shit deep in my mind so many times, I believed it myself.*

*Matt had gone to see her after I left, and her parents told him to leave. He had not seen her, and he told me to give her time. But, when he went back months later, he found out she left to visit her aunt. Then nothing, so I went on and did my service. I deployed for a short time, and I hated every minute of it. It was someone else's dream, no longer mine.*

*I did my time and as soon as I could, I got out. Sure, my father was less than pleased I did not make it my career choice, but I eventually stopped caring what he wanted. He's not me, and I am not him. Enough had been enough.*

*In all that time, I stopped using my damn name. I couldn't stand for any female to call me Micah, it felt like a betrayal. That was how messed up I was. A buddy of mine, Marcus, started calling me Ace and it stuck. The endless girls calling me Ace was easier to live with. I screwed every girl I could,* to try to erase her from my mind, but it never worked. I even had to close my eyes, dreaming of being inside the sweet little body that belonged to my pretty girl. Finally realizing no girl felt good anymore, I gave it all up. Cut out screwing easy girls, and just lived my life day to day. Maybe one day, I'd move on.

The day I finally got to come home it was like I'd hit the damn lottery. Five God damn long years had passed. Driving down our street, my first stop was her house. Overly excited at the chance of being this close to her again, I damn near couldn't contain myself. Her parents could at least tell me where to find her. I couldn't wipe the damn smile off my face the whole time running up to her front door. Her menacing looking father though was less than happy when he realized it was me at the door. Seemed leaving his daughter with little to no explanation was not a wise move on my part.

"What the hell do you think you're doing here, boy?" His voice was filled with contempt.

"Um...would Elsa happen to live here still?" I asked cautiously.

His snicker came across more like a sneer. "Got some balls to come here."

Okay, needing to step back. "Um...Sir, I just want to see Elsa. Just got home from the Air Force, and I really need to see her." I say holding my hands up, hell I'd pray if I thought that would help.

Appearing taller, he grimaces. "No.You.Don't. If you cared for my daughter at all, you would forget all about her. She doesn't ever need to see you again. She's moved on, so should you."

The door then slammed in my face.

*In utter shock, I was at a loss for words.*

"SHIT.DAMN.FUCK." I shout at my brother.

"Listen dumbass, I told you to calm the hell down earlier. But, NO, you just went on and on. Give her time, Micah." Matt said, raising his voice. The way he keeps moving his head from side to side, I can tell he's tense and worried. He's been making sure to let me know he was less than pleased with my rants from earlier. He told me he understood, but just the same, it wasn't my most shinning  moment.

We've spent hours looking for her, all the while he's been preaching to me. All I seemed to do was screw this whole situation up. Finding out you are a father to a child you never knew about is a totally blow your mind kind of moment. At first I was so disgusted, thinking Elsa had an abortion, but I should have known she'd never do such a thing. Adoption though?  Someone has my kid. Someone is raising my son... and it pisses me off. He should be my responsibility.

"Micah," my brother interrupts my thoughts. "Did you once put yourself in her shoes, man? Christ, did you see her parents? Hell, she had to live with THAT shit for years. Can you imagine what she had to deal with... all alone." Matt's on a roll, slamming his hand on the dash of my newly detailed Camaro. Yes, my other baby is my Cherry Red Camaro...call her El. Yeah, I know...I had my pretty girl, so my car goes by El.

"Matt," I grumble and moan. "I was way too mad to think about being rational. All I could think was I have a kid. A kid I never knew existed. Mom and Dad or even you never had a chance to raise the baby while I was gone. Hell, I would have stayed. I would have been back here for my girl, having our baby together." I'm so pissed, I'm yelling at my brother again. Just like with Elsa, I don't mean to take it out on them, but damn this sucks.

Matt stings my arm, smacking me with his hand. He's red in the face, shouting, "Jesus, I'm sitting right here. Stop yelling, because it's not doing a damn thing for you. Right now, you got your girl missing, and God only knows where she is, and what she is doing or with *whom*."

My head snaps at what he's implying. "What the fuck is that supposed to mean? She's not a slut."

A loud duh' escapes his lips. "I'm not saying she is—dude, but she's upset and alone...once again, all alone. Now if you're me, I would go drink...a lot. If I was as hot as Elsa, alone—and drinking, what would any guy try to do with that?" He says at me with a raised brow.

I'm damn near hyperventilating; I did not need that mental image he portrayed for me.

"Fuck, we need to find her."

The way I acted today it's like a stake in my chest, and the image my little brother planted in my head is pushing that stake in a little further. I screwed up, plain and simple. My girl is out there alone, thinking no one understands what she went through or how she feels, especially right now and she's right.

My pretty girl had waited five years before she was with another guy, and that alone makes my head dizzy. Nick, that little prick, slid his way into her good side. I had met him a few times when I was with Liza. Shit, at the time I was encouraging him to hit on Liza's roommate. The roommate I knew as Pip. Hell, I even questioned who the heck has a name like that.

I never pushed Liza about it, never cared, to be honest. The only thing I feel right now, is damn stupid.

Liza, is a cool chick and crazy in bed. She helped ease the pain. I escaped my inner turmoil to the one who got away from me. I was honest with Liza, and she knew I had some deep rooted feelings for a girl I was with long ago. I never offered more, and she never pushed. A major reason it worked for us. She liked to have fun, and I liked to party. Remembering back now, I wish I could have put the pieces together, but how? I never saw it coming. Liza's roommate, *aka* Pip, was my Elsa Winters...my pretty girl.

Slap me silly, this is some seriously screwed up shit. Add that to the realization that I was also a father to a baby boy we created back five years ago. Whose head wouldn't be fucked up? Oh man.

The one and only time I had made a girl mine, was the time that a condom had not worked, and because of that, I knocked her up. Even though I'm royally pissed off, it's not her fault. She most likely hates me after today, and that's not a great feeling to have to live with. I fucking love that girl. Knowing she was forced to go through all of that alone, that her parents disowned her, makes my skin boil. Her parents are pieces of shit in my by book. When they turned their backs on her, she had to be crushed and scared. A fucking testament to how strong my girl really is. I have no clue how she did it? But, because of her, our son lives and breathes.

I should have been there. I would have had the chance to hold her hand and kiss her forehead. Sure we were young, but I would have made sure we were together. All of it ripped away from us, a life experience we will never get back. This will haunt us for the rest of our lives.

Telling my parents, this afternoon was beyond painful. My father seemed almost as pissed as I had been. He was the one pushing me away from her, but now he's so furious he has a grandchild he will never see. Somewhere deep down, it seems he likes my pretty girl as much as I do. Well, maybe not that much. Though he acts different now then he did back then. My mom was shattered and in tears, and that crushed me even more. She was horrified to learn that Elsa's parents made her feel like an outcast. Hell, none of us could believe that one. She was alone, the whole nine months and during the delivery, too. Not knowing what a woman goes through during childbirth, my mom painted the picture and it down right frightened me. When I explained to my mom, I understood the concept of what actually happens, I was scolded for being insensitive to the many emotions a woman goes through. I kept my mouth shut from that point on.

Taking her word for it all, Matt and I, left canvassing the area for her Honda Accord. I called Liza dozens of times telling her what happened, it seems she was as clueless as I was about the baby. It seems like Nick had known all about it, and he made sure I got a play by play of how much darkness my girl has been in. He called me 'heartless' and a 'spineless fuck' for placing blame on her. The sick part is, I agreed with him. The bastard was right, I was a complete dick all the way, no matter how you looked at it.

I need to find her, explain how sorry I am. I swear I won't stop telling her and begging for her to give me a chance to make it up. I want to hug her and let her cry it out with me. We need to talk about the baby, I need to hear her story. No interruptions, no one around. Just us, like it should have been all along. If I'd only listened to her!

I fumble with the phone, dialing her number for the hundredth time, "Fuck, she won't answer me." Not even bothering to end the call, I throw my phone toward my brother.

"Shit, settle down," he fumbles around, trying to pick up my phone that is lying between his feet. "Between Liza, Nick and you and I, all looking for her, she'll show up. We'll find her, Micah. Just don't lose your shit again. When we find her, and we will, you better keep your composure and beg as if your ass depends on it. Because brother, I got to tell you, right now you suck."

Okay, can't argue with him on that, but I've never seen Matt so worked up over any girl I've been with before. I've always known he liked Elsa, took a liking to her right away. He also knew he better never try to make a move on her or else I'd beat his ass. It was a running joke between us back in the day.

Recalling our fun chats when it came to my pretty girl makes me chuckle. "Why thanks for your load of confidence, brother. AND thank you, Einstein, I know I screwed up today. I just need to find her safe and sound. The rest will be okay. My pretty girl will understand...she has to." My confidence is not what I'd like it to be, I just need to remain positive. If I let my insecurities creep in now, I will lose my shit all over again.

My phone, which is now lying in Matt's lap, beeps with an incoming text. I go to grab for it, but he has it already held up away from my reach.

"Christ Micah, eyes on the road. I'll read it to you." He huffs before running his fingers over the buttons and reads it.

"Says...oh, it's from Liza. Looks like Elsa went back to the apartment but left..."

I'm white knuckling the steering wheel, ready to turn back the other way to her apartment until he said she left. Now I'm looking at him, panicked.

"Left...what. What is it, MATT?" His eyes remain on the phone, but they are wide, and I'm not liking the unsettling feeling washing over me.

The way he's tapping my phone against his forehead is not a good sign. My eyes squint, my lips are thin, and I'm counting to thirty.

"Um...she says she left again...with Nick." That's all he says, and when he does, it's slow and drawn out, I can feel he's staring at me gaging my reaction.

I'm breathing heavy, mentally counting. Once I'm in the fifties I let out a big powerful sigh. To say I'm a bit angry is putting it mildly. I'm stark raving mad.

"WHAT? Why the fuck would she leave with Nick? Jesus Christ!" My mind is all over the place, and all I can see is him comforting her... my girl...my pretty girl.

"One finger, if he touches her with one fucking finger, I'll kill him. She's vulnerable, and if he takes advantage of it...Oh man. I hope like hell he is as smart as I think he is."

I have to trust my pretty girl, though. There's no way Elsa would allow that. She wouldn't do that. Not to me, not now. Her being pissed at me is one thing, but my girl would not sleep with another guy knowing I'm back and we're working things out. The idea of her turning to him for comfort...is like a kick in the gut.

"GOD DAMMIT."

"Micah, don't think the worst, man."

Slamming my hand against the steering wheel, I'm crazy with the thoughts that are playing out in my mind. The one guy she slept with after all this time, is now comforting her. That is the one thing that's killing me, she should have never needed to go to him, and that's on me.

I have to pull the car over on the side of the road, it's the only thing I can do to calm my nerves. With car in park, I lay my head back, rubbing my nose with my fingers. Breathing slowly, I grab my phone from my brother and try El one more time. Of course, it goes to voice mail. My once raging anger is now melting into anxious need. I need her, I want to be the one holding her.

I leave a message.

> *Elsa, please call me back, baby. I..I..I need to hear your voice. I'm hurting here, pretty girl, I'm worried and I have so much regret. I'm so fucking sorry for the way I acted earlier. I have left you so many messages. I get that you don't want to hear from me, but why him? Why Nick? It's me, Elsa. It should be me, not him. I need you just as much as you need me. Just call me... please, for the love of God, call me baby. I'll coming running to you, pretty girl. I swear I will. Just give me the chance.*

I press end call.

Without looking at Matt, I say. "She's with him brother, what does that mean for me?" Tears burn my eyes. "I really fucked up."

He sighs reaching for my shoulder, holding his hand there. "Look Micah, he has been the one who has comforted her for years. It's only natural she would turn to him."

They say the truth hurts, and I could not agree more right now.

"Let's go home Matt, she will call when she's ready... I hope."

"Give her time, just give her time." Matt says keeping his gaze out the window.

Nodding, I start up my car and pull away from the gas

station I ended up parking in. Home is our two bedroom house we rent together. This little house has been home to us for a while now. After coming back home, I refused to stay with my parents. Matt was a likely choice since I needed a friend, and we liked the idea of neither one of us living back at home.

\*\*\*

Before going to sleep, I call her yet again. No answer, no text messages and I'm dying on the inside. I thought I would have heard from her by now. Surely, she has to be home. This gives me an idea, I text Liza.

*Me: Hey Liza, El home yet?*

*Liza: Hell no, wish she was. Nick will keep her safe, but I wish she would call me. Her not calling me tells me how upset she is.*

*Me: Let me know when she gets home...The minute she walks in... please!*

*Liza: It's up to her, sorry no can do.*

*Me: It's that, or I come and sleep on your front door... take your pick.*

*Liza: Jesus Christ, wish you got this worked up over me when we were...shit...forget that.*

*Me: Don't go there, this is about her...not us. Please understand.*

*Liza: Going to bed...Later.*

I should have known she would not be much help, but this is not about us. I left her for El, her roommate. She has to understand the history Elsa and I share. Especially now, knowing we have a child out there.

"Hey, bro' any news before I turn in?" Matt asks appearing

in my doorway.

I shake my head before answering. "Not a word Matt, not a word."

Tapping his fingers on the wall, he's worried but trying to hide it. "Just let it be tonight, tomorrow is another day."

"Yeah...sure." I grimace.

Sitting alone in the dark, I replay my jackass behavior and then my mind wanders to the sounds of a baby crying. Tears fill my eyes, and I've never felt this helpless before.

I decide one last time to text her knowing I'll toss and turn all night with worry.

**Me:** *My sweet Elsa, please, just one word to let me know you are okay. Safe. I'm suffering like hell here, pretty girl. And I deserve it. I know I do. I deserve every bit of hell I'm going through because I brought it on myself. Just give me this, please? Are you okay baby?*

Nothing...so I wait...nothing again...so I wait...then nothing.

**Me:** *Please don't tell me I lost you...not again?*

# CHAPTER
## *Eighteen*

Elsa

*E*very part of my body hurts. My muscles ache, my eyes are puffy, and my head might split in two. I feel like the walking dead today. I've never cried so much in my life, reading Micah's last text had me rethinking my life and where it's heading. Never did it enter my mind that I could ever turn my back on him. Is that what I should do? Has too much happened between us? Will he always blame me? I can't imagine we could have a nice long life together while deep down, he has some resentment toward me. Hell, deep down a part of me resents myself.

Standing in the doorway to his bedroom, Nick stands, staring. "Hey sleepy head, how are you feeling today?" He asks smiling. "You sure as hell didn't sleep, I heard you crying all night. My shirt's still soaked." Glancing at his shirt I can easily see what he's talking about, there are patches of wet spots from where I held on tight, crying while he held me.

Lowering my head, I'm embarrassed this is where I ended up, but I needed him. Like always, my trusted friend put his feelings aside to comfort me. He listened, he wiped my tears and let me vent my frustrations. I owe him so much, and I know I don't deserve him. As if he can read my mind, he strolls over and sits next to me.

My smile hits his caring eyes. "I owe you so much, thank you for just being you," I say laying my head on his shoulder. "Wow, what a difference a day can make."

A sigh escapes his lips. "That's for sure." Adjusting our bodies so I'm leaning against his, Nick slowly rubs my arm. "You know you don't need to see him again, he doesn't deserve you. After the way he acted yesterday," he's struggling to find the right thing to say. "You deserve better, Elsa."

I heard it from him all last night. He sat and listed all the reasons why I should let Micah go. Unfortunately, my heart never believed in one.

"Yeah," I sigh. "Maybe you're right," I say it, but don't for one minute believe it. The only thing my mind is concentrating on is what he's doing right now. With every nagging thought, I bite my lip and wonder. "He has to be going stir crazy, he knows I'm with you, all night by now." I can only imagine how frantic he is.

Nick arches his eyebrow before letting out a chuckle. "I love the fact he knows you spent the night with me, serves him right." Of course he does.

Realizing I need to get this over with, I leave my dear friend, and head back home to face the music. All the way home I'm sick with worry. I have no idea what I'll come home too. Unlocking the door to our building, I look around for him, but I don't see him. I feared I'd find him camping out by my door or parked in the parking lot. Breathing a sigh of relief, I head to my apartment thinking so far so good.

Pushing the door open, I don't have to wait long to wonder where he is. He's here, looking disheveled. Eyes bloodshot, clothes wrinkled, he looks plain awful. He's sitting with a very pissed off looking Liza. Wow, can't imagine these two sitting together was a fun time.

Keeping my silence, I shut the door and quietly stroll over to the kitchen table and put my purse down. The eerie quiet from them both has me on pins and needles. Not sure what the hell to say, I decide not to say a word and walk to my room.

"Where the hell have you been, El?" He doesn't raise his voice, or sound mad, in fact, his voice is filled with so much regret and sadness. I've never heard him like this, well, that's not entirely true. Last night in his messages, he sounded pretty much with the same regretful tone.

I stop and turn back to face him, seeing him deflated and lost is not comforting at all. I should be the one who is pissed off, but I'm not. I'm tired and drained. Continuing to walk to my bed, I sit, and out a sigh. Lowering my head into my hands.

Micah joins me, kneeling in front of me settling between my legs.

"Pretty girl, why baby? Why go to him? Why spend the night with him?" He pauses when I partially close my eyes, knowing the tears are coming. "Me, Elsa, you should have been with me."

My nerves and lack of sleep have my tolerance at an all time low, and his remark has hit a nerve. "Really?" I say with a bit more sarcasm than I intended. He's taken back with it as well as his eyes winced.

"Hell yes, it's my job to comfort you. Not his." Clenching his fists, I can see he is contemplating his next words carefully. "Look, I screwed up...badly. Baby," he says, stretching out his hand for mine, "you just turned my world upside down. I didn't handle it well and took it out on you. I was so wrong. Please say you forgive me." His intense look and warm feel of his touch, softens all of my anger I had with him yesterday.

With his arms around my legs, he squeezes them tightly, laying his head in my lap. Not being able to stop myself, before I know it, I'm running my fingers through his hair. Comforting him, helps ease me in strange ways. The tears form and fall with ease, and it's not just my tears that are falling. With each tear that escapes his eyes, a part of my soul weeps. I can also feel my pants getting wet from the tears Micah is shedding.

"I'm so damn sorry, El. I'm hurting here...and I'm scared."

His apology is all I needed.

"About what?" I choke out.

"Losing you, babe. I can't lose you...not again. Put me out of my misery Elsa, will you forgive me?" Staring back, his eyes highlight his pain and agony, if he only knew seeing him this way is agony in itself.

Biting my lower lip, my tears fall faster. How I ever thought I could stay mad at this guy is beyond frustrating. If he only knew how much of my heart he owned.

"Can I show you something?" I shakily ask him knowing how significant this moment is going to be.

His head peers up. "Of course."

Not an easy task with him in my lap, but I finally stand. Pulling off my jeans to expose my hip, I reveal my tattoo.

Staring back to him, I ask, "What do you see?"

Hesitantly, his fingers gently trace my butterfly. He's

nervous, his eyes squint and the gentle shake of his head tells me he's taking it all in.

"Butterfly, honey. I see a butterfly...and the letter M."

"You're very observant. Can you make out two letters M's sideways to make the wings?"

"Yeah," tracing the wings with his finger, he parts his lips in a smile.

"Remember when I told you I named our son?" Saying the word son out loud causes me great pain.

The unrest in his eyes resonate with me, "Oh honey, I can..."

Sobbing my voice cracks, "Michael. I named him Michael. Micah and Michael, two names that start with the letter M. The two loves of my life forever commemorated by a simple butterfly."

My words must hit home with him, because he eagerly draws me into him. His cheek resting against my hip. He gently kisses my butterfly as tears continue to fall down his cheeks. Having his tears wash over my tribute to him and our son...there are no words to describe those emotions.

"I love you so damn much Elsa. Oh God, I'm so fucking sorry."

His words grip a hold of my heartstrings. Pulling me to him, my body crashes into him. His arms cradle me, so we are face to face, cheek to cheek our tears mix getting lost in each other's gaze. Pools of tears give way to the sweetest, most incredible tender kiss I've ever experienced. Our lips, soaked with salty tears, graze one another when we both halt our precious moment. It's a silent realization; iris to iris...we both feel it. No words are necessary, it's as if our eyes are in a deep conversation of their own.

A moment passes, a very monumental one at that. It's like our broken souls have finally found their way home. All the aches in my heart finally have this ease. To prove we were both thinking the same thing, together we mouth the words, "I love you."

Bruno Mars is filling my room with his sweet voice. *When I was your man,* is playing on my iPod. Pulling us off the floor I lay in bed cocooned in Micah's arms. Laying side by side, my play-list sets the mood. We take this time to hold one another, get lost in each other's eyes, while holding hands. I think we finally both found where we belong...home.

Before long, we both drifted off to sleep. Sleep did not come last night for either one of us, and now it has taken over our wrecked bodies.

It's the light whisper in my ear and the warm sensation spreading across my body that alerts me to the fact Micah must be awake. Before long, my shirt is being pulled up over my head. Surprisingly, my jeans and panties have already been stripped, and I have no memory of that happening. Right now, I don't care. A few moans suddenly escape my throat.

"Ssshhh, no words, pretty girl. Let me love you like you should be loved." He sweetly whispers in my ear.

Not wanting to ruin this moment, I silently nod. My arousal is on high alert and my nipples harden under the gentle grazing of his fingers. The way he is caressing me is a straight bee-line to my aching clit. Closing my eyes, I moan softly. Micah's arousal is evident as it's stabbing me in the lower back. I've also noted he has stripped himself naked.

Damn he is good.

I hope he doesn't flip me over. I'm desperate for him to take me this way. I want him to cradle my backside, mold his body to mine and enter me from behind. I need him to take me painstakingly slow.

Like he was reading my damn mind, he does just that.

"Yes Micah," moaning my approval. "Take me this way."

The moment I say this, he stops his rocking and it sounds like he's reaching for something. My groan, of course, is from his loss of contact, so I turn my head and look over my shoulder. "What are you doing?"

"Fuck, looking for a condom baby." He says while reaching for his jeans. Reaching my arm back, I grab his arm stopping him.

Shaking my head, I say. "No…I need to feel you." Swallowing loudly. "I need you just the way you are. No barriers between us, honey," I say lightheartedly. "I'm covered."

His smile widens. "Oh baby, I need you too. Good Lord knows I want to feel every inch of you around me."

His hips gyrate, like he's doing a salsa dance. It's amazing. Micah gingerly snakes his way behind me once again. Drawing my leg over his, he takes his knee and widens the space between my legs to give him plenty of access to unite us. Finding my entrance, he hesitates for a moment lining himself right where he wants.

I moan with anticipation. My eyes are clenched shut and I'm yearning for the moment I feel him slide inside of me. So slow. So perfect. Hitting spots he's never hit before. I suddenly realize he's stopped moving and is eerily quiet. I'm praying whatever has caused him to stop moving will pass quickly.

"Baby," he finds my ear breathing heavily. "Feel every hard inch of me as I slide all the way inside, making love to you." His words hitch slightly when he slides inside just like I wanted him to. Nice and slow, slick with my juices that have coated every inch of him.

"Oh pretty girl, hot damn, your body was made for me. Fuck... you feel so damn good." He says, grunting his words when his thrusts get more intense. Rolling my eyes in the back of my head, I enjoy the fullness of him. Giving into the sensation of how good it feels, I want more...need more.

"Oooohhhhh God, Micah. Please, please...do not stop."

"No, way." He grumbles.

With my head tilted back, I need more. "Harder...oh yes, harder."

"Fuck yes!" His voice is as forceful as his moves.

Cupping my shoulders with his hands, he's thrusting harder and faster. My leg over his thigh is bouncing with his swift movements. Not wanting anything to distract him from what he's doing, I hold my leg higher, keep it there to make sure Micah has easy access. I realize the harder I pull my leg back, the deeper he penetrates. The tilt of my pelvis in the perfect position. Oh so wonderful.

Eyes rolling in the back of my head. "Oohhhh, my... Godddddddd."

Moving in perfect rhythm, Micah's breathing and rapid grunts of pleasure escape his lips every time he's fully seated deep inside. Micah fits tightly inside of me, allowing me to absorb every part of him. The gentle friction of his body against mine sends shock waves throughout my entire body. Craving so much more, I let it be known how much I need him. My need and desire for him has no boundaries. When it comes to Micah, I surrender.

"Oh, baby." He moans with every roll of his hips, widening his circles as to hit my magical spot that heightens my arousal. Shit, I have no idea if he is hitting the infamous G-spot or not. The only thing I know is if that's what he keeps hitting, I hope like hell he doesn't stop. Let me tell ya, it's real, and it's fucking amazing.

My walls contract around him when the tremors of my orgasm start to come to life. I place my hand over my bare, very slick mound. He's so deep when he thrusts, I swear I can feel him in my throat. Every deep thrust has a slight sting of pain due to his size, but that same painful sting has me about crawling out of my skin in delight. Right now, I don't care how I feel afterward, I want him harder...and faster.

Enveloping my closeness, his wet tongue traces a spot between my neck and shoulder. Warm and wet, it's enticing. With an eager thrust, he pierces my skin with his teeth...hard. The eruption of his orgasm spurns on my release. His teeth penetrating my skin, at the same time his shaft penetrates my cervix is my undoing. I come...hard...loud...and I think the neighbors heard it all.

Both of us are breathing hard, and while he's still deep inside, pulling us into a tight embrace, he softly kisses my ear.

Breathless he says, "Love you El."

"Love you back," I say, panting for my next breath.

Still winded, he asks, "Tell me all about him pretty girl. Tell me all of it, I want to hear it from your point of view. I need to learn about...my son." He can barely say the words without losing it.

With our fingers laced together, I replay one of the worst years of my life. Bittersweet I guess, I lost so much in a year's time. Then again, I got the world's best present, Michael. He may have different parents raising him, but my baby has two parents who love him unconditionally. I don't hold back my anger, hurt, loss or betrayal as I shed my tears, telling it to

Micah. He's living it all as I take a stroll down memory lane.

By the time I am finished, I get up and find my only picture I have of Michael. I treasure it as much as the hat, the one he wore when I held him that night. I swear I can smell him today, by now his smell is long gone, but it doesn't stop me from remembering. Showing Micah the picture hits me so hard.

Holding it over my heart, I gaze into Micah's glistening eyes. This moment, the moment I swore would never happen is about to happen.

With a slight shrug of my shoulder, I nervously hand it to him. "Here's your son." Holding my nonexistent breath, I realize how monumental this moment is.

Micah takes a few deep breaths, shaking like a leaf. As he takes his first glance, the tears come out full force. Holding his hand over his mouth, I can clearly see his shock, and a hint of dismay. Moments later, his eyes show grief and loss.

With a heavy heart, he says, "My baby...Elsa, this is our son."

His words are etched with so much love and adoration for a baby he never knew existed until yesterday. In a whirlwind of rage and betrayal, it now gives way to sincerity and love.

Grasping my hand, he pulls me down beside him. We lay back, side by side and each stare longingly at our son's picture. My arms are seen cuddling this tiny miracle. To make this even more amazing, we can just make out his little hand holding on tight to my ring finger...the left hand of course.

Passionately, Micah whispers to me. "See him, El? He's holding the ring finger, the finger I'm going to use to make you mine. This is my sign, he's holding that finger, telling you to wait for his daddy. He knew back then that you belong to me."

Not even expecting him to say this, I close my eyes and let that idea and memory take center stage in my heart. Enraptured with his declaration, I can't help feeling euphoric.

Forever Micah, forever Michael. Both of these boys have enraptured my heart and soul forever.

# CHAPTER
## *Nineteen*

I spent the next week in a frenzy of disarray and commotion to say the least. I try to spend as much time with Micah as we caught up on each other's lives, and I'm amazed at most of the things he's been up to. Shortly after coming home from the Air Force, he decided to partner up with Matt and they are now operating a successful home based security business. Business seems to be booming so they were able to hire additional help. Their father's long line of friends and loyal customers with the McIntosh Group have been more than willing to support them and recommend the Taylor boys.

It was great up until Micah dropped a bombshell on me. It seems his plans now involve me leaving my current job to run their front office. Call me crazy, but I'm considering it. I asked him to give me a few days to think it over, though. Life with Liza has been a struggle. Eating, sleeping and working with her is not working out. Living with the daily struggle, prompted Micah to not only ask me to work with him, but to move in with him as well. If I had to bet, I'd say this worked to his advantage perfectly.

Living and working with him does solve the Liza situation entirely. On both fronts, it's a good idea. Moving too fast? Maybe to some people, but my heart knows what it wants, it always did when it came to him. So moving too fast? I think not!

"What can I do for you, Elsa?" Sitting across from my boss, he sits smiling at me, and I'm sure he's not ready to hear what I'm about to say. His desk is messy with charts, x-rays, and even plastic teeth. I'm going to miss this.

Even though I'm positive about leaving, I'm nervous facing my boss. "I have to give you my notice, I'm leaving Dr. Davis." Biting my lip, my leg bounces with nervous energy. God, I hate this.

Pausing he nods his head, but looks puzzled. "I see, can I change your mind?"

Shaking my head, I truthfully answer. "No, I'm sorry. It's not you or the office, I'm going to work for Micah." I know he has heard all about him and what he means to me. He's also noticed the coolness between Liza and me lately.

He eyes me, knowing there is not a thing he can do to sway my mind. "I figured as much, I don't like it though. You're an excellent member of this team, and you will be missed." Sighing loudly, he adds, "I also fully understand. Thank you for all the time you've given this office. It will be hard to replace you. I can contact the agency to send someone over."

I sat in disbelief. That was easier than I thought it would be. I had expected him to be upset, but he was quite the opposite. In fact, it bothered me a little. I'm not sure if I wanted him to fight a little harder to get me to stay, but I wanted something, at least. I know this is what I want, but I'm also leaving my friends and patients I've come to love and see on a daily basis. I've got to remember, it's for me and Micah. This is a good thing. Dr. Davis gave me a big hug and an open door to come back anytime.

Climbing in my car, I dial Micah to tell him the good news.

Answering the phone, he's as cheery as always. "Hey beautiful, what's new with you?"

Smiling from ear to ear, his voice alone sends my heart singing.

"Well," I teasingly say, "I'm about to make your damn day."

He chuckles into the phone. "You already do, pretty girl, but what did you do now?"

I don't hesitate. "Gave my notice, I'm now a week away from begging you to give me a job." I can hear his gasp, oh yeah, I surprised him.

"Oh baby, you've absolutely made my day. Excellent news, now move in with me and I'll have it all." He says eagerly.

I disclose my secret. "I'm ready."

"I'm sorry, did I hear you right?"

Chuckling, "Yes, Micah, you did. You were right. Living with Liza is not going well, and when I'm not with you, I miss you."

Going five long years without him was bad enough, but now, even going without him for one night, just seems wrong. I need to be where he is.

"You miss me giving you some loving, don't you?"

"Well, there is that..." I can't help cracking a smile.

As if on cloud nine, he says, "Dinner, my place around seven. I have some things we need to talk over. Saw my parents today, and we had a long talk." I don't feel great with the seriousness in his voice, but I'm sure it was a hard conversation to have with them.

"Everything okay?" Holding my breath, I'm afraid to even ask.

"Better than okay, they are happy we are together. Believe it, or not my parents love you. They want to talk to you about... well, you know." He pauses for a moment letting out a slight groan. "They are missing Michael as much as we do, and it hurts them."

Sighing, I can only shake my head. "They blame me, too, you mean?"

"Not at all, baby. Now your parents are another issue."

Oh yes, my *beloved* parents.

"Yeah, go figure." I can only imagine what his parents think of mine. "See you soon, I'm leaving work now."

"Later, pretty girl."

SHOWERED UP GRABBING my things to head over to Micah's place, I stop dead in my tracks when Liza walks inside the door. The tension is not getting any better between us. In fact, Liza and Nick are now best buds, and I'm on the outside. I need to get this moving thing happening sooner rather than later. For all of our sakes.

"Hey Liza, um...by the way." I'm struggling to find the words. "I'm going to move out soon, it's the right thing to do." Figured might as well come right out and say it.

"I hear you put in your notice today, too. Wow, moving fast to shack up with him, aren't you." Shaking her head back and forth, she lets out a grumbled laugh. "Good for you, I'd do the same thing given the situation and your history." She says with a slight chip on her shoulder. Her words are cold, like her posture. She's stiff as a board with a not so happy looking Nick. His stance mirrors hers.

I take offense with her attitude, biting my lip. "Look, this is not easy for any of us, I'm doing what I need to do to try to make it better."

Her annoying roll of her eyes, tells me I'm not going to be happy what she has to say next.

"I get it, okay? I tried to tell myself you both deserve one another, yadda, yadda, yadda. But, it still hurts and I'm trying not to hate you both, but right now I can't."

Her shoulders relax, and her eyes are endearing. Finally, she's admitting her real feelings, about time.

"I know, and I'm sorry," I say.

I lower my head when she grumbles, and walks by me. She goes to her room and shuts the door. My only thought is to tell Micah the sooner we can move me in the better...for all of our sakes.

Standing outside the little two-story house, Micah shares with Matt, I knock on the door.

"Hey little sis," Matt says opening the door. "Get in here."

Matt is the brother I never had. His messy brown hair flops on his forehead, so walking by I mess it up even more.

"Hey sexy, how are ya?"

"Yeah you got that right, all the sexiness went to this brother. Are you sure you don't want to switch Taylor boys?"

I laugh and punch his arm. Got to love those dimples he has. "Oh, I'm sure, poor ugly Micah. I feel sorry for his hideous looks, I can dump him now." My attempt at humor has Matt laughing, but Micah is not very amused, judging by the look on his face.

"My girlfriend is so funny, tonight. But seeing you smile is worth it, so make fun of me all you want. Matt, on the other hand, needs to watch his hands when it comes to my very sexy girlfriend." To make his point Micah stares at his brother.

Holding his hands up, Matt amusingly replies, "Options, I'm giving the girl options."

"Yeah, well flaunt yourself at another pretty girl, not mine." Micah side steps Matt to take me into his arms for a hug.

"Ah, thanks baby." Being wrapped in his arms allows me to take in his cologne, damn... pure heaven.

"Anytime, now give your ugly man a proper kiss."

His light laugh makes me blush, the idea of his name and ugly in the same sentence...no way. Micah is straight up every girl's dream guy.

"Not ugly sweetness, just pure male stud muffin."

"Oh God," Matt moans, walking away. "You both make me sick, truly it's not fair. Why can't I find myself an Elsa?"

Micah and I both agree and say in unison, "You will."

I'm impressed as I watch both boys making me dinner that consists of spaghetti and meatballs, garlic bread, and a salad. Looking at the food makes my mouth water, and I realize just how starved I am.

Sitting at the table, I take a drink of my tea and I envision myself living here. I can't help but question. "How is this going to work if I move in here, do you think it's enough room?"

Matt coughs, laughing looking at me surprised. "Micah did not tell you yet?"

"Shut it, Matt." Micah slams his hand on the table. His eyes are giving his brother a warning glare.

My eyes squint, wondering what is going on now. "Um... no, I don't understand what you are talking about," I say gazing at an angry looking Micah staring at his brother.

*Great, what now!*

I'm arching my eyebrow not sure I'm going to like whatever it is they are hiding from me. I hate surprises, always have.

"Look El," Micah says lowering his fork. "My dad and I were talking. Here, there's not a lot of room, it's only a two bedroom, and we need our privacy." Clearing his throat, he hesitantly looks at me then at Matt.

Matt winks. "Ah, you think I'm going to cramp your style, bro'?"

"Just want to be able to have El all to myself, and that means wherever I want her... whenever I want her." He said, with a devil of a smirk on his face.

I give him a piercing gaze to figure out where this is going. "Oh my God, can we just get to the part where you tell me what is going on?"

"Okay," Micah says holding up his hand. "I was going to ask if you wanted to get a place of our own?"

He says the last part very soft, just waiting to see how I respond to him. I don't get a chance to think it over as Matt interrupts.

Throwing his head back, Matt lets out a loud chuckle. "Bullshit. Micah, you are so full of it. Let me tell you how it really went, and Micah, you tell me if I've got it right. I believe it was more like, Micah put down a down payment on a place and hopes to hell Elsa is going to be okay with it!"

"WHAT!" I'm in shock. It's one thing to ask and another to go ahead and buy a place.

"And you wonder why I don't want to live with you any

longer?" Micah says to his brother who is smiling from ear to ear, loving to see his brother squirm in the hot seat.

I'm stunned. "Are you serious Micah? You found a place AND put a down payment on a house you only hope I will be okay with?" I question.

Looking at Matt, he has his eyes closed. I'm really praying he did not just blow up Micah's surprise for me. Micah's sitting back, arms crossed, and shaking his head. I can see the wheels spinning in his cute little head of his. He's nervous, and that alone makes me want to laugh.

"Babe, please don't be mad." Slowly inching his arms on the table, he holds out a hand. "Come on El, I wanted to surprise you. Matt," eyeing his brother, Micah takes a swing towards him. "Has a big mouth. I might have to shut for him."

"Hey," shouting at Micah. "I'm just keeping it real, bro'. Elsa's not mad at you. Jesus, do you even know your girlfriend at all? I don't even need to ask her to know what she is thinking. *That* is how sure of her I am. I swear I must be more observant than you."

"Yeah, right. Okay, big man, tell me what she is thinking and she will tell us if you are right." Micah challenges.

Matt looks at me and winks.

I bit my lip and laugh.

Arms crossed, I'm more than eager to hear what he has to say. "Go ahead Matt, what am I thinking right now." To be honest, this ought to be good, I squint my eyes just to prepare myself. I have no clue what might slip out of his mouth.

"Okay," he's smirking acting like he's my shrink or something. "You are no doubt nervous, a lot has happened very fast, but you love my brother, so there is no reason not to move in together. Although; while you're surprised that

Micah did this behind your back, you really don't mind. You are impressed he did this because he did it for you. The love you have for him...well...will let him get away with murder. Need I say more?" Holding up his finger, he cuts me off when I'm about to protest. "But you are somewhat sad with the fact you won't be living with me because you wanted to catch me in the shower butt ass naked. You are going to miss your chance for a peek at my goods." The sly fox says as slick as he can. And he sighs just to make me laugh even harder. Smooth talking Matt Taylor is a lady killer, and he's brought me to tears in a fit of hysterics.

Choking on my water, I have to wipe my eyes and my chin at the same time. Oh gosh, it just felt good to laugh. Only, Matt and I are the only one's laughing. Serious, Micah is so quiet and moody, and looking at him only makes us laugh harder.

"Very fucking funny," bringing his attention to me, he raises an eye. "Well my dear, how did he do? Minus the part about seeing him naked, of course. I know you do not wish to see, but just in case you did... do not tell me that."

Holding my stomach, I'm slowly recovering. "First of all," I say wiping my chin of any remaining water, "I am impressed with how observant Matt is. He's right on most of it, actually. I'm shocked, but also very impressed you did that for us." Reaching out I grab hold of Micah's hand. "I'm not sure what to say, we've not talked finances, yet Micah."

"Nothing for you to worry over," taking a hold of my hand, he squeezes it. "I got it handled. We'll sit down and figure it out, the first thing is to close on the house and then get you to work for us." He says, glancing at Matt.

"Thank God, Elsa can now take care of your unwanted attention you've been receiving lately." Matt says under his breath.

What, that got my attention.

Micah moans with his disapproval. "Matt would you shut your mouth, do you ever just stop saying shit you should not say?"

"Babe, don't listen to him. A few clients hang around more than they should. The great thing with you working there they will know I am with you and to leave me the hell alone." Micah rambles this out so fast, I'm not sure what he just said.

I took away from that admission that indeed, women were hot after him. Now I can't say I blame them for wanting him, he is beyond sexy. I just did not need to hear it.

Okay, I'm mentally seeing myself on a daily basis watching women hang on him...I'm not sure this is a good idea after all. Rolling my eyes, not liking it, I accidentally talk out loud. "Oh great, just what I need." I say it and the minute I do, I regret it.

Clearing his throat, Matt looks at me like I've grown ten heads. "Seriously, my brother only has eyes for you. Always has, always will. You are the only woman I can say with one hundred percent confidence that your man...my brother... would never cheat."

I sheeply reply, "Ah, thanks Matt. He knows better." I say with my butter knife in my hand, waving it around.

"Hey, I'm right here and I don't need anyone else. Five years ago you, ruined me for any other woman. No one compares to my pretty girl."

I hold my hand over my heart. "I'm one lucky gal."

"Not lucky," Matt's smirks. "I do think you have a magic... um... let's just say you must...yeah, I'm not going to finish that thought. I'd rather not get hit from my brother for less than pure thoughts of you, El." He lets out a quick exhale which sounds more like a snort.

I can't help but snicker. "You Taylor boys will be the death of me yet."

"Damn straight baby," Micah says with a head roll.

"The house is at the end of Park Street near Harrison Heights. It's perfect for us El, I took my dad there a few days ago. He liked it and to be honest," Micah says with a shrug of his shoulders, "He gave me the money for the down payment. I think it was his way of making amends."

I hate to tell him I'm not super comfortable with his parents yet. I've yet to face them now that they know about the baby.

"He doesn't need to do that Micah, even though it's beyond thoughtful. He has no reason to make amends with me, either." I don't need another reason to feel uncomfortable around him.

"Don't let it bother you, El. If he wants to help us out, let him. It's not like he's hurting for cash. My mother would string me up if I made him take it back. Just spend your time decorating it the way you want it."

The idea of decorating a place of our own is exciting. It's a lot to take in for the short time we've been back together. When has anything gone according to plan with me in my life? Never. Why start now?

The idea of finally being happy with Micah and us moving forward is like a dream come true. The only sad part of this dream is living my life without my parents in it. That part hurts.

"Why the sad face, beautiful?" He asks me, nudging my chin up with his finger so our eyes could meet.

"Nothing, forget it." My lack of a smile says it all.

Using his finger, he slides my hair from my face. "Not happening. Spit it out, El."

Wiping a stray tear, I try to shake my sad thoughts away. "Just thinking about my parents missing out on all of this. Growing up, I always looked forward to having them by my side in every facet of my life Micah, and none of it will ever happen. I now see them for what they are, and it kills me. To realize how much hatred they have for me, it's not love, it's sick."

After dinner we ended up sitting in his room. Needing a breather, I go walk back to the living room. I'm sick of crying and I need to get the idea they would be a part of my future out of my mind. They won't be there for me, not anymore. They stopped the minute they found out I was pregnant. A switch had flipped with them. I no longer held the same value in their eyes. I was pushed aside. Just like baby Michael, I was also swept under the rug.

I notice Matt sitting on the couch watching TV. I decide to sit next to him, he always could make me laugh...and right now, that is exactly what I need.

"Hey sweet pea," he can see my tense expression. "Oh no, what did my brother do now?" Of course, he thinks it's Micah's fault.

"No, not your brother...this time," I say with a smile. "Let's just say my parents suck. I'm the outcast and need to come to terms that they will never be by my side. They will miss out on all the beautiful things my life will bring." Placing my hand on his knee, he covers his hand on top of mine. "It's not a great feeling."

Taking a moment to let what I said sink in, he takes me by the shoulders and crushes me to him in a bear hug. I relish the comfort this crazy Taylor boy can bring me, he's the brother I've never had.

"You will be okay El, they are the ones who will miss out. You have your nutty boyfriend, my parents, and of course me. Now having me in your life, has got to rank right up there with number one." His sense of humor holds no bounds.

Of course, I agree with him. "Don't let your brother know that," I say laughing.

"Lips are sealed, baby."

And just like that, presto, my mood goes from sad to delight. Noticing movement out of the corner of my eye, I glance up to see Micah standing against the wall, watching us with such a sweet smile on his face. He enjoys the fact his brother and I get along so well. Sneaking a peek over Matt's shoulder at him, he winks back to me. My love for that man takes my breath away, to see him so strong and right in front of me is a magnificent sight.

I mouth the words, "I love you." Then give him a wink of my own.

Walking toward us, he sits with us. We spend the next hour watching whatever we can find. Relaxed, we all sit back laughing and talking like lifelong friends. It's a great way to pass the time, being here with the Taylor brothers is just what I needed. The rest of the night, not one time did I think of my parents.

# CHAPTER
## *twenty*

*M*icah's driving us to our new house today so I can get a look at where we will begin our future together. Arm out the window, he's bopping to the music like he doesn't have a care in the world. Me? I have one leg bouncing and I'm so nervous, I have to wipe my clammy hands on my pants. It's not so much I'm worried I won't like it, in fact, just the opposite. I'll love it because I'll be with him. The fact is his parents will be there, and facing them after all this time terrifies me.

As we pull up to the house, the lightness in my heart gives way to my wide grin. My pulse is racing, the house is beyond magnificent. The view reminds me of what you may find on the cover of magazines. I smile instead of speaking because Micah keeps asking me what I think. Wow.

It's slightly larger than he let on, it has arched peaks above the front door and second story windows. Two stall garage is trimmed in black which accentuates the incredible dark tan color of the house. There is an incredible winding walkway from the driveway to the front door. Noticing the color of the front door, I laugh and look over at Micah's beaming face. It's then he raises his eyes, and I know what may have sold him on this particular house. The front door is a beautiful shade of red. A nice match for his beloved Chicago Blackhawks. My man is a sports nut, lucky for him so am I. Yet, another reason we get along so well.

Holding my smile, I shake my head, noticing his parents are here. They open the front door to welcome us. Excitedly, I take Micah's hand walking to greet them. The quiver in my stomach is not helping my nerves.

"Hello sweet girl, come on in and see your new home." His mother Skylar greets me like we've been friends forever. No awkwardness at all, she takes me in for a hug and walks us through the door. She's just as beautiful as Micah. Both of Micah's parents are tall, light hair and blue eyed. No wonder they have good looking children. Micah and his dad share a few hugs and laugh following us inside.

Letting go of his son, David gives me a hesitant nod. "Hello Elsa, I'm so happy for the both of you."

Really! Nervously, I rake my hands through my unruly hair. "Thank you so much." It's barely a whisper, but I'm too busy swallowing more than usual. Damn nerves.

Wanting to avoid a conversation I know is coming, I look around the house, keeping my attention occupied on anything but them. My first impression is Wow! The inside is decorated with modern fixtures. Wood floors, gray, granite counter tops, and top of the line stainless steel appliances. A dream kitchen to cook in, yeah, I could see me baking up a storm in here for sure. Micah and his parents are busy chatting, so I continue exploring. A large brick fireplace is the central focus point in the living room. Even better, the fireplace has large bookcases on each side of it. Enough room to put my favorite books, note to self, need to buy many more books.

Walking behind me we venture up the staircase to the second floor. Each of them are pointing out different features they think I would like, it's odd I'm the last actually to view the house. In all honesty, I love everything about it.

Micah stands out in front of the doors to the master bedroom, it has two doors that are currently closed. The gleam in his eyes tells me I'm in for a treat. Opening them one at a time, he says, "this is the best room in the house, babe."

I raise my eyebrow at him, only to have him return it with a sexy grin.

Opening both of the doors, what I notice first is the view from the big, wrap around windows. The house backs up against a wooded area. The back yard is fenced and large, a great place for a dog and someday *children*. Okay, not letting my mind even think of kids. The attached bath is so big it's ridiculous.

"Holy crap, this is insane, Micah." Everywhere I look, it keeps getting better. This room is so large, it's amazing. Heck, I could even put a couch in here. That's how big it is.

"Great, isn't it?" The sparkle in his eye says it all.

"This house is perfect for you two, a lot of room to grow into," Skylar says while she rubs Micah's back. Both of his parents are commenting how much they love the house.

The house has three bedrooms in all, entirely decorated in neutral tones. I love it, not a thing I would change.

"We only need furniture to fill this house," I say not to anyone in particular.

"Oh honey, we will help with that," Skylar says mentioning

all the furniture she is going to donate to us. My head is swimming with how fast this is all going.

We spend the next hour walking around, talking all about the things Micah would change. I'm beaming with excitement, and nodding with my agreement. Of course I don't care what he does with it, leave me alone in the kitchen, and I'll be golden. Still can't believe we will be living here...as a couple. It's all so unbelievable, if this is a dream...do not wake me up.

His parents walk us out to Micah's car saying our good-byes. I thank them profusely for all they have done, but they keep telling me it's no big deal. Micah is happy, and that is the only thing they care about. It's then I find out we are having dinner at their house. Grimacing, I know what I'm in for... questions. Oh boy, time to relive it again as the day has come for the talk of their long-lost grandchild. I've avoided seeing them since I got back together with Micah. I know I can't avoid them any longer so we just need to get it over with. The sooner we do, the sooner we can all learn to cope.

WE ALL GATHER in the living room after dinner. At least I got to eat before the acquisition begins. Time to take some deep breaths and just answer them as honestly as I can, not sure what else they could want from me. I brought my picture of him to show his grandparents. They have a right to see it.

All eyes settle on me, and my mind is playing out worst-case scenarios. My irrational mind worries they will end up hating me. It's all I can think about and replaying the events that cause my heart to palpitate. Letting my eyes settle on each of theirs, I'm silently seeking reassurance that they will understand I only did what I was forced to do.

I start the conversation, fingering my necklace and shifting, unable to get comfortable. "I found out I was pregnant shortly after Micah left...not why or where he went. Not knowing how he felt, it never crossed my mind to come to you all." I say looking at his parents finally letting my eyes settle on Matt.

Mostly the question and answer part of the night went off with no yelling or shouting. They listened, cried and put themselves in my shoes. It shocked me, if I'm honest because Micah had a totally different reaction when he found out. Tears were shed, and regrets were shared, but we made it through. The picture of him is what caused his mom and dad to break down, and it tears my heart apart once again. Matt's face is just as shocked, only this time he is more agitated after seeing his nephew's picture.

"I want to find him, I have a right to find him," Matt exclaims.

The room goes silent. All eyes shift my way.

"I don't know the first thing about trying to find him, Matt. My parents, as you know, set it up, the only thing I know is Catholic Charities was the agency. Beyond that, nothing." My eyes widen and my shoulders sag.

Dave then spoke up. "What city did you give birth in, Elsa? You mentioned you gave birth while staying with your aunt, right?"

Nodding. "Yeah, I was in Waterloo."

"Then that is where we start. I know people who can help." Matt says while pulling out his phone. "I'll just text him to call me when he can, he does this sort of stuff."

"You mean Tyler?" Micah asks.

"Yep," Matt says while still texting, Micah just nodded his

head.

"Should we ask my parents for any documents, they have to have something?" I cringe even saying it. My parents are the last people I want anything from.

Skylar says unashamed, "I don't want a thing from those people, they have done enough to hurt my family. I'm sorry Elsa, but your parents piss me off. They should have told us... FIRST."

Can't argue with her there. I keep my mouth shut and just nod my head to agree.

Micah's rubbing my shoulders. "Ready, baby? Let's get you home."

Hell to the yes, I need to get out of here. Enough reminiscing about my past for one night. Great if Matt's friend can help, but I'm not fully convinced he can. Micah's been quiet on the subject of finding Michael, and I'm afraid to ask him what he thinks. I'm not even sure of my feelings. I've never even considered trying to find him.

Lying in bed at Micah's, neither one of us want to be alone. We need each other. We both work early tomorrow, but tonight is about holding onto one another. Micah cradles me under his chin, nuzzled up against his warm chest, his breathing calms my own. "Pretty girl, get some rest. You are beyond tired, and I know our evening was not easy for you. Hell, it wasn't easy on any of us. How do you really feel about Matt trying to find him?"

"I'm not sure, scared I guess."

"A part of me is scared shitless. I want to see him, but what scares me the most is that it won't change a damn thing. I don't have a right ever to get him back... is it better not to find him?" His voice softens to a whisper.

With a deep sigh. "Oh Micah, it's not a bad thing and I'm not sure myself. Are we better to just let it go? If we see him, we'll want him back, and that's most likely not possible. My heart breaks either way."

He gives me a gentle kiss and hugs me tight. A way to reassure me... or comfort me, either way it's nice.

"Will it ever get easier? Micah, sometimes I'm scared our damaged past will always come between us. We've both lost so much."

He lightly laughs, kissing the top of my head. "Were not damaged baby, we just have history. Some parts will always hurt, but we get to make our future. We will do it right."

Falling asleep, I'm praying he's right.

MY LAST DAY AT the dental office came and went. It was also my last day of living with Liza, she stayed away from most of the moving. Just when Micah, Matt and I were getting the last of the few boxes, Liza and Nick walk in together. We all pause, looking at one another. It's obvious no one wants to be the first to speak. So I do.

"Hey guys, just getting the last of my things and I'll be out of your hair." I say in a cheerful tone. Swallowing down how awkward this really is.

Liza merely nodded. "Um, okay. You do know I'll miss you, right?" Her voice is soft, and she's avoiding to look me in the eyes.

I'm a bit surprised, so I smile and give her a hug. "Yeah, I know. I'll miss you too, and when you're ready, if ever... we can do lunch."

"Do I get to come to lunch, or am I off limits to you, now that you are being back with him?" Nick chimes in, saying it in a not so friendly tone while he points his finger at Micah.

Standing in between them, I hold up my hand to Nick. "Stop it. I'm always going to be your friend, unless you don't want to be my friend anymore." It's not the time for Nick to go off, I'm sure Micah will no doubt respond.

Turning my head to Micah, I see he's fighting all of his urges. A bulging vein is pulsing in his neck. Good Lord, he's pissed.

Standing up taller, Micah inches closer. "Nick, do not give her shit. If you can't support us, stay the hell away. Simple as that." Micah and Matt share a look, both ready to beat his ass if need be.

"Do you speak for her now too, Micah? Should I just ask you for permission before I talk to her?"

"Fuck off, man." Micah's close to losing it with the way his fists are balled up. Just to keep the peace, Matt reminds Micah to chill.

"STOP IT," I shout, placing my hand against Micah's chest. Turning back to Nick, I snap. "God, what is wrong with you? Right now, I don't even want to be around you. You used to want the best for me, I'm sorry it's not you. But hell, you out of anyone knows how much I have always loved him. This is not new to you." I'm scrambling trying to reason with a head shaking Nick.

"Yeah, I know that, unfortunately. Too bad I went and slept with you right before the ass-hat came back into the picture." He says deadpan.

Ouch, that one stung. Raising my eyes to meet Micah's I'm about floored with the murderous glare he's giving Nick.

"Man, I will beat your ass if you talk to her like that again." Micah's patience is running thin. I'm amazed he hasn't hauled off and decked Nick by now.

Nick huffs a breath holding up his hand, "No worries, I'm out of here. Good luck with this, Liza." He says and walks out the door as well all stand too stunned to speak. I want to cry, but crying over Nick in front of Micah would be a disaster. Although he now knows how much Nick helped me over the years. I told him all about it.

"What a dick." Matt sighs.

Rocking in place, I'm biting my nails. "He's right, it's my fault. I hurt him, and he's pissed."

"Like HELL it is," Micah shouts.

Matt calmly adds, "Elsa, he fell for you. Right now, he can't be a friend, but with time, he will come around."

Leave it to Matt to find the right words to make me feel better. Liza clears her throat, eyes looking sympathetic. "Pip, give him time. I'm having a really hard time with this, too. But I do see how much you two love one another...it's great for you both. Unfortunately, he refuses to see it. He wanted it to be him." To shock me even more, she comes to give me a hug.

Looking over at Micah, she asks, "Take care of her, okay?"

"You bet I will, and Liza, thanks for everything. I know the whole situation is difficult on all of us. I hurt you , and for that I'm truly sorry."

They pause a moment, lost in one another. It's awkward, but I can't get upset. Finally Liza sighs and smiles. "Yeah, I know. Get going and get into the new place. I'll miss you at work too, Pip, but in time, I'll call you...okay?"

We share one last hug before we pack up the last of the boxes. Knowing I hurt my two best friends hurts, and I only hope one day they both can forgive me. I've got to learn to deal with it, my past is my past and that may include Nick in it. My future is sitting in his car holding my hand driving us to our new home. Its move in day!

Boxes are all around the house, we hardly have any furniture, but Micah's mom is on a mission to fill the house as quickly as possible. To be honest, having pillows around to sit on was kind of fun. We do have a bed, Micah had a king size bed and a top of the line mattress. It's like sleeping in heaven, mine was a queen and it's in one of the spare rooms.

Matt left after the last box was brought into the house, so it's just us. Micah orders Chinese and we are going to sit on our pillows and watch the TV, which is plugged in on the floor. Our first night, we are christening it with good food and hockey. Blackhawks are playing the Minnesota Wild, so to make Micah's night, I pulled out my favorite player's jersey. Yes, I've had it for a few years. Knowing it was my man's favorite team, I followed as well. I swim in the damn thing, it's more of a nightshirt. Jonathan Toews is my favorite player, #19. To add to Micah's entertainment, I strolled out in my jersey and black panties. Nothing else.

His mouth damn near dropped to the floor at the same time his fork fell to his plate. He stopped to give me a once over, well many times over actually. Sitting next to him on my pillow, I crossed my legs and can see him eyeing my freshly shaved legs.

"I see what I'm having for dessert," He says with a lick of his lips.

"Um, what is that? We need to hit the store tomorrow." I'm not paying any attention to his flirty side, I'm watching the hockey game while he obviously is not.

"Don't need the store, babe."

I happen to follow his eyes as they roam up my legs turning his head to sneak a peak under my jersey.

"Like what you see?" I ask raising my eyebrow.

Licking his lip, he wickedly agrees. "Do I ever. I knew living together was a fabulous idea. Even better idea that Matt is no where around to interrupt me doing many naughty things to you."

Licking my fork, I sigh. "Lover-boy, watch the game."

"Game now... Elsa later." He declares with a grumble.

The game was excellent, we won by two goals. And true to his word, Micah got his dessert. Our first night in our new home was christened properly. First the living room, then the master bedroom. By the time we made it to the bed, we were both too tired to give it another go around. That would have to wait for another night...just not tonight.

# CHAPTER
## Twenty-One

First day at Taylor Security, I'm taking in my new surroundings trying to make better use of the space they have with the reception area. To date, they've never had a front desk person, they've handled it all themselves as a two man show. In the short time they have been open, they are slowly getting busier which is exactly why they needed the extra help. The phone rings the moment I step foot in the front door along with a few clients who had stopped by for appointments.

"Oh hey Trevor," Micah greets a tall guy who walked up the hall towards us. "This is my girlfriend, Elsa. Elsa this is Trevor, one of our computer tech guys. Elsa will run the front office for us from now on."

The gleam in Micah's eyes when he introduced me as his girlfriend has me swooning. It's amazing to take in how genuinely proud he is to announce me as his girl let alone the person running the front office. Trevor seems more than thrilled. He has a buzz cut hair style, black framed glasses and is a walking stick. He's beyond thin, I'm not sure he ever eats.

"Awesome," Trevor claps his hands as his eyes squint overly joyed hearing this bit of news. "No more answering the phones. Good news, now I can concentrate on doing my job." And maybe eat.

On his way back to his office I presume, he slaps Micah on the shoulder muttering the word, "finally."

"Okay babe, lets get you started. I'll show you what we've been doing, and then you can change whatever you want to make it the way you want it." Micah's ushering me up the hall with a hand gently pressed at my lower back.

The office space is more than nice. There are big windows across the front of the building. The main desk itself is circular, and it wraps around to the hallway that leads to the boy's offices and the tech room. A break room is farther down the opposite hall. It's spacious for the few employees they have, but as they grow, it will be useful. All in all, the office rocks. I'm impressed. Now I need to figure out what my job requirements will be exactly, then I'll be able to relax a bit.

The phone rings and we look at each other, pausing. Lifting my hand up to Micah and Matt who has now just joined us, I might as well do my job. Matt goes to answer it, but I swat his hand away.

"Good morning, Taylor Security Elsa speaking," I say with my usual cheery voice, looking back at the boys. I can faintly hear Micah chatting with Matt. "See what did I tell ya? She's freaking perfect to answer the phones. Everyone will love her." Matt smiles back with a nod of his head.

"No doubt, brother. Plus she will keep you in line." Resting a hand on Micah's shoulder, his expression changes.

"Just make sure I don't walk in the break room and find you bending her over the table, I eat in there," Matt says it loud enough I can hear him.

Snapping my head in his direction, I see Micah just as he elbows his brother, and calling him a 'smartass' under his breath.

Since I'm on the phone with a client, the only thing I can do is roll my eyes and stick out my tongue. He chuckles faintly as I'm forced to listen to a female rant on about how she needs to talk to Micah over her installation date. Instead of writing it down, I glare pointedly at him.

"Yes, I see. Can you hold on a minute? I will check and see if he is available." I'm about to put her on hold when, she stuns me. She is asking me questions about who I am. I'm sure the stunned look of my face is one of bewilderment because both Matt and Micah are looking at me, wondering what the hell is going on.

"I'm sorry...um...well I was hired today. Yes...okay. How lovely for you." Eyes wide like saucers I'm biting my damn lip wanting to tell her where to shove it. How dare she grill me about who I am and what I do here. Not a great way to start off my first day. I can only assume this is what Matt was referring to with some of their clients wanting to stake a claim on my boyfriend.

Holding up my finger, I let her know my disdain with the clearing of my throat. "Please hold." Resting the phone on my chin, I'm counting to ten before I speak. "It seems a Carla Mitchell..."

"Oh shit." It's all Matt says, he seems to understand my odd behavior. It's then he whistles, giving Micah a strange expression.

"Anyway." Taking a calming breath, I focus on a nervous looking Micah. "She is on the phone for..."

"Micah." Matt shouts out slapping his brother on the back.

"Matt... shut it." My glare alone should tell him that this is not funny. "She was ill informed you hired a new front desk girl and is demanding to talk to you, Micah. I take it she is sweet for you." Plastering a fake smile on my face, I use the phone to tap my forehead when all I want to do is smash the damn thing.

"Babe," Micah says all comforting and sweet. "Don't even worry yourself, she is a handful, just ask Matt? He pushed her off on me, and now she won't leave me alone. I'll take it in my office, no worries." Micah walks back to his office, and I see the 'hold' button light go off so I know he's talking with her now.

Reading my less than thrilled attitude, Matt sighs. "El, don't let her bother you. You will meet a few clients who are taken with him." He says with a shrug of his shoulder.

"Yeah, sure. I left my job for this. Why did I do that, Matt?" *Seriously, what did I do?*

Walking over, he places his arm over my shoulder, Matt joking says, "So you can make sure women like Carla don't get their hooks in your boyfriend."

"Great. Super. I'm off to a grand start."

THE REST OF THE day was not so bad, a few more clients came in for their scheduled appointments. So far, only one female whose eyes I may have wanted to scratch out, because she drooled over Micah in front of me no less. He simply shrugged it off as no biggie. I, on the other hand, was not so dismissive of her actions. Matt spent the day laughing his ass off, watching me mostly. I had to admit, even with the few horrible women I had to put up with, it was fun.

After lunch, I had the front desk pretty organized. I was rocking it.

Filing the last of the orders coming up for installations, I heard a man clear his throat. Turning my head, I see a very handsome man eyeing me up and down. Oh great, this is just what I need to make this day even better. This place is worse than a bar. Pick Up Central should be its new name. Might have to bring that up at the next staff meeting. If we even have one!

"Hello welcome to Taylor Security, I'm Elsa." I say in welcome to *Mr. can't stop looking down my chest.* It annoys me so much, I glance down at my V-neck sweater to see if my chest is falling out. I am happy to see that it wasn't. Phew! Squinting my eyes, I make a point to look him dead in the eyes as if saying *caught ya!* He just smiles, not caring one bit.

"Well Elsa, I must say you are definitely a welcome addition to the office. I'm James Kirkland and I have an appointment in about," he looks at his watch, "ten minutes. I can chat with you until then." His smile tells me he knows how good looking he is and if I'm correct this sexy look of his must work on most women.

My fake smile and larger than life eyes have me jumping for joy, I get ten more minutes with this guy. I'm about to take my pencil and jam it in my eye, that's how excited I am. Mr. Kirkland does just that, he never left the front desk. Instead, he's chatting like we're old school mates. When I happen to catch sight of Matt and Micah walking my insides start doing somersaults. Goodness, get this man away from my desk. I'm hoping the boys get my drift with the less than friendly death glare I'm giving them.

Not even noticing my guest, they notice my desk instead. Everything has a proper place, no papers are presently thrown all over the place. I must admit, I've been a busy girl.

"Impressive. You are definitely what we needed to get this place in order." Both boys are nodding their heads.

"Yes," my guest adds his own input. "You gentlemen have got yourself a winner, here. She not only brightens up this office, but her voice alone makes me want to stay here all day and chat with her." Mr. Kirkland eagerly says, tapping his finger on the counter. Licking his lower lip, his eyes dart downward to my chest once again. Giving him a pleasant smile, because he is a client after all, I cross my arms to hide my chest from his vantage point. I noticed Micah's smile fade when it instantly turned into a menacing glare, lips tightly pressed together, I take it he too noticed his client eyeing my chest.

"Well James, you might be advised as to *who* she belongs to." Micah grimly adds with a slight lean of his head in my direction.

Taking the challenge to Micah, he replies. "Is that right? Do I dare ask?"

"Now James, let's not upset Micah. He's most protective of his girl." Matt chuckles with a laugh but is eyeing his brother just to make sure he wont need to break up a fight.

I must be staring like an idiot because Matt sighs waving his hand to get my attention. "Don't worry Elsa, James goes way back with us. Old friend," Matt then looks back to his dear old friend. "You may not stay Micah's friend if you do not take your eyes off of her."

My mouth falls open when Micah steps behind me, pulling me against him. Slowly turning me around, he cusps my jaw in each hand and lays a kiss on me that damn near melts my panties. Wanting it to go longer than it should in a place of business, Micah opens and thrusts his tongue inside of my mouth. I do the only thing I can, I hang on for dear life. I forget we have company because as soon as his lips caress mine... I'm a goner.

"Oh for fuck's sake Micah, I get the picture." James huffs.

Breaking the kiss, he gives me one last peck on the lips. Keeping his eyes trained on me, he speaks to James. "Make sure you get that loud and clear James, this pretty girl is mine."

Micah then winks letting me know all is okay. He may be, but I sure as hell am anything but, I'm frustrated, embarrassed, and now my panties feel like they are on fire.

Sitting, I run my fingers through my hair, messing it up more than it already is.

Matt slaps his hand against the counter twice "And this is why working with her is going to be so much fun. I'm taking bets on how soon before Micah loses his shit and beats one of our clients, or better yet, how soon it will take Elsa to beat a bitch who is in heat for my dearest brother." His face is bright a shade of red, actually enjoying this nonsense.

Slapping James on the back, all three walk down the hall chatting and sharing laughs. "Either way, it's pure entertainment. But mostly she knows her shit, and we need the help." Matt turns around looking back at me with that sexy as hell smile of his.

"Love you, Elsa girl."

Yeah. Such a smart ass.

"Hey Elsa, can you help me a minute?" Trevor breaks up the awkward moment, wanting me to come to his office.

"Um, sure whatever I can do." I happily get up and walk to his office.

"Do you think we could find a way to organize these orders with the equipment that has come in, and then organize it based on their appointments? I'm so behind, and could use the help."

Eyeing the stacks of papers on his desk, it's no wonder he's confused and behind on work. Not only papers, there are boxes opened and a few unopened. I'm not sure how the hell they kept it all straight this long.

"Sure, bring them up to me and tell me what pile to organize them in."

He mouths 'thank-you' while gathering up the papers.

"How the hell did you ever get any work accomplished?" I ask looking briefly at the stacks of paper.

"I didn't, but you are the saving grace I have been praying for." He says, with his hands laced together like he's praying when a few papers fall to the floor. We both end up laughing.

By the end of the day, order has been restored and I'm super impressed I got it done. The loose papers are filed and labeled. I'm marking names on few of the boxes of equipment when I notice Matt approaching me.

"Holy crap you have been busy today. Run away with me now, Elsa. Leave my brother for the younger, better looking Taylor." His sexy eyes sparkle as he crosses his fingers.

"You never give up, do ya?" I can't take him seriously, he just cracks me the hell up. I love him all the more for it, because he brightens my day. Just like a brother!

"Me," he says pointing a finger at his chest. "Never, it's too funny to watch my brother get pissed off at me flirting with you." His humorous smirk fades the instant Micah comes up to stand behind him.

A loud huff escapes his lips before he rolls his eyes at his brother. "Still hitting on my girl, I see."

Matt happily agrees. "You know it, one day she will see for herself. I'm just better looking than you." He adjusts his shirt and ducks out of arm's length of his brother. Good idea, considering Micah is bigger than Matt. Never know when Micah might throw a right hook, jokingly of course.

While I enjoy this fun banter between them, I throw my hands in the air. "You two. I swear, one day, I might turn lesbo and leave ya both." Figure I might as well have some fun myself.

Suddenly a loud laugh comes out of nowhere. "Oh shit, that one burned." Trevor walks up throwing his head back, laughing as if that was the funniest things he's heard in a while.

"Well I, for one, am glad the day is over. El, my love, let's get out of here." Rolling his shoulders, Micah looks tense, he totally disregards my attempt at humor.

"Sore shoulders?" I ask.

"Yeah, want to rub them for me?" Micah walks to me and wraps me in a hug.

"Oh Jesus, you two never quit." Matt uses his hands to break up the sexy gaze between his brother and me. "Hey, that reminds me, I got a call from Tyler." He snaps his fingers like he totally forgot.

The instant that name leaves Matt's lips, I tense up and my eyes freeze on Micah. I notice his body stiffens, as well.

"What did he find out?" Micah quietly asks, no emotion

behind his words. I realize he might be just as nervous as I am with Tyler finding Michael.

"Not much," Matt says with a shoulder shrug. "He will stop by soon if he gets any more information."

"Did he find anything?" This time it's me asking.

"Yeah, I guess the town you had him in was small enough, so he quickly found the building of public records. Found the day Elsa gave birth, lucky for him, even though the records were sealed, he got the information he needed to start with. Catholic Charities was not much help, but he has resources. We'll see." He says with a shoulder shrug.

Sitting here listening to the possibility of us getting closer to finding out where our little boy may be living upsets my stomach. The sudden retching of it sends me barreling to the bathroom to toss my lunch.

"Baby." Micah gently knocks on the door. I can tell by his voice, he's more than concerned.

Opening the door, my eyes rest on a worried looking Micah while Matt's pacing in the other room. Micah kisses my head as I walk out. There are no words to describe how I'm feeling. On one hand, I want to know where my baby is, how he's doing. On the other hand, I'm scared of what it will do for my already fragile heart.

"I'm okay." Whispering to Micah. He sways us back and forth, I try to reassure him.

Matt tenses and hesitantly approaches us. "Elsa, are you okay with Tyler trying to find him?" He just comes right out and asks. To be honest, it's rather nice he's thinking of my feelings when he's got his own to contend with.

Micah stops rocking us so we both can face his brother.

I sigh, not knowing what to say. "I'm not sure, Matt. Don't

get me wrong, I would love nothing more than to find him, but then what? It changes nothing. He's been adopted into a family. I just don't see a happy ending here. It's selfish on my part, I had to give him up once and doing it again might just kill me." In all honesty, it will.

Fingers tighten around my shoulders when Micah's hands freeze. Knowing how badly he wants to see his son, but knowing it won't change a damn thing hurts me and him beyond belief. I can't tell them not to try to find our son, this is his right, after all. I can't deny him what he wants.

"Oh El, baby, this is killing you. Let's just see what happens. We can always find out and leave it at that." Not sure if Micah is trying to convince me or himself, but it does sound like a plan. It also gives us time to figure out what we will do if given the chance to see him.

"I have no fucking clue what is right or wrong here." Matt's frustrated, running his hands through his hair before he storms off. I get it, but I have no words to comfort him. I can't even console Micah. Feeling useless is not a feeling I enjoy. In this situation, we have three complete different emotions and ways to look at it, when it comes to Michael. I'm the one who gave birth and had to let him go. Micah's his father, and he never had a chance to see him. But all the same, he can't change what happened. Being his father and trying to do what is best for him should be his only concern. Matt, on the other hand, is his uncle and he looks at this differently. I'm not the girl he left to have a baby alone. He's not the father, he's the uncle who wants to get the chance to see his only nephew.

With what sounds like a frustrated sigh, Micah said, "Let's go home."

I concur. What a first day!

# CHAPTER
## *twenty-two*

The next few days were pretty much the same, although I had the office running like a well-oiled machine. Trevor is off and running, finally able to concentrate only on his job duties. In doing so, it has taken a lot of pressures off Matt and Micah. With me running the front, everyone's morale seems to be on the upswing. Every day I've feel more comfortable in my role at Taylor Securities, finally letting Micah, and I relax for a change. I had no idea all the cool things our company has to offer and what different types of security we provided to our clients. It's impressive and a big change from dentistry.

Today, is a day I'm dreading. Micah had to be in the office early for an appointment with a client. I told him I'd rather come in later when the office opened. We've been riding together every day, but I just needed some time to myself, because today will be hard enough for me. I have yet to tell him, and I'm not sure if I even should, at this point. Some reminders are just too painful.

Taking my time walking into the office my cell rings, digging in my purse, I find it and press call without even looking at the caller ID.

"Hello."

"Hey, El." A voice I flatly did not expect to hear hits me until I realize what this day holds for me. Why am I surprised to hear his voice? Of course, he'd reach out to me.

"Hey Nick, it's nice to hear your voice." I stop walking and slide against the wall, I'm left breathless just hearing the voice that has been my calming force for so long.

"Just wanted to say I'm sorry for the way I acted, I've been going back and forth with myself if I should even call you today. I guess," his voice trails off but I can hear his deep breathing. "I'm just thinking about you."

I have to sniffle, as a big lump forms in my throat.

"That is so sweet of you, and I appreciate it. I'm lost here." I hate to admit it, but when my hands start to shake, I'm overcome with the urge to run and find a place to hide for a while.

"Does he know?"

"No." My sigh comes out with a half hazard laugh. "I've yet to tell him. Not sure any good would come of it."

"Elsa, I have no answer for that. To be honest, when it comes to him I couldn't give a shit. For you, I'm wrecked. I know how hard this day has been for you. Even after all this time."

Wiping away a torturous tear, I head straight for the bathroom. Undoubtedly at the same time, Micah walks out from his office with a very tall, voluptuous, blonde beauty. His smile from ear to ear is the first thing I happen to notice.

Secondly, the way her hand is gently resting on his shoulder, in a way that implies she's familiar with him, does not sit well with me. He's yet to notice me, so I rush to the bathroom, hopefully going unnoticed.

"Shit," I whisper.

Hiding out in the bathroom won't help me one bit, but it buys me time to gets my wits about me. I spend a few minutes convincing Nick I'm okay, and I'll chat with him soon. That satisfies him, so I'm off to start my day.

Rounding the corner to sit at the desk, I see Micah chatting with the same blonde, still smiling ear to ear only now he's put distance between them. He's behind the desk, and she's enthusiastically leaning over it, exposing her chest. My immediate reaction is to gag, but instead I walk up putting my arms around him, staking my claim. Work or no work, she needs to realize he's not available.

That does the trick because her eyes narrow, shooting daggers straight at my smiling, perky face.

"Hey babe, I was wondering where you were?" Micah sweetly says turning to give me an affectionate hug. If I didn't know any better, I'd say he was trying to send a message to his overly eager client, too. Either way, it works for me. I'm the one who he has his arms wrapped around tightly.

"Micah, you never said you had a lady friend." With an eyebrow arched, she questions him in a less than warm tone.

What? Who the hell says lady friend now days?

"Well." Micah shifts his weight a few times looking extremely out of his comfort zone. "It never came up because Elsa is my personal life, and is none of your business. We only discuss business Carla."

He says matter of fact, and I have to say, he handled her

perfectly.

"Oh, don't play cool because she's standing here." She says way to condescending for my liking.

I'm not sure if she's trying to get a rise out of me more or him, but I swear I can see her daggers coming out.

Her grin mischievous. "We both know differently."

Her first attempt did not draw a reaction, so she just had to try again. Only this time she's tapping her red nails on her lower lip.

Coughing or choking, I'm not sure which, but Micah had to take a minute to respond.

"Excuse me?" He's face reddens when I pat his back trying calm him before he goes off on his client. It would seem she views her working relationship quite differently than Micah does.

"Micah, seriously forget it. Let's talk installation dates?" She's dismissing her inappropriate comments, with a subtle shrug of her shoulder and an eye roll to boot. My mouth is hanging open. I stare at her wondering what the hell? I slowly slip around Micah, distracting myself by filing the latest papers on my desk.

"Okay, let's keep our conversations strictly business and we'll get along just fine." Micah says matter of fact.

Not sure if she can notice, but she just dodged a bullet, if not from me, definitely from Micah. He shrugs off his anger looking for dates to install her new security system.

"Whatever." She says with an annoyed sigh.

AN HOUR LATER, I get a phone call from my mother wanting to

see me. Odd, since I've not spoken to either of my parents since that dreadful day. I realize why she's calling, and I decide it's a battle I don't want to have with her today, so I agreed to meet her over lunch.

"Are you sure you don't want me to come with you?" Micah asks me again for the tenth time.

"I'm sure, let me find out what she wants. I'll call you later."

He knows my mood is off today and that something is bothering me. He's annoyed because I won't talk about it with him. To be honest, I just want to forget it. Unfortunately, Nick's phone call does nothing to help me forget, even though his heart was in the right place. Can't fault the guy, he has a big heart.

"Mom, where are you?" I call out entering the house. It's so quiet, it's downright eerie.

Walking to the kitchen the first thing I see is their mail spread out on the table. But, no mom! No noise. It's as if she's not even here. Getting myself a glass of sweet tea, I'm sitting at the table looking at a magazine, wondering if I can find ideas for my new home. I could surprise Micah with a few great decorating ideas.

An envelope slips from the magazine, falling to the floor, I almost missed it, but what catches my attention is the odd shaped envelope. It appears to have some photo's inside. Picking it up, I notice the name scripted on the front. "That's just plain odd," I mutter with a sigh. The name on the return address is from a Carla Mitchell.

Wait a minute, that's the name of the dragon lady drooling all over Micah, earlier today. The same woman who was rude as hell to me on the phone the other day? It's too much of a coincidence not to be the same person, is the only thing I can think. Totally intrigued, I tear it open, without another thought. Not even thinking anything of it. My mom's not here to ask, so why not?

Upon opening the envelope, I see a letter and a few pictures. How bizarre would it be if this is the same Carla Mitchell? Wanting to see if she is in the photos I inspect them carefully. Okay, I see a black lab puppy sitting with a little boy. Cute. Looking at the next few it's more of the little boy but not one of Carla Mitchell. Huh! Not thinking anything I read the letter.

*Dearest Cindy,*

*Just wanted to send you a few pictures so you can see how he's growing. It's amazing how fast time goes. Just got settled into our new home, I'm a bit of a nervous nelly, so I called a security company to install the security alarms for us. Dan is gone all the time for work, and I get lonely and a bit scared at night. Will send more pictures when I can.*

*Love,*
*Carla*

Well, that answers that question, this is the same Carla. I now know she's a lonely housewife looking to get my boyfriend to give her some wanted attention. Too bad for her, I will rain on her parade...soon if need be. What is weird is the fact she knows my mom. Were they old friends, or what?

Just then, my mom comes down the stairs looking a bit worse for wear. Wow, I can't help thinking I've never seen her look so distraught before.

"Mom, are you okay?" I damn near jump out of my chair to give her a hug when she motions with her hands to stay seated.

"Hey sweetie, I'm not feeling the best. Better now that you're here, though."

Her eyes trail to the mail on the table. Her face freezes as she eyes the letter and picture in my hands.

"Wh...what are you doing with my mail?"

Looking at my hands, and slightly embarrassed she caught me with her mail, I let out a slight laugh.

"This is so weird, but your friend here is a client of Micah's. I met her today and let's just say she's taken with my boyfriend."

"What?" Her shaking hand lingers over her mouth as every bit of color drains from her face.

"How do you know her?" I had to ask, this was just weird not to know.

"Um...I've known her for a few years. I didn't know she contacted Micah, guess I had no idea he ran a security company."

Yeah, I spend the next half hour filling her in on all the new things happening with me. Starting with the fact I'm now living with Micah. She spent the half hour looking like a deer caught in a headlight. I'm not sure she even heard half of it, but it was one of the most uncomfortable talks ever. We've not had a close relationship over the years and right now she seems very interested. Whatever!

"Mom, what did you want when you called?"

"I wanted to apologize and wanted to...tell you something, but now I'm not sure." The way her words trail off I continue to look at her, wondering what the hell I missed. She's just not acting right. I hope she's not sick and afraid to tell me.

"Okay, well if that's it, I need to get back to work."

"Elsa, I know what today is... how are you?" Okay, now I

realize she's not sick this visit was more of a fishing expedition.

Oh God, I just knew this was coming.

"Mom, I'm fine. It's over, and I'm happier than I've ever been."

"Three years ago today you weren't. This happens to be the day I thought we lost you...for good."

Not the time or the place and I'm not in the mood for a stroll down memory lane. I've had one reminder with Nick's phone call, and now my mom. She takes Carla's letter and photos from me and stuffs them in her purse. I make a mental note to talk to Micah about this lady. Wasted lunch trip, I head back to the office without even bothering to call Micah. I'll see him soon enough, this just gives me a few more minutes to listen to music while driving back to the office. Upon getting out of my car, I don't even get my door closed, and Micah comes storming towards me.

Holding his hands up, he's visibly upset. "Elsa, no more messing around. Tell me what's bothering you and what the hell lunch was about?"

Well, no time like the present.

"Okay." Biting my lip, I'm frantically searching for next words carefully. "Three years ago today, my parents found me unresponsive. I ended up in the ER and was watched over for a few days."

"What the hell?" He definitely was not expecting that I'm sure. To lighten the moment I let out a hint of a laugh.

"Listen, it's not what you think. Everyone thinks I tried to end my life, but that is not true. I took some pills to get rid of a migraine, only I took my dad's pills from his cabinet. I took the wrong ones and nearly overdosed."

"Baby, please tell me you didn't..." I can see it in his eyes, and I hate it. This is the one reason I never wanted to tell him.

"No, Micah, and don't look at me like that. My migraine was so bad I accidentally picked the wrong bottle. I knew my dad had some powerful pain medications for his back. Honestly, I picked up the wrong bottle. I read the dosage wrong and took more than I should have."

It happened so fast, he grabbed me, instantly crushing me in his arms, asking me if I'm telling him the truth. I tell him the whole story of how my parents and even Nick did not believe me. They seriously thought things got too hard, and I wanted to end my suffering. Not true, but how many times can you continue to say the same things only to have no one believe you.

What started out as a quick discussion ended up being a four hour long ordeal in Micah's office while Matt and Trevor covered the phones and clients. Most of the time, I spent crying, trying to convince Micah how much of a mistake it was. A costly mistake but a mistake nonetheless. Pity was the last thing I wanted, especially from him. I got that from Nick and my parents for a long time afterward and if he dares to pity me, I might lose it all together.

Sitting on the small couch in his office, I decide to change the subject.

"Hey, did you know Carla Mitchell is a friend of my mother's?"

Micah does a double take. "What? Um, hell no."

"Yeah, I saw a letter and pictures she sent my mom. What a coincidence."

"Weird, I was thinking of turning her back over to Matt to handle for the installation." What a relief.

"Good idea."

It sounded good until Matt laughed and explained it was a big enough job it would take Micah and Trevor's help to get the job done. I swear Matt loved to see his brother squirm, he made sure to point out once she laid her eyes on Micah, it was lights out for Matt. He held her attention up until that point. Trevor, the poor soul, made it known how sad it was that none of the ladies were ever hot after him.

I gladly told him he could have Carla if he wanted. They all laughed, thought it was funny. I, on the other hand, was serious.

# CHAPTER
## twenty-Three

Carla Mitchell's installation day was today, and it was an all-day install at that. All three of the guys were busy getting it finished making sure it met her time schedule. Poor Trevor spent his day going back and forth from the office to her house troubleshooting with replacement parts. It took him several trips back and forth throughout the day. Now, it was after hours, so I agreed to take the last few items they needed to her address.

I did not want to see this lady, but the job needed to get done. I wanted to get home with Micah. It's a Friday night, and we had a quiet evening planned for the two of us. Driving up to her address I could see our company truck out front. Matt happened to be outside the front door, messing with a camera he was installing. Having no idea where Micah could be, I startled Matt when I walked up with the two boxes of wires they needed to finish up the job. Instead of being happy to see me his face shows the exact opposite. Not at all comforting.

"Where the hell is Trevor?" His eyes are searching behind me, expecting Trevor to show his face.

"Um... back at the office waiting for you to finish up. I told him I'd bring these over instead. Why, what's wrong?" Holding the boxes, I don't see the issue with me being here.

Lowering his face, he sighs. "Nothing, it's been a really long day. Why don't you leave the boxes and head back and tell Trevor we need him."

"Okay, where's Micah?" Looking around the bushes for some reason, thinking he's somewhere outside I ask Matt. It's dark out, so it's difficult to focus.

"Um... he's inside finishing things up." He says without looking me in the eyes.

The way he's fumbling with his words raises red flags. My insecurities start to boil, and the only thing I want, is to find Micah and let him know I'm here. It's been hours since I've heard from him. Suddenly hearing loud voices coming from inside I snap my head back thinking how odd it was that someone would be raising their voice at all.

My eyes swiftly shift back to Matt only to find him covering his face with his hands, lightly cussing to himself.

"Listen El, let us finish up so we can get done with this install. He can explain later, when he sees you." He looks wiped out, like he'd rather be anywhere but here.

"No, don't think so," I say with a sneer. "I want to see him now."

Instead of waiting for his answer, I walk right into the house calling out Micah's name. No need to wait long, I instantly see him holding a child as he's in deep conversation with...*Carla Mitchell.* How wonderful and completely bizarre.

"What's going on?" I say louder than necessary.

Micah stiffens. "Elsa, what are you doing here?" Saying he was surprised to see me is an understatement. I believe the word uncomfortable is how I would describe him at the moment.

Really? "Um...my job. I brought the last few boxes you needed and left Trevor back at the office. Now, is there a reason she's raising her voice, and you are holding her son?" I point from Micah to Carla.

Micah shrugs his shoulder. "He was fussy, came to me, so I picked him up. For some reason he got quiet when I held him, so I'm taking advantage of the time now that her son is quiet to explain. She was talking loud because he was fussy."

Glancing from Micah back to Carla, I feeling like I've entered the twilight zone. She's holding the manual looking frazzled and asking him questions. Not giving me a second thought. Micah looks so uncomfortable, I would laugh if I wasn't so upset. I keep telling myself it's silly, but for some strange reason, I don't feel like I want to kill him. I know deep down he would never cheat on me, and my insurance is knowing Matt would never allow it to happen. An added benefit of Micah working with his brother, I guess.

Walking over to Micah, without a second thought, I hold out my arms and the little boy comes willingly. I never bothered to ask Carla if it was alright to do so. She doesn't seem bothered that I did that. She just continues with her many questions, holding Micah's undivided attention. Either she doesn't have a clue how to use her new system, or she's using it as an excuse to keep Micah longer than necessary. Well, guess what, I'm not leaving until he does, so she might want to take notes.

The little boy is really quite sweet and seems more than comfortable in my arms. At first it was odd, but after a few minutes I swayed him back and forth and before long, he drifted off to sleep. So many different emotions flutter in my head and my heart.

Carla lets out a 'huh.' "I'm amazed, he was so fussy. Once Micah held him, he completely stopped, and now you put him to sleep. I might need to borrow you both at night, he keeps me up to the wee hours of the morning." *Yeah, I bet she would like Micah here at night with her.*

Poor baby, he's totally fine right now. Maybe it's his mother.

"How do you know Cindy Winters?" I blurt it out, not even thinking if it was proper or not.

"What?" She tries to act surprised, but the look she's giving me tells me she almost expected the question. Odd!

"Well, she's an old friend," she nervously plays with her shirt sleeves. "Why do you ask?" Her mouth keeps moving, but her eyes won't acknowledge me.

She's not a good liar.

"I'm her daughter." I say it slowly.

"Oh...I see." It's all she says, continuing to keep her hands busy. Turning her attention back to Micah she decides she suddenly understands how to use the new system and that her husband should be home tomorrow night. He would be in touch if they needed any further instructions or questions. With that, she eagerly wants to dismiss us.

She takes her sleeping son from my arms and he stirs. Upon opening his eyes, I notice how beautifully blue they are. He's so unbelievably breathtaking. A look of terror washes over his face as he wails. Loudly. Matt walks in with an odd expression on his face. He gives Micah a nod before letting Carla know he's finished. With a crying son, she pushes us out the door, wanting to put her son to bed.

"Good Lord, that was weird." I can't help saying.

"Yep, sure was." Matt can't help chuckling.

Wrapping his hand around my shoulder, Micah whispers in my ear. "Let's get the hell out of here."

Matt drove the truck and Micah came home with me. The rest of the night, Micah's quiet, and it leaves me with an unsettled feeling. Something doesn't seem right. In fact, the night ends on a quiet note. I let it go...for now.

Saturday morning, I'm barely awake and feel cold. It's obvious I'm alone in bed. No wake up kiss or anything. Stumbling from our bedroom, I hear Micah having a conversation. Apparently, he's on the phone. Keeping his voice hushed, he sounds tense. I find it odd and unsettling, especially with his odd behavior last night. Walking closer to the living room, my stomach flutters anxiously when I notice Micah hunched over sitting on the couch.

"No man, what if he's wrong?" Stretching his head back, he rubs the back of his neck. Yep, he's tense.

"Hell if I know, he's the one that needs to make sure before I go telling her a word."

I must have made a noise because Micah turns his head feigning a fake smile. Rolling my eyes, I give him a look like really?

"Got to go." He says switching off his phone.

"Hey babe, how long you been up?" He fails miserably in his attempt to cover up his conversation.

"Don't you mean how much did I actually hear?" I correct him.

"Shit," he lets out an angry sigh. "This is exactly what I was trying to avoid."

"What are you trying to avoid?" I ask, not moving an inch.

Holding out his hand, his fingers move and welcomes me. "Come here."

Sitting, I'm forced to listen to a very sordid story and I'm in total disbelief. I can't begin to comprehend what he's saying. Tyler, the man Matt hired to help him, was either a miracle worker or he was just plain nuts. My mind's spinning, and I'm not sure what to think. I soon realize there is only one place I can go to get the answers I need. It's the last place I want to get them.

Driving to my parents, I'm silently shaking my head that any of this holds much truth. All this time, how can this be? Could they have known all of this time? Why? It makes no sense.

I walk right in without even knocking, I'm shouting my parents' names, as I sprint through the house looking for them. Micah hasn't said a word since we left our house, a part of me wanted to come alone to get my answers, but I needed him here. This concerns him as well.

"Mother!"

"Dad!"

No answer.

"Jesus Christ, where are they?" I shout again a few more times, this time I go straight to their room. Knowing my mother, I know where she most likely keeps things. Her private things, she stores in her closet in a box way in the back. Funny how I seem to do the exact same thing.

Finding the black velvet box, I'm afraid to open it. I'm afraid what I'll find. My hands shake as I slide the box between my legs. Taking a breath, I look over my shoulder to Micah, who slowly sinks to his knees behind me.

My hands shake, my breath halts. "Well, let's see if there are any secrets in here."

I only get a faint head nod from him. His eyes tear up, not knowing what I might uncover. Cautiously lifting the lid, it has blue tissue paper covering it. It seems my mother keeps her things neatly stored.

Moving the tissue back, I notice the stack of envelopes, and my heart plummets. I'm hesitantly moving the tissue back careful not to rip it. Sure enough, I see the name I feared I would find. Sometimes, it hurts even more to be right. At the moment I wanted to be wrong. But I was disappointed once again, knowing what I may uncover makes my heart skip a beat or two.

"Carla Mitchell," I say thumbing through every last one. "They are *all* from Carla Mitchell." I'm in total disbelief.

I say it, but don't even look back at Micah, because he knows it as well. We both realize what I'm about to uncover.

I look at the dates on the envelopes, praying they don't date back to around four years ago, but to my astonishment they do. Somber filled tears stream down my cheeks. The letters are in order from newest to oldest. I slowly read the dates, feeling sick. I feel betrayed and downright lied to. At the bottom of the box is a thicker letter that catches my immediate attention. It reads *Contract*.

*What the hell?*

Holding the letter so Micah can get a better look, he reads the words, wondering what they mean. I don't wait, I open the damn thing. Scanning the document it looks legal, it has names, dates and oh my God!

NO!

NO!

NO!

How could they?

My fingers freeze and I'm holding this piece of paper in an iron grip. Seething mad, idle threats escape my lips as I read the details word for hurtful word. *Said minor Elsa Winters is willingly giving said child to Mark and Carla Mitchell for adoption.* Reading further, I'm morbidly stricken to find out my parents got compensation for the adoption. I'm definitely going to throw up. I'm frantically trying to comprehend that they took payment for my child. The document is notarized, but no mention of a lawyer or Catholic Charities is ever mentioned. Hell, I'm not sure this thing is even legal. As I toss the papers to the floor, Micah is quick to pick them up reading them. He's not saying one word and the fact he is dead silent terrifies me. I'd rather have him screaming or throwing my mom's shoes. That way I'd know what he was thinking or feeling right now.

Rocking from side to side, my tears slide faster, when I hear the first sob escape Micah's throat. How is it even possible? My parents lied to me all this time, never saying one word to me. They've been getting letters and pictures of a child they never wanted a thing to do with from day one. They treated me so poorly, and what's worse is they made *MONEY* off of me!

Nauseated and weak I say, "They got paid twenty-five thousand dollars for my son. How the hell could they?" Dropping the last page I can't help feeling numb.

"I've got no clue, but I *will* find out answers. They *will* explain themselves." Rubbing my shoulders, Micah lets out an uneasy sigh. "While digging in your past Tyler found the name Carla Mitchell. He never found a trace that led back to Catholic Charities anywhere. I just wanted to make sure before I said a word to you." He slowly lays his head on my back, and I understand why he would want to make sure before he said a word to me. He'd never want to upset me unless he absolutely had to.

Micah explained that he found this out right before her scheduled install appointment. It's the reason he never asked her to find a new security company. He needed to make sure it was indeed *this* Carla Mitchell, who had our son. The same Carla Mitchell, who was so called friends with my parents.

What a small fucking world.

We hear a noise coming from downstairs, we go meet my parents in the kitchen their hands full of groceries.

"Well hello," my mom says before her eyes go wide. "Oh, Micah you're here, too?"

"That I am." He says with obvious distaste.

I'm holding my mother's box containing the letters and photos. As her eyes focus on the box, she drops her bags of groceries. My dad curses, looking at the broken spaghetti sauce, not at what I'm holding in my hands. Taking a minute to try and regain her composure, my mother cautiously raises her eyes to see me glaring back at her. Without words, I'm mentally asking my mom how she could do this. To me, her daughter. Turning back to look at Micah, his arms are crossed, and I swear his are pressed together so tightly, they are turning white.

"Well, I see we need to talk." My dad finally acknowledges my angry stare, now that my focus is centered on him.

"I'm all ears," I say trembling.

"What do you know?" He asks all rational and reasonable like.

"Enough, why don't you start from the beginning?" Both Micah and I say for a lack of better words. My dad realizes he not only needs to answer to me, he needs to answer to Micah, as well.

"Let's go and sit in the living room." My dad says as he ushers his hand to lead the way.

My parents are on the couch looking uncomfortable. Micah, and I sit in the newly upholstered loveseat. It's the perfect place to sit since it's directly across from them. My leg bounces so violently, Micah has to put his hand on my knee to contain it. I never put the box down, I just hold it.

"We wanted to tell you, your mother and I. It just got too hard, and we were so disappointed in you." My dad says with such lack of authority, he's totally withdrawn. His words are shallow and empty.

My mom sits, crying and fidgeting with the hem of her dress. Her eyes are everywhere but on me. My dad continues to tell his story of how my aunt Peggy had a friend of a friend who was desperate to adopt a child, the only problem was the agencies said it could take years to find a suitable child. My aunt, to my utter shock, facilitated this partnership with my parents. It was never even legal. The Mitchell's had a criminal record, so they never stood a chance at getting a child through the legal channels. Some sort of felony fraud crime that would have stopped any chance they ever had of adopting a child.

My parents overlooked that important, fine detail. I think they felt overjoyed finding a solution to my problem, no *their* problem. Much to their surprise Carla insisted on sending pictures and letters, letting my parents know how grateful she and her husband were.

"The money. Why the money?" I can't wrap my head around the fact they profited from it.

"We felt they should have to pay something, and decided we could set it aside for you, Elsa. We just didn't know how to give it to you without an explanation as to where it came from. To be honest, we thought it would be wiser to make sure he went to college, instead. The Mitchell's don't know this, but it's another reason we liked being in contact with them. It's a way to make sure we know he's doing okay and then someday, we could help pay for his education." My mom's lost her mind. She's smiling like this is good news!

"Are you serious right now?" I'm damn near left speechless, hearing this so called plan they had.

Micah's coming unglued, the moans escaping his throat are more of a growl. "How the hell could you sell my kid and never tell Elsa any of it? You treated her so badly, yet you took the money? What kind of sick people do that?"

"Listen here boy," My dad scowls.

"Don't you *boy* me, you bastard." Micah jumps to his feet. "You're lucky I don't haul off and kick your ass, old man."

"Stop! I can't have you fighting. Tell me the rest. I want to know it all." I'm all but yanking Micah to sit back down. If forced to, I'll sit on his lap to keep him from mauling my dad. Well at least until I hear the rest of their story.

Over the next hour, we sat and listened to my parents explain the why's and how's of what took place. It was more than a shock when my mom found out Carla was using Taylor Security for her services. She knew right then and there I was going to find out the truth. The hardest part was listening to the way Carla had taken the news that the girl working for

Taylor Securities was actually her child's birth mother.

Carla took the news hard only because while she didn't see me as a threat to her plans to seduce Micah, her baby was my and Micah's biological child. That devastated her... and her wild fantasies.

"Are you kidding me MOM! Did you even stick up for me in your sweet talks with Carla-I-want-to-sink-my-teeth-into-Micah-Taylor? He's with ME! And she has MY SON! Where is your loyalty to me?"

"I don't know Elsa, I'm just telling you the truth." *Oh finally, it's only five years too late but hey, who's counting?*

Biting my lower lip, I shake my head in disbelief. "I held him you know?" No idea why I care if she knows this, but GOD ALMIGHTY maybe if I can find a way to break into her icy cold heart, she might begin to understand how I'm feeling.

"What?" All the blood drains from her face.

"Yeah Micah held him, too. He took a liking to him during her install." I'm taken aback, realizing we both held our son, but never had any idea. No words can describe the emotions running through my body.

"We held him El, we held our son." As if he's just now realizing this, his hand trembles against my shoulder.

*Oh Micah.* There are no words to even begin to describe how epic a moment we had and never knew it. I simply say, "I...know."

Tears and sobs overtake my weary body, I'm a mess, and once again, I'm totally broken. Lost and hurt at the hands of my parents. Just when I thought they could never top how much they've hurt me...they do again.

"Did you ever file it legally?" My overactive mind takes over, wondering just how legal this adoption actually is.

"No," my mom says, shaking her head. "We did it under the table but did write up a hand written contract. We thought it would work."

"Wow, you people disgust me. Trust me when I tell you that Elsa will no longer have anything to do with you." He's standing gathering his coat at the same time pulling me, to get the hell out of here. I'm sure he's already thought of ten different ways to take out my parents, but they're not worth it.

"Now wait..." My dad is standing pointing his finger.

"He's right, I'm done."

I have no fight left in me. Going on six years with my parents of living this elaborate lie, is just too much of a pill to swallow. They have damaged me for the last time.

Micah storms out the front door with his phone in his hand. I'm sure he's calling his dad. With the connections he has, he will know what to do.

"I'm taking the letters and photos, you don't deserve them." There is no way I'm leaving them with any of these things. This makeshift contract is the only thing I have that this farce of an adoption even exists.

"Wait...that's my grandso..." My mother starts to say.

"Don't you even finish that sentence! He's nothing to you just like I'm nothing to you. He's mine, he always was mine." I spit out every word with venom.

Micah comes barreling back in the house, pulling at me and this time, making sure I leave this God forsaking house for good. I stayed back, making sure to grab all of the envelopes as Micah went out with his phone. On the way out the door, Micah makes it known his parents would be in contact. He also told them to never contact me again. If they ever did, it would not be pretty, he'd make sure of it.

# CHAPTER
## *twenty-Four*

*T*wo weeks had passed since that day in my parent's living room. Tonight we're at Micah's parents' house for a family meeting. Matt and Tyler were already here by the time we showed up. A short time later the Taylor's lawyer, Mr. Hamilton, showed up. I'm not sure if I'm more elated or scared, watching his less than animated reactions. He gives nothing away, a mild eyebrow raise here and there, all the while intently taking notes.

I had to share the whole story with the many letters and pictures I took from my parents. Matt takes it pretty hard, knowing this is his nephew. Skylar, Micah's mom, has been crying, but shows excitement knowing we've actually found him.

I kept quiet most of the night, just looking at Michael's pictures. His changes from infant to toddler were incredible to see. I'm thanking my lucky stars I even get the chance to see them at all. The resemblance to Micah was unbelievable. I can't believe I didn't see it that night I held him. When he opened his eyes, the familiar baby blues should have been my first clue. Who knew?

After that night, we've all tried to live our lives as normal as possible. The Taylor's lawyer told us not to contact the Mitchell's ourselves, to let his firm handle things going forward. Knowing the whole adoption was not legal in the eyes of the law, he said he might be able to scare them into handing him back to us with no issues. It was a long shot, but we were willing to do whatever was necessary to get Michael back.

I no longer held onto the idea that I would just let him be with his adopted family. Knowing all the facts now, they don't deserve him. I've never forgotten him, and now I won't stop fighting for him.

It happens that luck may be on our side. Mr. Hamilton, called, wanting to schedule an appointment for us to come talk with him about the progress he has made since we last spoke. Wednesday after work, Matt, Micah and I met his parents at Mr. Hamilton's office.

Sitting at a long conference table, another gentleman, Mr. Reid, was also present. He explained he was working alongside Mr. Hamilton on what he called "a most sensitive case." Micah holds my hand in his as we sit quietly, his dad's taking the driver's seat, and asking the tough questions.

"We have several things in our favor with regards to the 'adoption' that took place." Mr. Hamilton flips through his stack of papers. Pushing his glasses higher up on his nose, as he begins to walk us through all he has learned.

From what I've seen so far, Micah's mom, Skylar was a strong woman who loved her family fiercely. I see this first hand as tears of hope fill her eyes, her once look of loss when we spoke that one night is now edging on hope. Now that there is a possibility that she may get to see her only grandson grow up. Looking at her, I get a real look how a mother should act, loving her family and stopping at nothing to get what her family needs and wants.

Once again, I can't believe all of this pain and suffering is at the hands of my mother and father. The old saying you can pick your friends but you can't choose your family? Pretty much.

Lost in my thoughts, I don't realize I'm crying. My face shows no emotion. I should be listening, but I just can't find it in me to concentrate. When I happen to look up, I realize, all eyes are centered on me.

"I'm sorry." Not sure if they asked me a question or what I've missed.

"Oh dear, you have nothing to be sorry for. We are all worried about you honey, that's all." Skylar holds her hand over her heart. Her face tightens and fresh tears descend once again. I'm astonished with the love this lady has for everyone around her.

"Baby, you okay?" Micah asks.

Looking up into his comforting baby blues, I lay my head on his arm, nodding my answer. Kissing my head, Micah reaches around the chair and pulls me against him. We stay seated like this for the rest of the hour.

We learned several things at this meeting. For starters, their contract was not legally binding and would not hold up in court for a number of reasons. My parental rights were never terminated in the eyes of the law. Micah's parental rights weren't terminated either. Nor had either one of us signed our rights away, voluntarily. The hand written contract between my parents and the Mitchell's would be considered a high risk in the legal system. We were informed every state had their set of rules when it came to adoptions.

In our case, it appears not all legal requirements were ever established, and that alone gives Mr. Hamilton, and Mr. Reid hope we will win this case. Micah's dad had contacted a few of his friends who were circuit court judges and was pushing hard to make sure we had the letter of the law on our side. He was adamant that no stone be left unturned. Having friends in high places does have its advantages.

Leaving the law office, Micah and I headed home holding on the hope that we'd get Michael. Not only are we just back together, but now we might be parents. Are we ready? Can we do this?

"Micah, are we ready to raise our child?" I ask, panicking with the doubts my parents have drilled in my mind over the years.

"Babe, we will do whatever it takes. We may be young, and just finding our way back to one another, but after I found out I had a son, I could not stop thinking about him." Pulling the car over on the side of the road, he puts it in the park and sits back, looking ahead at the road. "If I never would have left, we would be the ones raising him. It literally kills me knowing that even though we created him, he's living with strangers, and not us."

Sitting back, it's easy to see that he is deep in thought. Reaching across the seat, he opens the glove box and pulls out a small bag. A hint of a smile crosses his face before he closes his eyes and takes a calming breath. When he opens his eyes, they sparkle as they dance over my face. His infectious grin makes me giggle but then he pauses and his lower lip began to quiver.

"Do you believe things happen for a reason, El?" Micah's voice cracks when he says my name.

I answer with a nod, unsure where this is heading.

His breathing slows before his eyes settle on the road the look on his face looks like he is trying to remember something. "What did you tell me all those years ago?"

"Not sure what you mean?" I can't help smiling back at him feigning ignorance. Even though I have an idea what's he's asking me.

He lowers his chin. "Yes, you do."

I'm more than happy to go back and relive this part of our past, so I tell him what he wants to hear. "That you're my soul mate, and I knew it by the way I felt about you all the way to my bones."

"Exactly." His body relaxes. Reaching over, he gently cups my jaw, and runs his thumb across my cheek. Closing my eyes, I am resting my head in his hand. His touch alone could calm a thousand storms.

His smiles then lowers his eyes to my lips before settling back on my eyes. "Baby, do you still feel that way?"

Reaching up I cup my hand over his, lacing our fingers. "All the way to my bones, Micah, and I've never stopped. Once you give your soul away, you can't take it back. It no longer belongs to me. It belongs to you and it has since the day my eyes collided with yours five years ago."

His eyes shimmer with the tears that fill his eyes. Leaning in close, he keeps his eyes locked on mine, even as our lips connect. Holding my head in his hands, Micah deepens the kiss by tilting his head. Breaking our kiss for a fraction of a moment, a breathless Micah rubs his nose against mine in a butterfly style kiss. I normally would giggle, but this moment is anything but funny. The endearment in his feather-like touches and sweet kisses is what makes life worth living.

"Elsa." He whispers, as his lips caress mine in slow circles.

"Micah." My reply is more of a whimper.

"Baby, look at me?"

I do, opening my eyes, the first thing I notice is how piercing and commanding his eyes are. He gives me two more quick, passionate kisses, and then stops. He smiles, but still keeps his lips lightly pressed against mine.

"Marry me, baby?"

My eyes widen in surprise. I'm not sure I heard him right. I don't even have time to answer him because right after he said those words, he crushed his lips to mine in a powerful, thundering kiss that rivals all kisses. The windows are fogging up and before I know it, I'm in his lap, running my hands through his hair and pulling on it with everything I've got.

"Is that a yes?" He struggles to say the words because my lips are now taking ownership of his.

Out of breath, I lay my back against the steering wheel and let out a quiet chuckle while wiping my lower lip. "Are we really doing this?"

With a nod of his own, he winks. "Yes, we are." He says with confidence. I love that about him, but I'm a bit skeptical.

"Are you doing this because it's what you want, or because of there's a possibility we may get Michael? It's important for me to know."

"I bought the ring a long time ago, actually, it was over a year ago." He says, then holds up the bag he got out of the glove box with a sheepish grin on his face.

"What?" I'm stunned speechless. *A year?*

"I'm not kidding. I saw it in a window, and It reminded me of you. I knew one day, if ever given the chance, I'd put it on your finger." His pained expression is mixed with the fact he is getting his chance to do just that.

"What," I say in utter shock. "What if you never saw me again?"

Winching for a brief moment, he raises his eyes from the ring box to me. "I would have kept it locked in my safe. No other women would ever have worn it, if that's what you're wondering. I would never have given it to anyone else, this one was only for you. A reminder of the girl who stole my heart all those years ago."

Opening the box, I gasp!

It's the single most beautiful ring I've ever laid eyes on. The center square stone is laying with tiny diamonds around it. Each and every one sparkles as the moon's light hits them. I marvel at its beauty and can't help but cry, because this moment is really happening.

"I have no idea what to say." To say I'm surprised is an understatement, but what a pleasant surprise. With a shrug of his shoulder, he replies. "Simple, say yes."

Our eyes sparkle when the moon lights up the inside of the car. It's romantic and it's the perfect setting for this moment. A few sighs escape my lips, while I gaze into Micah's dazzling white smile. Making him wait for his answer is slowly driving him crazy, so I look up, pretending to ponder his question. He goes to tickle my sides, so I give in.

"Yes.Yes.Yes." I lean into arms, never letting go of my ring.

"That's my girl." With one last kiss, he takes the ring from the box and gently places it on my finger. And just like us, it's a perfect fit.

WEEKS AFTER WE got engaged, things moved pretty fast. Mr. Hamilton quickly reached a settlement with the Mitchell's and had even dragged my parents to several long meetings behind closed doors. I eventually found out Micah's parents were present at every one of them. Thankfully, they kept most of what was said to themselves. I know Micah had been well informed of what all had taken place, but I explained, I had no interest in knowing the details.

No longer did I want to be hurt by any news or actions from my parents. Skylar and Dave let it be known they were taking over the role of my parents. My family now consisted of the Taylor's. Two weeks after that announcement, we were in our lawyer's office, signing a stack of paperwork. And by the end of the meeting, Skylar and Dave walked in with Michael. I'll never forget it as long as I live. Micah grabbed onto my hand and squeezed my fingers until I no longer could feel them.

I couldn't believe it was happening, but I've never been so happy. We were going to be a family from this day forward, and ready or not, this was happening. Micah and I both had smiles plastered on our faces. There wasn't a dry eye in that room. We all were a bit nervous how Michael would act around us with him not knowing we were his real family. To him we were strangers. But you would have never known that, he came to us willingly. No tears, no hesitation. I think we all breathed a sigh of relief that this transition was going to be better than expected. Michael is four now and there was never an ounce of fear in his eyes. He willingly came to Micah and I like we were familiar to him all along. It was the first day of the rest of my life. I'm not sure who left that building happier that day...Micah's parents, Matt, or us. The one thing I do know, is that Michael will never have a moment of peace with this loving family he has now.

We quickly established a routine. Literally a few days was all it took for Michael to feel completely comfortable with Micah and I. Out of the three of us, it took me the longest to feel some sort of ease. Every waking moment, I was afraid he would be ripped away from us...again.

It took Micah several long talks with me to soothe my fears and wipe my tears. All three of us would sit for hours at a time, just getting familiar with one another. We rarely let Michael out of our sight. And to my pleasant surprise, we had house guests almost daily. The Taylor family had a new member who was beyond loved and cherished.

# CHAPTER
## *Twenty-Five*

Epilogue...

"*D*o I look okay?" I nervously ask Skylar, who is standing in the doorway fighting back her tears. She's frantically fanning her face with her hands.

"You look perfect." She says, giving me a watery smile.

Gazing in the mirror, I can't help letting out a nervous laugh. I'm finally dressed, in this fabulous, form fitting white dress. The instant my eyes landed on it, I had to try it on. There was no need to look any further, and it only took one shop, and under an hour. A very successful shopping day indeed, the minute I stood in the floor length mirror and saw myself...I knew it was the one. Looking behind me at Micah's mom only confirmed it if the flow of tears and her hand covering her mouth were any indications. She loved it as much as I did and the poor sales lady was busy handing us tissues. If she only knew my story, I'm sure she'd be in tears as well.

The strapless white mermaid style dress had a form fitted

lace corset accentuating every curve. The black lace details enhanced the corset and the back of the dress all the way down the train. The dress was simply gorgeous.

"Micah will flip out when he sees you." Wiping her eyes, she's holding a box out for me to take. I chuckle at her remark slowly opening the box. With nervous energy running wild throughout my body, I can't believe this day is finally here. Having Micah's mom help me get dressed makes it that much more special.

"This is your something old. Now, please breathe for me, so you don't pass out." Her humor helps calm me some.

I let out a few laughs and she soon follows with a few of her own.

"Okay, this locket is the first present Dave ever gave me. I've had it for over twenty years, and now I'm giving it to you. I had this locket custom made, especially for you."

Opening the locket I see two pictures, one on each side of the heart pendant, both are baby pictures. I can only assume they are both Micah since they are strikingly familiar to one another. It's incredible, and I start to weep, gently tracing my finger over his cute face. *My sweet Micah.*

"The one on the left is Micah and the one on the right... is Michael. I found this picture in one of those letters you collected from your mother, and had it sized to fit the locket. This heart locket now holds your whole heart."

"Oh my God!" It's perfect and beyond beautiful. Skylar helps me put it on and it falls against my neck, lining up perfectly with my dress. We both stay silent a moment, with tear filled eyes in awe of how amazing it looks with my dress. This locket completes my dress...just like Micah and Michael complete me. The silver chain runs through the top of the locket. It's simple but elegant. Holding the locket in my fingers, I thank her a few dozen times for a gift I never thought I'd have.

"Dave is downstairs with my over anxious son, and he's more than ready to claim you as his wife. You know, back when you both were in high school, I knew it then. I saw it in both your eyes, and I knew that one day, we'd be right here as we are now. You are becoming my daughter, and I couldn't ask for a better one. Now we need to help Matt. His choice in girls is not so great." We exchange a laugh because she is spot on. Poor Matt needs a good girl in his life. I realize just how lucky I really am with Micah and his parents.

"After all this time, I'm so glad I get you as my mother. A bit funny seeing I have a vacancy for one of those nowadays." I use humor to ease my pain when it comes to my current relationship with my mother. I will never be able to forgive what she did, and that really hurts.

"Oh hush, don't give it another thought. You have a mom and dad who love you dearly now. Dave would have knocked Micah on his ass if he didn't marry you, but we never worried too much. Our son has been in love with you forever."

Both of us are crying and laughing when a loud knock on the door startles us. It's my soon to be husband, all dressed up and looking hotter than hell. His eyes travel up and down my dress, taking in every detail. I'm not sure, but it looked liked his knees buckled a little.

"Mom, leave me with my bride, please." He asks breathlessly. "I want a few minutes with her before we get started." Micah is talking to his mom, but his eyes stay glued to mine. Oh boy, he looks at me like he wants to devour every inch of me.

Jokingly rolling her eyes, she gives her son a dismissive nod. "Okay son, hold on." To add to her annoyance she swats her hand towards him playfully.

Giving me one more look over, she seems satisfied as she gives me one last kiss on the cheek. Fully opening the door, my man walks in dressed in his black tux. And to my surprise, he's not alone. Walking in beside him is our son dressed in a tux just like his daddy's. The resemblance between them is remarkable. I'm not sure who could win a contest between these two. They both look stellar right now.

Micah lifts his eyebrow. "He wanted to see his mommy real quick before he has to sit with Uncle Matt and grandpa."

Michael, who is looking so comfortable next to his daddy, is a truly a sight to behold. Fitting, seeing as though they are both Taylor boys. We changed Michael's last name to Taylor as soon as he was legally ours. It was Micah's first official act as his father. For Micah, his son needed to have his last name. And after today, it will also be my name. Looking at them now, it just feels right. Nothing could make this day any better.

"Wow, my two boys look fantastic." Both smiling from ear to ear, they look at me with the same sweet smile. In a short amount of time, Michael is mimicking his daddy's every move and quirks. *Lord, save me now.*

Not able to help myself, I lean over to pick him up to kiss his plump cheeks and when I do my nose is engulfed with a manly scent. He smells of Micah's cologne, and I have to giggle knowing Micah took pride in getting his mini me ready for today. Standing behind me, Micah engulfs the two of us in his arms, and we stay like this, silently. This feeling right here, right now, this is what life is all about. A day I never could've imagined happening is about to finally be here. It's a powerful thing and I'll never take it for granted...ever.

Kissing my handsome son one last time, Micah seems anxious to get our wedding started. A movement catches my eyes when I noticed Matt strolling in the room. When Matt notices his nephew, he wastes no time in taking our son into his arms. It's pretty easy for us to notice how eager Micah is. Matt chuckles enjoying his brothers nervously behavior. It's pretty cute.

"Okay, Uncle Matt," Micah says as he hands Michael over. "Take your buddy downstairs so I can have a moment with his mommy."

Matt eagerly holds his hands out to receive his nephew, but not before he notices me in my dress. He lets out a loud whistle. And my face turns completely red.

"Hey buddy, let's go pick up some chicks for Uncle Matty." Matt says playfully. From the moment Michael came home with us, Matt has been on cloud nine. To say he spoils his nephew is an understatement. *I love it.*

The instant Matt playfully said the words, he knew it would bother his dear brother. Micah couldn't help but groan in displeasure.

"Do *not* use my son to pick up dates, please?" Micah says it in such a sweet voice, I had to do a double take. Even Matt looked at Micah, somewhat puzzled. It seems today, my future husband is all serious and maybe even a little nervous. Matt opens his mouth to say something but doesn't. He just shakes his head instead and I raise my eyebrow at him. I can tell he wants to say make a joke at Micah's expense, but he holds back. Today is his brother's big day, after all.

Biting his tongue, Matt replies hesitantly. "Yeah, whatever. Come on little man, let's party and leave your daddy to it."

The way Matt interacts with a very receptive Michael, warms my heart. Michael seems eager to get down and run around. He doesn't like to sit still for long in one place. If I only had the energy my son has. Speaking to Micah, I whisper, "Matt loves him, dearly."

Nodding his head, Micah responds. "Everyone loves our boy. What's not to love?" We watch as Matt tries to keep up with our son, who is already out the door.

*Can't argue with that.*

Turning his attention to me, Micah lets out a long, low whistle, again eyeing my body up and down. Now that his son has left the room, Micah's naughty side comes out to play.

"Can't wait to get you out of this dress, pretty girl. Damn shame too, because you look so freaking beautiful in it." His dazzling smile turns mischievous the instant his eyes blaze with desire.

I've planned our wedding night well. I decided to spice things a bit, and spent a small fortune on undergarments. Since Michael has been home with us, we are more careful when it comes to our love making. Sex, is only happening in the bedroom now—a shame but with an active four year old, we have to be creative. I want tonight it to be all about desire.

"Oh, just wait till you see the surprise I have on underneath?"

Raising a brow, he traces his finger along my breast line. "Tease. Good thing Grandma and Grandpa are taking our son for the weekend. It may take me all that long to thoroughly enjoy my surprise."

I'm mentally melting with anticipation. First, we have a wedding to attend. Leaning into him, I let out a slow yearning moan. "Kiss me and get out, I'll see you shortly." Hell, I need to calm my raging libido now, before I go downstairs and pledge my vows before God and everyone else to Micah. I'm afraid everyone might be able to read my mind if I walk down the isle with flushed cheeks. It's going to be hard enough standing so close to Micah with the way he looks, then keep my hands off of him. I can tell he sees me struggling, because his evil grin shows it.

"Yes ma'am." Kissing me one last time, he does the one thing I knew he most likely would. He tells me in my ear how happy he finally is. He began whispering all these keepsake moments he wants to remember about today and he kept on until my mascara was streaking down my cheeks. I had to look like a raccoon.

Once he left the room, it ended up taking me ten full minutes to clean it off and apply new makeup. *Darn that boy!*

When I was just about fixed up, I hear a light tap against the door. Finding it odd since it was almost time for the ceremony to start, I walk over to the door and, I open it slowly.

"Liza."

My eyes go wide is shock, I can't believe she's standing here, all dressed up. She must sense my disbelief.

"That man of yours is very persuasive when he wants to be." She says, looking at me sheepishly.

"Micah." I say, smiling. Like I even need to ask.

"Who else? I've come to realize not having you in my life hurts much more than accepting you and Micah. Plus, it took you two getting back together for me to find my own great guy."

The surprises keep coming. It's a bit odd, I don't know what is happening in her life anymore. I've been busy, but I've spent many times wondering show she was. Many times

I wanted to call her for a friendly chat. I push those feelings aside because she is here, with me now, dressed ready for a wedding. This feels right.

"That's awesome to hear, Liza. I've missed you so much." Not holding back, I hug her, tight.

She squeals. "Okay, that little boy of yours is such a little Micah. Good Lord. He's a doll, and I'm going to spoil him rotten. How does aunt Liza sound?" She says, staring at the ceiling thinking just that as my mouth is gaping wide. All of sudden, it's as if a heavy weight has been lifted off her shoulders.

*Aunt Liza, wow. Things have indeed changed since we last talked.*

We end up hugging each other hard we both get teary eyed, but I pull back dotting my eyes. I have no time to fix them again. She stayed and teased my hair, straightened my dress and handed me my bouquet. It was like old times again. I must remember to thank my man, once again, for always looking out for me. Is there anything that man wouldn't do for me? I hope I never find out.

Liza hesitates, and her eyes dart everywhere but me. "So, I wanted to let you know Nick is downstairs." She definitely appears nervous.

My body tenses. "Shit, are you serious?" My mind is playing out some shouting match between Nick and Micah. Not good. I'm not paying a bit of attention to what she is hinting at.

"Yes, but it's okay," she uses her hands to cup my shoulder. "He's with me."

My body halts. I'm frozen in shock at what she just hinted at. When my eyes hit hers, her face lights up in one of the biggest smiles I've ever seen on her face. She can't contain it any longer.

"You aren't serious?" I didn't mean it come out like that, but it slipped out anyway. I'm happy just a bit taken back.

"Yep, and it's awesome. We get along great. Elsa, this is the way it should have been. Micah even had a long talk with Nick, and they can be in the same room without wanting to kill one another, so it's progress."

Progress, yes, I would say. Knowing Nick is busy with Liza is the only reason why I'm sure Micah is so cool with this. I did not see this one coming, that's for damn sure, but it makes sense. They've been friends for years, if it's meant to be...it's meant to be.

Our lives have taken so many twists and turns, my head can't keep up. All I know right now is I'm needed downstairs I hear my music alerting me it's that time. Hugging Liza one last time, we make our way down, to find Dave at the bottom of the stairs. I come to a stop and he gives me a wink.

"I need to walk my daughter down the aisle." He's so confident in everything he does. Not a hesitation on his part, he offers up his arm for me to take.

Soaking in the sight of him extending his arm, I'm visibly shaking, in awe of Micah's father. This day just got a whole lot better. Wiping a single fallen tear, I have a hard time finding my voice. "I was so scared to ask you." And I was. For weeks I wanted to ask him but for some reason, I just couldn't do it. Micah brought up the subject several times, only to find me full of doubt. More scared then doubtful, though.

He gives me a smile that I feel all the way through to my heart. "No need, I would have done it anyway. Now, we better hurry up. Your son is acting up, and my son is anxious to claim you as his wife."

I chuckle, knowing how true that is. "Well, that's two Taylor boys I need to take care of for sure."

Dave pats my hand that is laced over his arm. "All the more power to you little lady." We share one last sweet exchange before it's show time.

Walking side by side we follow our makeshift isle that leads to the back yard. I can see it's filled with friends of Micah's parents, a few buddies from the Air Force and my friends from work. It's just perfect. The closer we get to the front, Michael looks over Matt's shoulders and locks eyes with mine. My heart beats faster.

"Mommy." He mumbles, reaching his arms out for me. Everyone openly sighs at the sweetness his words hold. They all know our story, and I don't believe there will be a dry eye by the end of this ceremony. Since I only smile back to my sweet boy, he then decides to see if he can get to Micah.

"Daddy." He suddenly says, trying his best to get into Micah's arms instead.

"Hang on little buddy, need to marry your mommy first." Micah says wiping a bead of sweat over his eyebrow. I'd say my man was nervous and anxious. The way Micah interacts with our son, is not only amazing, it's spectacular.

We all laugh and glance at an anxious little boy who now seems content when he eyes his Grandpa. We are at the end of the isle so grandpa is able to take his grandson. Taking his seat, Michael settles in his grandpa's lap. He is more than content since he now has both his grandparents fussing over him.

Both Micah and I exchange a smile before the minister clears his throat, alerting us it's time.

"Dearly beloved, we are gathered here today to join this

man and this woman in holy matrimony." Our minister announces and shivers run down my spine. I'm marrying the boy who walked into my life years ago and just like I knew he'd change it forever, he sure did.

Not everyone's journey in life is ever easy, many are hard. My journey to finding Micah only to lose him was one of the worst in my life. Giving Michael away? Well? No words can describe that. I once said I found my soul mate at sixteen and indeed I had. I may have lost love, hope, and all the dreams I once envisioned. But knowing it would lead to me being here today marrying my soul mate while having our son with us...I'd live with that pain all over again.

I've made my peace knowing my parents can no longer hurt me, I've not spoken to them and I'm not sure I ever will again. They are the ones who lost out.

We exchange our vows, pledge our faithfulness, and love and promise our future will always be with each other.

"Ladies and Gentlemen may I introduce to you, for the very first time, Mr. and Mrs. Micah Taylor!"

In true Micah fashion, he kisses me hard and picks me up, walking me to stop where Michael sits. Plopping me to my feet, he picks our son up as we walk down the aisle to the cheering of our friends and family.

The party is in full swing, the country club had done an amazing job setting up this magical day for us. All black and white with red accents. The night is settling on us, and it's time for the first dance. A song starts to play, and I can't help smiling over at my new husband. He'd picked our song, and his choice was, *All of Me* by John Legend. Pulling me in his arms, we slow dance, getting lost in each other's eyes.

"Elsa Taylor. It suits you baby."

"I think so too, husband." I say lacing my fingers behind his neck.

His smile goes mega wide. And he says, "Wife, oh man, that is what I have always dreamed I'd call you one day."

My chuckle is followed by one of his own. "I'm glad. It's too late to change it now." I say, jokingly.

We laugh a few more times, and holding on to each other we glance over at the table where Micah's parents are sitting, enjoying themselves. Matt is holding on to Michael. He tries to eat a bit of cake for himself, but his nephew is demanding that he gets it all. Taking this quiet moment, we both just watch them all interacting with one another. Not much more in life could get any better than it is right now. I happen to catch Liza and Nick talking with the girls from the dental office, laughing and totally carefree. Both Micah and I shake our heads at the idea of Nick and Liza as a couple, but hey, I'm happy for them.

Smiling, Micah leans into my ear, giving it a sweet kiss and he whispers.

"Elsa, thank you for never giving up."

My heart skips a beat when a final tear escapes my eye. This last, lingering tear was indeed for the part of my soul that never let me give up, no matter what. Holding onto my locket, I bring it to my lips to seal those words with a kiss.

Our night comes to an end with the three of us dancing together. Who would of thought we all would find a way back to one another? I sure didn't. I wonder how our lives would be if we had all been together from the beginning. Would we be just as happy as we are now? Who knows? One thing for certain is how incredibly blessed I feel having both Micah and Michael back where they belong...with me. Forever.

*The End!*

# Acknowledgments

I am very thankful and lucky to have surrounded myself with individuals who helped make my dream come true. First my amazing family, your support means the world to me. My loyal friends, you have done more for me than you will ever know. To my beta readers, you helped me so much with making sure Micah and Elsa's story came together perfectly. I'm so blessed to have your support. A special thank you to Emma, Joanna and Cassy. I could not have done this without your special talents with what you do. To my readers, thank you so much for reading Never Give Up. I really hope you enjoyed this story. It's a very personal story to me. Writing this book, I've cried, laughed, and fell in love with Elsa and Micah. Please take the time to leave a review. Without you, I would not be able to do what I love to do. Thank you!

# About the Author

Heidi grew up in the Midwest, but currently resides with her husband and four children in the Pacific Northwest. Heidi most enjoys spending time outdoors with her family. Between raising her children and obsessing over her favorite reads, she has let the storyteller within herself come to life. With the love and support of her family, she is following her dream while teaching her children how important it is to follow theirs. She prides herself in believing that anything is possible, the first step is believing in yourself. Heidi's passionate and loving style in which she lives her life comes through in her writing. Her heart has led her down the genre path of a contemporary and suspense romance writer, but she has plans to extend her vision into other genres as well.

# Follow the Author

You can keep in touch with Heidi about her upcoming books and giveaways on Facebook and Goodreads.

https://www.facebook.com/pages/Author-Heidi-Lis/360554554103550

https://www.goodreads.com/author/show/13933067.Heidi_Lis

# Other Books by Heidi Lis:

**Defying Fate**

Printed in Great Britain
by Amazon